TEMPLAR'S BANK

AN ARCHAEOLOGICAL THRILLER

DARWIN LACROIX ADVENTURE SERIES
BOOK 3

DAVE BARTELL

TRIPLE SHOT PRESS

To my daughters Kelly and Sara who fuel my imagination.

PROLOGUE

Paris, France
15 April 2019

P ierre Laporte walked into the raging inferno. Across the river Seine, thousands had gathered. They sang and prayed, witnessing the unthinkable as Notre-Dame de Paris glowed like a stage designer's depiction of Hell.

Ten minutes earlier, the commander had radioed to ready the water cannon. They needed to cool the stone walls to prevent a collapse. Despite the structural engineers saying it could be suicide for anyone to go inside the weakened structure.

Earlier, Pierre had taken part in a human chain, saving relics from the cathedral, but as a lifelong Parisian, he knew the prize was the building. Notre-Dame de Paris had stood at the heart of France for nearly a thousand years.

He had followed generations of his family in joining the *Brigade de sapeurs-pompiers de Paris*, the Paris Fire Brigade, to protect the capital city's monuments. He knew the risks, but he also knew he could not live without trying. His grandparents had been married in Notre-

Dame, an honor bestowed for their service in the Resistance in World War II. He would not fail the memory of their sacrifices.

A knack for technology had led Pierre to work in the Robotics unit, which tackled the most critical situations. Tethered to the control box hanging from his chest, the water cannon robot, nicknamed Colossus, faced the cathedral. The red machine, a meter wide and twice as long, moved on thick rubber treads like a miniature tank. Its stout barrel moved hydraulically by an armature within its frame. Two high-powered spotlights periscoped from its center and a water hose trailed Colossus like a massive tail. At twenty-five hundred liters per minute, Colossus could fill a third of a million water bottles an hour.

"Are you ready?" asked the fire commander.

"*Oui.*"

The commander placed a hand on Pierre's shoulder. "*Va avec Dieu,* go with God."

Pierre nodded and his colleague, Antoine, adjusted the straps holding the robot control box and opened the valves on the breathing tanks. The wide, clear mask pressed Pierre's wavy dark hair against his forehead. His hazel eyes rapidly scanned the open portal behind Antoine.

"Can you hear me?" Antoine tested the communications one more time.

"*Oui.*" Pierre locked eyes with Antoine and slapped his silver helmet. *Allons-y.* Let's go."

Colossus moved forward. Around them, twin-tone sirens reverberated through the neighborhood. Pump engines roared as they sucked water from the Seine into a dozen hoses streaming onto the burning roof. The crowd cheered when it saw the robot advance.

Pierre guided it toward the cathedral's three arched portals, each containing two doors outlined with dozens of carved figures. He eased Colossus through the left door in the center portal, known as the Last Judgment, careful to avoid scraping the centuries-old carvings. The wind howled as the inferno sucked him through the opening.

A moment later, the wind died down and the outside noises fell away. An eerie silence settled inside his full body suit as a scene of utter devastation unveiled. The enclosed space reverberated like the low breathing of some inhuman beast. He looked up and gasped. *"Mon Dieu!"*

The collapsed vault exposed a semicircle of flames, like a monster's open mouth. Wicked orange teeth danced and embers rained like flaming spittle. He stopped and guided Colossus past the racks of prayer candles toward a massive pile of oak beams, once part of the roof. The bonfire risked superheating the central stone walls and columns to dangerous levels.

"Now!" yelled Pierre. Water surged from Colossus. A bright white arc crossed the black space into the hideous orange maw. Steam billowed, followed by a massive hiss. Pierre guided the stream side-to-side as the flames took the moisture like a parched serpent. Sweat beaded on his brow and the inside of the suit stuck to his skin.

"Pierre. Talk to me. Are you okay?" crackled the voice of his commander.

"Oui, oui. It's working," said Pierre. Hearing the voice gave him a surge of confidence.

Twenty minutes in, he leaned against one of the massive columns as protection from the heat wave as he oscillated the cannon back and forth, back and forth. He knew it would not extinguish the fire but could hopefully cool the superstructure. He prayed as the water moved. *Please stay up. Please stay up,* his incantation willed the stone.

Suddenly a body rushed past him, stopped, and turned back.

"Pierre! Some idiot ran in. Do you see him?" shouted the commander.

"Oui."

A man of medium height with shoulder-length blond hair looked about as if not sure which way to go. Pierre kept his fingers steady on the robot's controls but trained his powerful helmet lamp to see the stranger's face. His green eyes, set between a hawk-beaked nose, were wide with fear. As Antoine moved toward him, the guy took off up the cathedral's north aisle.

"He's running toward the north rose window," shouted Antoine.

"Let him go. It's probably some nut who wants to die with the cathedral," said the commander.

"D'accord." Pierre watched the man stop in the transept, just meters

from the flames. He turned the water jet to shield the runner. The flames lowered. The man, shielding his eyes with a forearm, studied the floor. Then knelt, crossed himself, and pounded the marble tiles.

What the hell?

The figure threw broken marble aside and lifted a small cylinder. He held it aloft a moment, then stood and ran from view. Pierre leaned forward as if the extra few centimeters would help him see where the man went.

"He went out the side door," said Antoine.

"*Non!* He went into the tombs beyond. I am sure," said Pierre. As he spoke, another section of the roof dropped to the floor in a fire-bomb. Heat surged toward Pierre, who shoved Antoine behind the closest column and curled himself into a ball to minimize exposure. It passed, and they returned to operating Colossus.

When the danger of the cathedral's collapse had passed, Pierre withdrew the robot. He sat on an ambulance step, breathing oxygen and drinking a third bottle of water. His mind kept coming back to the man's face before he ran to certain death in the conflagration. The teams outside the north side door and Porte Rouge confirmed that no one had exited. Pierre replayed the memory multiple times, even asking Antoine if it had been an illusion. He confirmed seeing a man, but not his face.

Long after sunrise, Pierre wandered about the scene of devastation as his adrenaline dissipated. Eventually, he was sent home, where he tried talking, but his throat hardened with grief.

"Shh." His wife held a finger to his lips and continued, "I was so afraid of watching you on TV. But I am so proud of you for saving Her. Come." She took his hand and helped him undress for a shower. A half hour later, he lay in bed as fatigue pulled him deep into the sheets. The scene of the man played one more time before sleep took him: the crazed look, the pounding of the marble.

What did he take from the floor?

F ive months later, on a crisp September morning, Pierre enjoyed brunch with his wife and children at a café on Île Saint-Louis, one of the two islands in the Seine that formed the heart of Paris. Notre-Dame was on Île de la Cité, the larger island just across a short bridge. He had not returned to the cathedral since the fire and told himself, *Don't look, not yet.* His wife had encouraged him to go on the outing. She promised the kids ice cream at Berthillon a block away, then they would walk by the cathedral.

In the days following the April fire, Pierre had insisted on seeing where the man had run—if nothing else but to confirm his own sanity. But the fire inspectors allowed no one in the cathedral. They had found no human remains, and the floor was so badly damaged there was no way to confirm whether a person had cracked it. "He was a lunatic. Pierre. Forget about him," the commander had said at the ceremony where they gave Pierre a medal honoring his bravery.

The waiter delivered a glass of Chateauneuf du Pape as Pierre's wife organized the kids coloring on the paper placemats. The wine's earthy aroma reminded him of summer and eased his mood. He leaned toward his daughter, who was drawing a cat. She pointed to it, sitting across the narrow Rue Saint-Louis en l'Île. He looked up. The cat shone in a halo of sunlight reflected from the restaurant window, and he picked up his mobile to capture the moment.

A man walking along the street stepped out of the shadow just as Pierre snapped the photo. He was annoyed at the ruined image and moved to delete it. His thumb froze over the icon. *Mon Dieu! It's him—the man from the fire.* The three-quarter profile showed the same green eyes and a prominent nose that he remembered from the fire. The man's shoulder-length blond hair confirmed it. Pierre was certain. He jumped from the table and rushed to the front door, his wife asking what was wrong.

"*Hé!*" Pierre yelled, emerging from the restaurant's side door. The man had stopped at a corner shop and turned at the shout. When he saw the prominent sapeurs-pompiers logo on Pierre's polo shirt, he ran onto a cross-island street toward the river's Right Bank. Pierre got momentarily tangled in a purse strap hanging on a chair of one sidewalk table.

"*Desolé*," he said, checking that the woman was okay, then resumed his chase. The man had gained ten meters during the brief encounter with the chair, but Pierre, in top condition, began closing the gap. The man reached the intersection. Pierre sped up to overtake him on the Pont Louis-Philippe, where the vast space on the bridge would yield more options to confront the man.

But just as the guy reached the bridge, ten horses from the Republican Guard trotted in side-by-side formation across Quai de Bourbon. Pierre slowed, assessed the horses' speed, and looped around their rear. The detour took moments but was enough for the man to extend his lead. Pierre dug deep as the man reached a group of electric scooters-for-hire parked at the bridge's far side.

"Stop him!" yelled Pierre.

People looked up, but in the time it took for them to figure out what was happening, the man had unlocked the scooter with his mobile and pushed off into the traffic on Quai de l'Hôtel de ville on the opposite bank. Pierre stopped and bent over, hands on knees. After a minute, his breathing settled. He strolled back across the bridge while phoning his wife.

An hour later, as the kids enjoyed their ice cream and his wife ducked into a shop to look at a scarf, Pierre looked at the photo. He zoomed in on the man's face. Green eyes stared at the camera from an unshaven face, drawn and with lines betraying middle-age. There was a definite scar across the man's forehead that looked recent. He messaged his brother, a police detective, with the man's picture.

Can you find this guy? Call me later. I'll explain.

1

Corsica, France
October

Darwin warmed his hands on a porcelain mug and sipped the triple-shot cappuccino. Autumn came earlier in the Corsican mountains, the temperature reminding him of foggy mornings in Berkeley, California, where he had earned a Ph.D. in archaeology.

He sighed into the cool air; the coffee's heat increased the mini cloud that dissipated into the gorge. A breeze wafting up the canyon ruffled his hair. He brushed back the unruly mass and reminded himself to visit the barber on his next visit to Ajaccio, the capital city of Corsica.

His wife, Eyrún Stephansdottir, had suggested they take a break from the stress of their back-to-back explorations and live like ordinary people—although, so far, their life together had been anything but ordinary. Each of their previous explorations in Iceland and Egypt had resulted in significant archaeological discoveries.

To get even farther off the grid, she had convinced Darwin to remodel his family's mountain house at the foot of Monte d'Oro. His grandfather, Emelio, still lived in the family mansion in the port of

Ajaccio, where the Lacroix family's Genoese ancestors had built their shipping empire.

Corsica lay at a strategic point between Italy, France, Spain, and North Africa. Its woodlands had provided timber for shipbuilding, and natural harbors created hubs for shipping. The island's near-impenetrable mountainous core made it a hiding place for bandits and a locals' refuge to avoid pirates.

The Lacroix family built the mountain house in the late 1700s as a summer retreat during their shipping empire's zenith, when the contracts from transporting armies for Napoleon, a childhood friend of Darwin's great-great-grandfather, filled the family coffers.

The house occupied a ridge set back from the road that ran from sea level in Ajaccio across Corsica's spine into the northeast port of Bastia. While just over thirty kilometers to the harbor in Ajaccio, a round-trip drive averaged two hours.

Pages flapped in an open book on the table behind Darwin as another gust swirled up the canyon. He turned and closed the diary, written by his great-great-grandmother, chronicling the family's history in southern Corsica. He and Eyrún had unplugged from the world here, choosing to read, hike the surrounding mountains, and learn to cook the local cuisines.

"What a gorgeous day," said Eyrún, walking onto the patio, toweling her long, dark-brown hair. She had showered first after their morning yoga and mixed-martial-arts routine. The morning sun radiated off her pale Nordic complexion and accentuated her glacier-blue eyes and natural beauty.

She smiled at him and said, "It's all yours. Get in before Luka shuts off the water," referring to the Croatian contractor remodeling the kitchen and baths.

"Thanks, Love," he said.

"Did you figure out what your *grand-mère* meant about the secret hiding places?"

"Not yet. I'll have to ask Emelio."

They watched a truck on the road far below snake its way up the canyon. A red-and-white checkerboard pattern covered its passenger door—a nod to Luka's homeland.

"That's Luka. You better get in the shower now." She pressed a finger to his sweaty shirt, pushing him toward the bathroom.

"You could join me."

"We don't have time."

"I don't need much time." He grinned.

"Go." She spun him around.

Before showering, he shaved. Three day's growth was the limit for Eyrún. "After that, you need to grow it out or shave it off," she had said three weeks earlier as they were packing up to leave Egypt.

Placing both palms on the counter, he studied the mirror.

Was it only three weeks?

The skin down to his neckline was a deep bronze: the result of the Egyptian sun combined with his family's Mediterranean and Caribbean heritage. His mother, Carmen Méndez, hailed from a family of doctors and judges in Puerto Rico. She had met his father, Olivier, while both worked on archaeology Ph.D.s. Darwin, born in Paris, had lived all over the world due to his parents' teaching and research.

Summers spent with their grandparents in Ajaccio was the one constant as Darwin and his sister Marie grew from innocents into adolescents, testing the boundaries of youth. Later, the family settled in London, where both finished schooling in French before going to university. The traveling and cultural mashups had given Darwin fluency in multiple languages.

Earlier in the year, his discovery of the lost Library of Alexandria at the Siwa Oasis in Egypt had elated him, even though he'd nearly been killed in the process. The Egyptian Ministry of Antiquities asked him to stay on and supervise the library's curation. Then it falsely accused him of stealing a scroll—a treasure map drawn by Alexander the Great. Darwin was sure the ministry's corrupt officials took it for themselves because it had not yet shown up in the published catalog.

He looked down at his white knuckles, squeezing the sink. Then he let go, physically and mentally. *This is why I'm here.*

He inhaled and sighed. Amid the past year's heaviness, he also had many splendid memories of living at Siwa Oasis. He grinned, and smile lines replaced the frown. His green eyes sparkled in the glass.

He stood under the shower awhile before remembering that the temporary hot water tank did not last long. He quickly soaped up and rinsed off as the water turned cool, then toweled dry and was rubbing lotion on his arms when Eyrún knocked at the door.

"Darwin."

"Almost done. Tell Luka I'll be right there," he said.

"It's Emelio. He's here with a man from the Vatican."

"What? I'll be right out." He wrapped the towel around his waist and walked to the bedroom. Three minutes later, he was dressed and in the kitchen, where Eyrún was brewing coffee.

"Darwin," greeted his grandfather Emelio. "I've been trying to reach you for two days. Richard called, and then this man showed up. The Pope wants to see you."

"Darwin Lacroix?" asked a tall, middle-aged man standing beside Emelio. The contrast of his dark suit and tie against the casual mountain backdrop added tension to the unexpected visit.

"Yes," he said, shaking the man's hand.

"I am Adolfo de Mandato of the *Corpo della Gendarmeria dello Stato della Città del Vaticano*. The Pope requests that you visit him at your earliest convenience to discuss a private matter."

Darwin's eyes widened. He looked at Emelio, who shrugged.

"What's it about?" asked Eyrún.

"This is my wife, Eyrún," said Darwin. "You can share anything with her."

"Unfortunately, I don't know what His Holiness wishes to discuss," said Adolfo, "but I am under strict orders to accompany you to Vatican City as soon as possible."

"Is he under arrest?" asked Emelio.

"No. Nothing of the kind. I only understand that His Holiness wishes to keep the matter private, which is why they sent me to relay the invitation in person."

The coffee was ready, and Eyrún suggested taking their cups onto the patio to sit more informally. Adolfo commented on the spectacular view and, when everyone had settled in, added, "I understand that your family has made important discoveries."

While Emelio launched into a response, Darwin looked out over the gorge, knowing his grandfather could talk for hours about ancient Rome. Seven years earlier, Emelio showed Darwin an ancient box that had survived the eruption of Mt. Vesuvius in 79 CE. Inside were scrolls, written by a man named Agrippa, that described lava tubes used by the Roman military for secret troop movements and by Emperor Nero to hide gold.

Several generations of Lacroix men had fallen prey to searching for the Roman lava tubes, and Emelio had thrown away a stable academic career chasing phantom clues. Darwin's father had warned him not to get sucked in, but Darwin took the lure, pausing only to pursue a Ph.D. at the University of California.

Emelio had started on the minutiae of Roman military conquests in Gaul when Darwin saw Adolfo look at his watch and suppress a yawn. He interjected, "Adolfo, how did you know where to find us?"

"Your friend Father Ndembele told me," said Adolfo, jumping on the question.

Richard Ndembele was a personal assistant to a cardinal. They had met three years prior when Darwin broke into the crypt below a cathedral where Richard served as a priest. Rather than turn him in, Richard helped shape Darwin's moral compass—or, at least, helped him become more thoughtful about his ambitions. Their friendship had deepened, and Richard had officiated Darwin's and Eyrún's wedding in late August.

The conversation had shifted to the goings-on in Vatican City when Eyrún asked if Adolfo wanted more coffee. He used the opportunity to press them on a response about travel.

"We'll go," said Darwin. "But it's a long way back to town. And we need some time to pack a few things and make arrangements."

"That won't be necessary," Adolfo said. "I have chartered a helicopter service. It's on standby to take us to a private jet waiting in Ajaccio," said Adolfo.

2

Over the Tyrrhenian Sea

That afternoon, Darwin gazed out the window of the six-passenger jet at the whitecaps racing across the Tyrrhenian Sea thousands of meters below. He had heard tales of the rough waters and shoals between Corsica and the Italian peninsula. An oil painting in Emelio's house in Ajaccio depicted one of the Lacroix ships lost in this notorious section of the Mediterranean.

Earlier, while packing, he and Eyrún had speculated on the reason for the Pope's requested meeting. He had a suspicion but kept it to himself, not wanting to get his hopes up. Now, with Eyrún and Adolfo engaged in their own conversation, his thoughts drifted back to March, a month before the Notre-Dame fire, when he stood in the basement of the Vatican Apostolic Archive.

He had gone to Vatican City in search of a diary written by Hypatia of Alexandria. The Pope had granted him unique access to a secret vault in the Archive, where, two days previously, Darwin had located the diary. After scanning and deciphering it, he had replaced it in the drawer, next to its index card that read:

```
380 AD +/- 50, carbon-dated in 1983.
Language: Greek. Unknown cipher.
```

He was tempted to edit the last two words on the card when the man with him asked, "Don't you wonder what's in that Knights Templar package?"

Darwin stood after closing the low drawer and studied Franz Erhle, the head librarian of the Vatican Apostolic Archive. When they had first met a week earlier, Franz had seemed anything but curious. The man had even disparaged Darwin's idea that they would store a diary written by a pagan in the Archive.

"It couldn't hurt to look again," said Franz, raising shoulders and eyebrows.

Darwin, an archaeologist more akin to an entrepreneur than a curator of potsherds, knew the look: people who had no guts to do something but thought they could persuade him to do it. He sized up Franz, whose BMI heralded a cardiac event. *His last risk was probably choosing peach gelato over chocolate. But still...* Darwin glanced at the drawer in question and pulled its handle. Its half-meter-wide tray opened silently, and they both looked at a small paper-wrapped package.

```
Codex returned with the Papacy from Avignon.
Language: Old French. Found in a chest with
other documents marked Templar.
```

Darwin had picked it up on his first visit while searching for the Hypatia document, but the Pope had only given him permission to look for a document relating to the lost Library of Alexandria, so he had put it back in the drawer.

Now holding it again, he balanced it on his palm, gauging its weight. It was heavier than a modern book of similar size. "Must be vellum and bound in leather," he said, slipping into a university lecturer's voice. "The Papacy returned to Rome in the fourteenth century. The size shows it belonged to an individual; that is, it's not a volume that would rest on a lectern. But we'd have to read it to know if it's important or just a simple knight's diary."

His fingers ran across the paper. *It has to be important. Otherwise, why would it be here?* The Knights Templar's vast hoard had never been found, and he wondered what the wrapped codex might say about the Templars' last days. *Could this point to their lost treasure?*

His breathing stopped as he pulled at the string. A knock on the door caused him to jump and reflexively set the package back in the drawer. Someone outside called for Franz. Behind Darwin, Franz pushed the drawer closed and said, "It's time we should be going."

They exited and found a research assistant waiting by the door. "The person you are expecting has arrived," said the young man, dressed in a black suit. Franz and the assistant carried on a conversation as they walked out of the basement, but Darwin tuned them out, his mind still on the mysterious codex.

The Knights Templar never gave up their secrets. If the Church powers moved it here from Avignon, it's got to be suspicious. As he followed Franz through the subterranean stacks, a question arose.

Why have they not opened it before?

3

Vatican City

The day after their flight from Corsica, Darwin found himself in the Pope's antechamber, one year after his first visit. This time, he felt more at ease and held Eyrún's hand as they sat in a waiting area.

"You look lovely," he said.

"Thanks. Is it always this quiet here?" she said, smoothing the hem of her dress over her crossed legs.

Richard Ndembele, who had escorted them from the security entrance, was about to answer when the inner door opened. Miguel Suarez, the head of Vatican security, stepped out to welcome them.

"Nice to see you again, Miguel," said Darwin, introducing Eyrún.

"It's a pleasure to meet you, Madame Lacroix. Please, if you would all follow me," said Miguel, closing the door behind them. Darwin had met Miguel earlier when the Pope initially granted him access to the private collection in the Vatican.

Eyrún's heels clacked on the diagonally laid black-and-white marble tiles until they reached a carpeted area in the room's center. Six wooden armchairs were arranged around a low table with a coffee service.

A moment later, the Pope entered from a side door. His erect posture and full head of black hair displayed a vigor harkening back to his days on the Italian national rugby squad. "Darwin and Eyrún! I'm so pleased to see you again. And congratulations on your marriage. I understand it was quite a unique ceremony with Richard officiating the vows, but in a traditional Siwa Oasis setting."

"It was," said Darwin, taking his iPhone from his suit pocket and showing the Pontiff a wedding photo.

"My goodness. Eyrún, the dress is beautiful. Was the jewelry heavy?" he asked, referring to the head-sized silver disc around her neck and chains hanging from her braided hair.

She touched her chest as if remembering the disc's weight. "About a kilogram, but fortunately, I only wore it an hour."

The Pope asked everyone to sit, and they continued the polite conversation while an assistant served coffee. When everyone had their coffees, the server departed.

"Thank you for coming on brief notice," said the Pope when the side door had closed. "I need your help in a delicate matter and require your assurance that our discussion will not leave this room."

"You have my word," said Darwin.

"Mine too," said Eyrún.

"Good. You handled the situation competently with Hypatia's diary, but we needed to cover the formality. Have you told Eyrún about the special vault where you found the diary?" asked the Pope.

"Yes. We keep no secrets from each other," said Darwin.

"That's fine. I just needed to know how much ground to cover." The Pope nodded and sipped his coffee before asking, "Do you remember the other document you looked at?"

"Yes. It was hard to put down," Darwin answered, pulse racing and nearly levitating from the chair. "Do you want me to look into it?"

"In a word, yes. Someone removed it without my authorization," said the Pope.

"What?" Darwin sputtered through his coffee.

"Miguel, perhaps you can best explain."

"Certainly, Your Holiness." Miguel looked across at Darwin. "Sometime during the month after you deciphered the other codex, the head librarian, Franz Erhle, removed the Templar document."

"You said at the time that no document could leave the room," said Darwin, now on the edge of his seat.

"That's correct," said Miguel.

"But how—" Darwin burst out of the chair.

Richard leaned forward, both hands motioning him to sit. Eyrún reached for Darwin's hand.

The Pope took charge of the conversation. "As best we can tell from reviewing the video, Franz swapped the original codex with a fake the last time you went in with him. Do you remember Franz asking about the Templar document?"

"Yes. I thought about unwrapping it when someone knocked at the door," said Darwin.

"I would have been tempted to look myself," said the Pope, smiling.

"But I put it back."

"We know," said Miguel. "When Franz's assistant knocked on the door, one of my people also distracted me with a question, and, during that moment, I looked away and Franz made the switch."

Miguel produced a tablet and played a video. The overhead camera showed Darwin putting down the package and turning toward the door. As soon as his head turned, Franz took a package from a jacket pocket with one hand as he simultaneously lifted the Knights Templar package from the drawer with his other. They had to watch the video several times to catch it, since Darwin's body blocked most of Franz's movement.

"Why would he do that?" asked Darwin, sitting up straight.

"We've learned that Franz is sympathetic to an ultraconservative Catholic group," said Miguel. "One that actively seeks to remove His Holiness from office."

Merde. As much as Darwin liked this Pope, he could see how the constant barrage of malicious attacks would age even the most courageous leader. He had read rumors suggesting that the previous Pope had been corralled into resignation by insiders who did not support his reformation attempts.

4

That same afternoon, the Vatican Apostolic Archive head librarian, Franz Ehrle, left his office, explaining to his assistant that he was going out to get fresh air. He turned left out the building's side door and walked along the outer wall and border of the Earth's smallest country. Warm afternoon sun radiated off the wall as he followed the path into the extensive garden.

Franz did not enjoy the outdoors and flinched as tiny insects swarmed to investigate his cologne. He swatted at them and sped up, hoping to get away from the horde. A minute later, he had closed the gap on the purpose of his venture outside.

"You wished to see me, Your Grace," he said.

"Walk with me," said Cardinal John Keenan, a tall American. His red cassock billowed with his long strides.

Franz fell in beside him, beads of perspiration blossoming on his forehead as his shirt dampened in the unseasonable heat. *Why're Americans so obsessed with exercise?*

"I've always loved autumn," Keenan said. "The heat subsides, and you could smell the harvest coming in and the apple pies our mothers would bring to the church picnics… It was a simpler time."

Franz had first met the cardinal a decade earlier when Keenan had arrived from his native Alabama and joined the deeply conservative Catholic faction of which Franz was a part. By now, he knew that Keenan liked stage-setting, to have people yearn for better days gone by, whether or not true. Franz understood the power of nostalgia and had read about Keenan's rise in the church.

The only son of rural farmers, John Keenan was raised Catholic. His Irish father, having fled religious conflict in the north of Ireland, landed in a hotbed of civil rights. His mother, a Baptist, switched faiths and together they raised John in a God-centric hard-work ethic.

Keenan grew into a gifted athlete and leader, captaining both his high-school and university football teams. He accepted a junior executive position for the local Montgomery office of a national company, where he prospered. At twenty-seven, he took over the family farm when his father died of a heart attack. He expanded the farm but became deeply troubled by the late 1960s shift in society. This led to his election to the town council in 1969—to, as he said, "return a sense of decency to the community." But when a stoned-out-of-her-mind driver killed John's mother, he withdrew into his faith and eventually sought the priesthood.

He championed a conservative interpretation of Catholicism and had little patience for the continual broadening of church doctrine. The same work ethic he had brought to sports and farming in his early life, combined with the leadership of a large parish, had seen him rise to Bishop of the Ecclesiastical Province of Mobile when Vatican leaders recruited him. In his current role as Camerlengo of the Holy Roman Church, he administrated the global church properties and revenue.

Franz knew Keenan to be a savvy politician who was gathering the necessary power to enact a more conservative pivot in the church. He organized his thoughts, knowing that a question was coming. Yesterday, when Keenan had asked for an update, Franz had messaged that they were still looking for the clue's location. The Camerlengo responded with "two p.m.," meaning that Franz was to meet him here at two o'clock.

"What's taking so long?" asked Keenan.

"The location inside the Beziérs Cathedral is not clear. It's been extensively remodeled since the Templar clue was placed," said Franz.

"How're they solving it? I don't want another incident like Paris."

"That wasn't us. We just took advantage of the situation," said Franz, now sweating heavily. Despite the heat, a shiver ran through him as he remembered the cardinal shouting, "Tell me your idiots didn't burn down Notre-Dame!"

The idiots that Keenan referred to were members of Action Française, a political think tank that championed a return of the monarchy. Franz considered this a fantasy not worth listening to, but they were strong Catholics and were willing to do the dirty work. If they failed, Franz knew they would be dismissed as nut cases, and he could quickly distance himself from their lunatic fringe.

The cardinal stopped and, turning to face Franz, said, "I should hope not. His Holiness is planning another conference on diversity. I hear he's considering an announcement on women in the priesthood and allowing priests to marry. It's an abomination. We need those words of Christ to support us." He was referring to a papyrus mentioned in the Knights Templar codex.

"My librarians have found an old floor plan of the cathedral," said Franz, "and I sent two researchers, saying the Apostolic Archive is updating its records and checking on the condition of ancient texts."

"I don't care how. When will they find the next clue?"

"I can't say. You know the challenge of finding centuries-old documents."

Keenen strode, hands clasped behind his back, eyes elevated as if in thought. After a long minute, he asked, "They're sure it's Béziers?"

"Yes. Yes. Be patient, Your Grace. We'll find it."

The cardinal's mobile rang, and he withdrew it to look at the caller ID. "I need to take this. Leave me," he said, answering the call.

5

Following their meeting with the Pope, Darwin and Eyrún followed Miguel to his office for a deeper run-through on what Vatican security had learned about the theft. Darwin placed a water glass on the small conference table. Eyrún took out a small notebook. Miguel opened a folio and spread several documents across the table. To Darwin, it looked like the case files he had seen in detective shows, with photos paper-clipped to pages.

"Bear with me, as it's somewhat long," said Miguel, spinning around a page that listed a timeline. "On March twentieth, you and Franz went to the secret vault to return the Hypatia of Alexandria codex. Franz persuaded you to open the drawer with the Knights Templar codex and distracted all of us for a few moments while swapping it with a fake. After leaving the vault with you, Franz went directly to his office—where, we presume, he hid it.

"Two days later, you left for Alexandria, where I lost track of your project. Within days of your departure, Franz emailed the scans to a firm in Zurich to decipher the Knights Templar codex."

"I thought you didn't allow electronic transmission of sensitive documents," said Darwin. "You made me hand carry paper to the University of Newcastle to decipher Hypatia's codex.

"That's correct, but Franz worked this personally. My team first noticed it on June third, during a security audit. The firm flagged a large email attachment outside the Vatican Archives' information security policies. I opened it and was stunned to see a translation of the Knights Templar codex from the private collection."

Darwin sipped his water to mask impatience.

"I confronted Franz privately about the improper email attachment," said Miguel.

"I don't like that he used Darwin to steal it," said Eyrún.

"Me, either. When I pressed Franz about it, he stood looking out his office window where I couldn't see his face, but I had the feeling he was trying to hide a lie. At that point, it was a matter of disciplinary action and out of my hands."

"I thought the Pope had to grant access to the secret vault?" asked Eyrún.

"Technically yes," said Miguel, "but Franz is the head librarian and has broad access and control over the Archive. I wrote a security briefing of the incident for His Holiness." He slid pages toward Darwin and Eyrún. They read the highlighted paragraph in a longer document and a separate double-sided incident report. Darwin looked up, and Miguel continued.

"The Papal office never commented on the report, and I forgot about it."

"What's in the codex?" Darwin shifted to the very edge of his chair as if ready to jump over the table to the folder on the seat next to Miguel.

"I was getting to it," said Miguel, moving the folder onto the table but leaving a hand on top of it. "The codex is written by the last Grand Master of the Knights Templar during his imprisonment after the thirteen-oh-seven arrest. Most of it is history, but the deciphered section mentions the location of what the Grand Master calls the Templars reserve bank."

"Where?" asked Darwin, like a boy just told his father had brought home a puppy.

6

Rome

Late that afternoon, Darwin and Eyrún sat on their suite's outdoor patio and reread the Vatican documents. Miguel instructed them to review the codex, and he would answer their questions when they met on Tuesday. The next day, Sunday, the Vatican offices closed for its holy day of the week, and Miguel took Mondays off.

A plate of olives, meats, and cheeses lay half-eaten on the sun-streaked glass tabletop. Darwin refilled their glasses with a robust Tuscan red. Aromatic smoke from a nearby pizza oven mixed with the fragrant rosemary hedge that surrounded the terrace. He sipped the wine and reread the document a third time.

The translation that follows is from a codex assumed written by Jacques de Molay. He does not name himself but makes claims as a Grand Master of the Knights Templar and refers to his second in command, Geoffroi de Charny. Both men faced execution by the French monarchy in AD 1314.

The codex was returned to the Vatican from Avignon, France, in or about AD 1387 following the Papacy's move back to Vatican City. It was in a chest with other documents marked "Templar."

We speculate the ciphered pages are the core purpose of this codex. Most of the document describes the order's operational details before highlighting an encoded passage that makes up the last pages of the codex.

Note: The deciphering required both identifying the cipher keyword and the language. The Vatican team collaborated with the Google Brain team, an artificial intelligence and machine learning project. By instructing the algorithms to use a broad collection of Knights Templar documents as a reference, the algorithm arrived on the keyword YESHUA and the LATIN language to produce the following text:

(BEGIN TRANSLATION)

It is clear what I must do now that Pope Clement has disbanded our Holy Order. What I write is known only to myself and Geoffroi de Charny. When one of us dies, the survivor must share the knowledge with another. This is how it has been for two hundred years.

But, we are sentenced to die together by the hand of Philip, the corrupt King of France, and have no one we trust to whom we can pass the knowledge. May God help you find the key to read what follows.

(BEGIN DECIPHERED SECTION)

You are now the Grand Master of the Poor Fellow-Soldiers of Christ and the Temple of Solomon. Discharge your duties with care. Honor the sacrifices of the Brothers who have gone before you or answer to God for your sins.

Our predecessors protected pilgrims traveling to the Holy Land, but we became greedy over the centuries, building for our own glory. Popes and Kings fought to seize our riches and power. This is not the world our Saviour wanted for us. We cannot hide our lands, but there is other treasure.

The Knights Templar operated a Reserve Bank to support pilgrims traveling to the Holy Land. It contains the gold backing the transfers. Roger I of Trencavel discovered a cave network. He feared our order could suffer the same persecution as the Cathars and proposed we move our Reserve Bank into the caves.

Roger developed a strict hierarchy of secrecy and access to the entrances. Only Geoffroi and I know the location of the cave. We have no use now for this Earthly fortune, but neither do we wish it used to decorate the walls of Papal palaces or the ghastly dwellings of Kings.

However, the Reserve holds a more valuable treasure than gold.

In the year before His death, Jesus of Nazareth chronicled what He wanted for us. We found His Gospel in Joseph of Arimathea's crypt deep beneath the Temple of Solomon. A sealed clay jar lay between His bones. It contained a papyrus written by our Lord in the language of the Jews.

We encased the papyrus in lead and stored it in a special vault within the Reserve Bank. This is the True treasure.

I care not about the gold and suggest you disperse it in a manner that benefits His kingdom on Earth. Would that we could distribute it to the poor... But we must answer to our fate.

Three steps lead to the Reserve Bank, each one reveals the next.

First, go to Notre-Dame de Paris and stand in the transept beneath the boss. Traverse the black tiles northward until directly under the north transept vault.

Step two lies beneath your feet.

When you align the clues, you will find the cave.

May God guide you.

(END DECIPHERED SECTION AND TRANSLATION)

D arwin set down the pages and swirled his wine before sipping. He had filled the page margins with questions, but mostly about Notre-Dame. Finding anything in the floor depended on its condition after the fire. The biggest problem was likely the collapsed transept vault.

"What's a boss?" asked Eyrún, looking up from the document. She read the pages as he put them down.

"The jerk who writes your review," he said, turning around. She frowned, and he added, "It's the stone that joins the ribs in a vaulted ceiling, like a keystone in an arch.

"Isn't that the part that fell?"

"Yes."

"I watched it on my mobile. It was so sad." She paused, as if reliving the moment, then said, "Tell me again about the Templars. How does the Papacy in France fit in?" she asked.

Darwin ran through a brief history of the order's rise in Jerusalem following the First Crusade. "As the Saracens repelled the Europeans from the Middle East, the Templars retreated to southern France, where they administered their massive holdings acquired during the Crusades. At the same time, the catholic church was feuding with the French kings, saying it had dominion over all earthly realms, including kings themselves.

"Philip the fourth said, 'Hell, no' and used military power to move the Papacy to Avignon. He then had his puppet pope disband the Templars, so he could seize their wealth. But, he never found it and died a few years later.

"After that, the Templar treasure was forgotten. Between the Hundred Years' War with England and the Black Death, the French population was decimated. There's a lot more detail, but that's the basic story," he finished.

Eyrún's mobile rang. "It's Stevie!" She walked to the terrace railing to talk with her best friend. Darwin refocused on the document and became immersed in its mystery as Eyrún's voice lilted in the background. *The starting point's Notre-Dame. "Beneath your feet" has to mean under the floor. And, with all the construction, now's the best time to look for something.*

"How are you? Where are you?" asked Eyrún. She had been friends with Stevie Leroy for years, ever since they met while on a two-week exploration under an Iceland glacier. They were the only two women on the expedition, which surprised neither of them, since both followed paths in male-dominated professions. Stevie's vocation as a cave biologist took her all over the world, and she regularly went underground and out of touch, so when she called, Eyrún answered, knowing it might be weeks or months before her next contact.

This time, Stevie happened to be calling from her house in Orange, near the Chauvet Cave. As they caught up on news, including Stevie's American boyfriend Zac coming to visit, Eyrún's thoughts drifted. *What're we doing in Rome? I'm supposed to be off-the-grid, remodeling my house in Corsica. Hiking and reading.* While she appreciated the Vatican's trust in her husband, they had been married for less than three months, and she was looking forward to the chance to relax. *He's frustrating as hell when he gets on a task.*

"What? Oh, sorry, Stevie—I got distracted. No, we're back in Rome."

Darwin jumped up and joined her at the railing. "Can I talk to her?"

She glowered at him, and he mouthed, "Sorry."

"Hang on, Stevie, I'm putting you on speaker." She placed her mobile on the railing.

"Hi, Stevie," said Darwin.

"What's so important that you butted into our call?" Stevie asked.

"How close is your friend Aya to the restoration of Notre-Dame?" he asked.

"*Je ne sais pas,*" she said. "Last I talked to her, they were still cataloging all the pieces. There are big tents in the forecourt. Why?"

Darwin explained what the Pope had asked of them and the need for secrecy. Both he and Eyrún trusted Stevie with their lives.

"Do you think we could meet with Aya?"

"*Mais oui!* We haven't seen you since Egypt. When will you come?"

"Maybe Wednesday? We have to meet someone on Tuesday," said Darwin.

"*Très bien.* I'll let you know Aya's schedule," said Stevie.

7

Barcelona, Catalonia, Spain

J acques Bourbon watched two women stroll by his café table on Playa de la Barceloneta. The early October sun remained strong enough to warm his skin, but a cool breeze fluttered the women's dresses and caused one to grab hold of her hat. He smiled at them, but each was deeply engrossed in her mobile.

His hand moved toward his own resting on the table but was diverted as the waiter delivered another plate of boquerones. There was something about the fresh white anchovies that never tasted the same outside of Barcelona. He had tried them in Paris and in the French Riviera cities, but they were not as satisfying.

The mobile vibrated and he looked at a new message from Franz:

Need to talk. Call me.

I'll bet you do. Jacques refocused on the boquerones, gently bringing one to his mouth and leaning it in to prevent olive oil from dripping on his shorts. A sea wave of flavor broke on his tongue, and as he bit down, the vinegar tickled his palate. He chewed the soft flesh several times before washing it down with a mouthful of rosé from the Codorníu Winery. Local to the Catalan province, its floral blend was a worthy chaser.

His mobile vibrated from an incoming call. It was Franz Ehrle. He reached for it and stopped, reminding himself that he had walked away from the project. He turned toward the beach and unconsciously rubbed the scar on his forehead, a burn where he was struck by molten lead that had poured through Notre-Dame's burning ceiling.

The stakes had become too high. What started as a quest to find Templars' gold had led to a near-death experience followed by a fruit-less search for the second clue. Worse, the fireman who saw him enter the burning Notre-Dame had recognized him two weeks prior in Paris. Jacques was sure he had seen the man take his picture. He left France the next day and had been in Barcelona ever since.

Unfortunately, his welcome at a friend's apartment was running out, as was his cash. If Europol was looking for him, pulling money from a Spanish ATM would land him back on their grid. The brightly painted table vibrated again. He picked up the mobile this time.

"Hola."

"Jacques? Where are you?" asked Franz. His voice was hushed as if not wanting to be overheard.

"On holiday."

"We need you back in Béziers."

"You don't tell me what to do, Franz," said Jacques.

"But we found the location." Franz explained that his researchers pored through the cathedral's records and found construction notes documenting changes to the crypt.

"It can wait."

"No, it can't. Someone else knows about the Knights Templar codex."

"But they won't know about Béziers. We got the only clue from Notre-Dame."

"Don't be so sure. Vatican security discovered someone deciphered the codex. Finding it has become a top priority."

"A priority for whom?" asked Jacques.

"Someone higher up. That's all I can say," said Franz.

Jacques waited for Franz to continue. *If someone higher up's involved, this must be worth a lot more.*

"Jacques?" Did I lose you?" asked Franz.

"No. I'm here. Listen, this is costing me a small fortune to travel between Paris and Béziers, and I'm no closer to this treasure you keep alluding to."

"I can transfer another ten thousand euros to your account."

"Make it a hundred. If it's important to 'someone higher up,' then it won't be a problem. Text me when you've made the transfer. Bye, Franz." Jacques ended the call, switched the phone to do-not-disturb, and refocused on his meal. The waiter had just delivered the monkfish.

8

Later, Jacques went to a movie to kill time. It was an action flick, more nonstop exploding car chase than plot- or character-driven. Predictable, but a decent distraction. In one scene, the protagonist ran into a burning building. Jacques shuddered.

Early in the year, he had been so desperate for money that he considered selling family heirlooms. He was then introduced to Franz, who claimed to know of a treasure and needed the right scholar to find it. Jacques thought him crazy, since people had hunted Templar treasure for centuries—until a courier delivered a plain envelope.

It contained instructions to a floor tile in Notre-Dame's north transept; he was curious. Jacques visited multiple times, but with crowds always present he could not open it. The instructions also detailed a way out through a tomb and secret tunnel. Jacques worked out the reverse directions and, entering through a Metro tunnel, found an iron door leading under the Seine.

The door was braced shut from the cathedral side, but it aligned with Notre-Dame as best he could tell. For days, he wandered the cathedral's surrounding streets pondering how to get in; once he hid after closing, but the guards ushered him out.

Three days later, the fire had propelled him to act. Sheer terror seized him after running into the conflagration. Death loomed as he pressed against a column, the fire roaring like an underworld demon. But the pompier's water cannon kept the interior flames at bay and cooled the air enough to breathe. He loosened his grip on the warm stone and moved along the north wall.

The blaze was confined to the roof and a pile in the transept. Something seared his forehead. Sweeping it away, he stepped back from the freshly splattered lead. No blood on his hand. He kept going and counted the tiles from the instructions. Digging a hammer out of his coat, he smashed the correct tile and lifted out a small lead tube. He felt around, confirmed there was nothing else in the hole, and tossed the wood-handled hammer into the blaze.

A larger stream of lead began pouring onto the floor, and he moved farther into the dark, smoky structure. The water cannon lights slashed around the interior columns and glowed like street lamps in a deep fog. He coughed. Sucked in a more massive breath and coughed again. Pulling up his scarf, he found his eyes flooded as he gasped through the wool. A long moment later, dizziness subsided, and his breathing stabilized.

He looked at the Porte Rouge, the fastest way out. His pulse raced as he took a step. *No!* He froze—*the police. Get to the tomb. It's right there.*

He willed himself to the tomb five meters distant and felt around its carved edifice. Following the instructions, he pushed against the foot end. He slipped on the ash-covered marble and wiped the area clean for traction. He shoved again. Three tries later, it moved enough for him to peer in. Steps receding in his light beam confirmed a way out.

Jacques pushed once more, and the marble rotated. He stepped into the tomb and moved down the stairs under the marble. Looking at it from the underside, he saw large iron handles. Bracing himself on a step, he pushed up and sideways, moving it back into place.

Following the tunnel to the left, he went downstairs and below the river level, where he found the door. It was braced shut on this side with two iron bars. He tried to lift one, but it was frozen in place by rust. He pulled up a granite block from the stairs and used it to pound the bars free of the brackets. He moved quickly through the door and, would have been out to street level within twenty minutes, but he made a wrong turn and was lost three hours before finding a marker pointing to a Metro tunnel.

Jacques's attention now returned to the movie, where the protagonist and leading lady were engaged in a passionate tangle following a gun battle. The memory of the fire had left him dry-mouthed, and he sipped his beer.

An hour later, Jacques emerged from the theater and checked his mobile. His stomach dropped as he saw a red-dot alert on his banking app. They had been after him about a delinquent loan. He checked a message from Franz first.

Agreed. Half now. Half when you recover clue.

He whistled. He would have done it for ten thousand. Asking for a hundred was part negotiation, but more to learn how important this was to the Vatican. *That was fast. Who's the higher up? The Pope? No, he wouldn't dirty his hands in this.*

He opened the app and confirmed that €50,000 had been deposited. *Christ, they must really believe in this Templars' story. How much farther would they go?*

He looked around at a sudden sense of being watched, realizing that people had been killed for less money. Up to now, he had only considered the upside of finding a treasure.

What if I find it, and they also don't want anyone to know? Ever!

He started walking toward his friend's apartment, glancing over his shoulder before reading the other messages from Franz:

Get to Béziers ASAP. Someone will call you with new instructions
for the tomb. We have a competitor. Get there before they do.

Jacques: On way to Béziers

His pace quickened as he skirted the Plaça de Catalunya and crossed the Gran Via. He fantasized about finding the treasure as he navigated the octagonal intersections in L'Eixample neighborhood.

To hell with any Jesus papyrus. Half the scriptures are riddles with contradictions. More words to fight about. But gold...

Gold would give him power. Donations to the party would get him recognition. He envisioned handing checks to the director of the Rassemblement National at a fundraiser and him weighing in on party decisions.

He turned into a local bar and saw his friend drinking with neighbors.

"Jacques," he yelled. "Join us."

Jacques slid into a chair and ordered a round for everyone.

9

A little before ten the next morning, Jacques stepped out of a taxi and entered the flow of people into the Barcelona-Sants train station. *"Con permiso,"* he said, pressing the shoulder of a man who had abruptly stopped to read the train status board.

He had just enough time to get a coffee and, seeing the independence pin on the barista's apron, ordered in Catalan. *"Un tallat si us plau,* Espresso with milk, please." He slid a ten-euro note across the counter in a gesture of solidarity to help shrug off the yoke of Spanish domination.

"Gràcies," said the young woman, who hurried to get his order.

He grabbed the paper cup as soon as it hit the counter and hurried to track seven. He sipped the beverage on the escalator down to track level and walked toward the far end of the platform where a conductor confirmed his first-class ticket. Mounting the steps, he navigated the aisle to his single seat on the left as the brakes hissed, and the carriage jerked into motion.

He dropped into the seat and cradled his pack like a pillow. Last night had led to one too many bottles of wine. Fortunately, the milk was settling his sour stomach and the caffeine smoothing the sharp edges in his brain—until a moment later, when bright sun flashed in as the train broke free of the platform. He grunted, eyes squeezed shut. As the train gathered momentum, he shifted sideways, and the rhythmic rocking lulled him into a lucid dream from the previous summer.

He had joined a rally of more than a hundred people on Pont Neuf in Paris to celebrate the Duke of Anjou's returning as the French king Louis XX. Jacques, a Bourbon whose own heritage linked to the Sun King, Louis XVI, supported a return to a constitutional monarchy. He had no desire to see the abusive feudalism of the ancien régime. Still, he argued that the French Republic's current state was so fractured that the president was no longer elected by a majority, especially given the disenfranchised who no longer voted.

He had published an essay for the right-wing Rassemblement National party before the rally, calling for the French monarchy's reestablishment to reunite the country's divisions. Few took it seriously, but he knew of polls that showed more than ten percent of the population supported the idea. In an interview before his election, even the current president had said that French politics was missing the figure of a monarch. Jacques felt the idea was ripe and needed the right kind of promotion.

In his dream, he found the Templars' bank. The accrued wealth allowed him to build a platform where he advocated for a Sixth Republic: a clean break with the corrupt European Union, a more powerful France to lead the European continent and rival the United States and China. Let Germany deal with the beggar states. England had already retreated behind its moat.

He awakened at the sound of glass rattling in a cart that had bumped his seat. "*Buenos días,*" said an attendant, laying a white cloth on Jacques's table, followed by a tray with a tostada with crushed tomatoes and Iberian ham, and an almond croissant.

"*Gracias,*" he said as she moved up the aisle.

10

Vatican City

Darwin awoke on Tuesday morning to find Rome under thick rain clouds. The dim light had confused the street lamps into switching on. After breakfast, he and Eyrún caught a taxi to Vatican City, where they had an appointment with Miguel at half-past ten. His assistant brought them cups of espresso. They sat at a round work table in Miguel's office, where he opened a manila folder and turned its top sheet toward them.

"This is Jacques Bourbon, a French national, the man who ran into Notre-Dame," said Miguel.

Merde! Darwin studied the photo of a blond-haired man and passed it to Eyrún.

"On September eleventh, I got a regular weekly report from Europol. It's part of my review of potential threats and criminal activity that might affect Vatican City or its properties. The report had a photo of a man the French police want to question regarding events on the night of the Notre-Dame fire.

"On a hunch, I called my contacts in Paris and learned several pompiers reported a man running into the cathedral the night of the fire. But no one saw him leave and assumed he perished in the blaze.

"Then, one of the pompiers saw Jacques in Paris and took the photo you're holding. I went to Paris to interview the fireman. He had thought it a suicide event until he saw the man lift an object from the floor, then run deeper into the building."

Miguel described being escorted into the burned cathedral and finding a broken tile in the north transept, but the hole had been filled with ash. The sheer volume of water used to extinguish the fire obscured any evidence. Unfortunately, they would not allow exploration of the hole beyond visible inspection, since the French state owned the cathedral and tightly controlled its restoration.

"Where is Jacques now?" asked Darwin.

"He vanished again."

Darwin sat back and crossed his arms while looking up at the ceiling. Faint traffic noises came from the street below Miguel's office.

"I'm confused. Yesterday you told us Franz stole the codex. Is there a linkage between this guy, Jacques, and Franz?" asked Eyrún.

"Right." Darwin sat up and scanned through the papers on the table. "You said Franz took the codex that mentions the clue in Notre-Dame. How did Jacques learn about it?"

"We suspect Franz is working with Jacques but can't prove it," said Miguel. "I know from the French police that Jacques Bourbon's a devout Catholic and a member of a group that wants to restore the French monarchy. I mentioned yesterday that Franz belongs to an ultraconservative Catholic movement. Both seek a return to a more authoritarian government and church that adheres to strict doctrine. Jacques is building a platform inside the French right-wing National Rally party. Franz supports ultraconservative groups in various countries, including the US and France. Overall, the global movement is gaining power."

"They sound like nutcases," said Eyrún.

"On the contrary. The groups are well-formed and with strong, albeit still minority, support," said Miguel.

"Why do you want us? It sounds like you need a detective," said Darwin, standing and walking to the window. The rain had stopped, but a wind had picked up, and the pedestrians gathered their coats against the damp chill.

"You have proven, unique skills at finding lost ancient treasures," said Miguel.

"You could shadow Jacques and take the treasure when he finds it," Eyrún offered.

Darwin turned back to face Miguel. "Right, why the urgency? You flew us here in a hurry."

"Eyrún, I'll address your comment in a moment. Darwin, the urgency is the late-stage planning of a series of conferences to make the church more open and inclusive. His Holiness is the sponsor, but some cardinals and bishops in the US, France, and Brazil vehemently oppose the idea. They talk about it as even more radical than the liturgical reforms of the Second Vatican Council.

Miguel continued, "The ultraconservatives want a return to more traditional positions: no divorce, no support for women in the priesthood, excommunication of homosexuals, and so on. They fear what Christ might have written. Remember, in the Gospels, Jesus accepted everyone and forgave sinners. If words in Christ's own hand were to confirm this, then the conservative positions would fall apart. The Pope wants the church to continue its current path of reconciliation and acceptance."

"We understand the church's internal strife and appreciate that you admire our skills," said Eyrún, "but others have the same skills. As I suggested, why not follow Jacques?"

Miguel made eye contact with each of them before answering. "His Holiness thinks there are insiders, much higher up in the church hierarchy, who are working with Franz. He needs this matter handled with discretion and has great faith in your principles and abilities."

Darwin gazed at a painting behind Miguel that depicted a scene in Christ's ministry. *My principles? How does the Pope know my principles?* Darwin had been raised Catholic, and France remained majority Christian and Catholic, but he had never thought about his principles. He looked at Eyrún, who shrugged as if to say this was his call.

He refocused on Miguel. "Let's say we accept. The codex mentions the clue in Notre-Dame, but Jacques took it, and he's missing. Where would we start?"

"The French police say Jacques has an alibi for the night of the fire, but they aren't convinced. They've been tracking his mobile and told me he's been to Béziers four times since the fire," said Miguel.

"Maybe he has friends there," said Eyrún.

"I don't think so," said Miguel. "While the French won't share all their data, I started surveillance on Franz's mobile. Jacques's number appears eighty-seven times beginning in March. Also, Telecom Italia alerts me about any traffic between these numbers. Let me show you."

He swiped to a document on his mobile and scrolled to the latest entry. He went rigid.

"Shit! We need to move now!" He showed them the last message from Franz to Jacques yesterday:

Found it. Get to the cathedral. Someone will call you.

11

Béziers, France

J acques stood mid-courtyard looking up at the western frontispiece of the Cathédrale Saint-Nazaire et Saint-Celse in Béziers. One of his hands soothed his neck from the heat of the late-afternoon sun as the other pressed the mobile tightly to his ear, listening to a Vatican librarian's instructions. A breeze swept the courtyard from the bluff overlooking the river Orb behind him. The waterway elbowed through Béziers on its way to the Mediterranean Sea, a mere ten kilometers distant.

"*Oui, oui,* I know the door. Just tell me which crypt," he said. He squinted at the front arches with carvings of the usual saints and, above them, a round stained-glass window in the thirteenth-century style of Notre-Dame de Paris. Towers rose on either side of the window, but the church-like appearance ended there, for a parapet capped the walls, making it a rampart where defenders could protect themselves.

This was Cathar country, a gnostic version of Christianity that had thrived for centuries until one Pope called for a campaign against its believers. The Albigensian Crusade, as it was known, began in Béziers.

Across town, the crusaders burned the church of Saint Mary Magdalene, massacring thousands of men, women, and children who sought sanctuary inside. The crusaders also burned Cathédrale Saint-Nazaire, and Jacques imagined cries of "never again" as the locals restored it to fortress conditions.

When the librarian had finished relaying the directions, Jacques pushed through the left of the twin front doors, its hinges groaning against the weight of thick oak. Sounds fell away as the door thumped softly behind him. His eyes adjusted to the dim light streaming in through tall windows in the apse. Its ten-ribbed arches supported colored glass panels.

He moved toward a devotional stand, dropped a one-euro coin in the slot, then removed a small candle and lit it. He knelt in prayer, asking for guidance on his quest. This was his fifth trip to the cathedral, and he had low expectations of a different outcome.

His mobile vibrated in his pocket and he read Franz's message:

Did you find it?

No, idiot. I just got here. Jacques slipped the device back into his pocket. A scuff of wood on stone alerted him to the only other worshiper, an elderly woman, balancing against a chair as she departed. She ducked under the velvet drape that hung over the side entrance, and silence returned in the cool stone building.

He waited a full minute while watching dust particles play in the light, then moved toward a doorway beside the pulpit. He pretended to read a small sign before looking around the church to confirm he was still alone. He stepped through the door and walked down the crypt stairs.

12

Eyrún drove their rental car out of the lot at the Béziers Cap d'Agde airport as Darwin gave directions. The tires squealed on the tight arc of the airport exit road as she accelerated toward Béziers. Darwin grabbed the handhold with his right hand and held his iPhone in the other.

"Go right on to D612," he said. "From there, it's a straight shot to the cathedral. About… fourteen kilometers. Light traffic."

Eyrún made the turn but pulled in behind a caravan. "Shit, we'll never make…" She moved across the center line to get a view down the road.

"There's a passing lane one kilometer ahead," said Darwin.

An hour earlier, a mid-flight message from Miguel via the jet's Wi-Fi had increased the urgency of their arrival at the cathedral.

Intercepted another text from Franz. He told Jacques to be in front of the cathedral at 4pm

Darwin estimated they would reach the cathedral a few minutes before five o'clock. Eyrún reached the passing lane, and they rocketed around the caravan.

"Where did you learn to drive like this?" he asked.

"Rally driver. College. Got real fun in the winter months. Dark and slippery."

Merde. What else don't I know about her? They had been married two months after living together a year and a half. She swept back a lock of hair and downshifted to pass another car. Scanning the road, she smiled like a kid just let out on recess.

"Roundabout," she said.

"Take the second exit—612B toward Narbonne. Aim for the Carrefour market," he said.

Horns flared as she passed a car on the left, then swept right to make the turn by the big box store. A few minutes later, they reached the older main section of Béziers, and Darwin directed her through its narrow streets. Although it was mostly a straight route, she had to navigate the traffic furniture.

"I hate those things," said Eyrún, steering hard around a fountain in the intersection of Avenues Gambetta and Maréchal Joffre. Fifty meters later, she yelled, "Darwin!" as the road became one-way traffic coming at them.

"Left. Left. Go left there." He pointed, almost poking her in the nose. The road narrowed after turning. "Go right at the restaurant."

Eyrún nudged the wheel, and their tiny car shot up Rue des Docteurs Bourguet, built when donkey carts were the largest rolling stock. Darwin squeezed his knees together as they passed two couples pressed flat against the buildings.

"Look out." She stomped on the brakes to avoid kids playing football. She sped away as one kid thumped the ball off their side window and yelled. "What did he say?" she asked.

"Nice lady driver."

"Right! How close are we?"

"Less than a kilometer. Stay on this road."

"Whoo. I forgot how much I love this," she said, slamming into first and diving into a tight corner.

Darwin braced against the dashboard and twisted to see a seam of blue sky three stories above. The deep shadows made it feel like twilight, but sunset was still hours away.

Suddenly, the road opened. Cars parked on a diagonal lined the edge of a plaza where dozens of people enjoyed late afternoon drinks. Large trees shaded the area. A massive gothic structure emerged as they drew level with the crowd.

"Go right. Follow the building. The entrance is ahead," he said.

Eyrún swept around the plaza, then left along the cathedral's side.

"Park there." Darwin pointed to a chained-off pathway near a row of cars. Eyrún stopped behind the last car—not a legal space, but enough room for people to access the path. He swung the door open and jumped out as Eyrún stopped the vehicle.

"Which way?" she asked, falling in next to him.

"This way." Darwin jumped over the slumped chain, Eyrún following him, and they ran beside the stone structure onto the promenade in front of the cathedral.

"It's beautiful," said Eyrún as their view spread out above the river, some twenty meters below. Beyond its far bank, lush hills, punctuated only by terra-cotta roofs, rolled toward the distant horizon. She followed the pull of his hand into the cathedral's darkness. Bells tolled as they crossed its threshold.

"*Merde.*" Darwin's watch read five o'clock. "Look around. Does anyone seem suspicious?"

A lone worshipper knelt at a shrine opposite them.

"What are we looking for?" she whispered.

"There. C'mon." He walked toward the pulpit, moving up the left aisle and crossing the transept to a heavy door set beside the pulpit.

"This goes to the crypt," he said.

Eyrún pressed the lever atop a handle but met resistance from a deadbolt. "It's locked."

Darwin removed a small pouch from his pocket and withdrew two tools. He inserted them in the lock and, in less than a minute, opened the bolt.

"Where did you learn that?" she asked.

"Here and there."

She stared at him.

"What? You're a rally driver, and I'm a closet cat burglar. Let's go." He shouldered the door open and closed it behind them. He unclipped a chain across the downward steps and led them below, their shoes scuffing against the smooth stone.

"Creepy. Do you think he's here?" she asked.

"It's possible. Be on guard."

Less than twenty steps and one revolution, they reached the bottom. An iron gate filled an arch leading to a space about half the size of the choir space above them. Eyrún blocked a sneeze.

"Bless you," said Darwin. He beamed the iPhone's light at the tombs.

"Look," said Eyrún, pushing around him. "One's been opened."

Dirt spread on the floor below one tombstone that stuck out two centimeters on one side as if someone had not been able to push it back in. Darwin held the light to the engraving on its face.

ROGER I TRENCAVEL

AD 1099–1150

"*Merde*," said Darwin, running his fingers over a carving of two knights on a single horse. "It's Templar."

"Open it," she said.

He handed her the iPhone. "Hold this."

He stood to the side and grasped the edge of the tombstone, sweeping grit away with one foot and bracing himself to pull the stone.

"*Arrêtez!*" commanded a voice behind them.

13

F ive minutes earlier, Jacques had stepped out the cathedral side
door, dropping the crypt key in a planter, as a white Renault tore
around the corner and parked by the chained-off promenade. A couple
ran from the car along the cobblestone walkway toward the front
entrance. Jacques turned toward the plaza and walked to the hotel,
where he had a room for the night. He messaged Franz:

Got it, was in the eye socket, disgusting

Franz: what's it say

Jacques: not opened yet, too fragile, will do in Paris

Franz: fragile?

Jacques: best to open with the proper tools and setting

Franz: fine, when do you reach Paris?

Jacques clicked the mobile's side button, darkening its screen. *What a pain in the ass,* he thought while pocketing the mobile in the rear of his jeans. He then slipped the hand into his jacket pocket and grasped the cold tube. The lead cylinder warmed as his fingers probed its shape. A block later, as he walked toward central Beziers, an idea formed. *If the Vatican codex is correct, then this tube will tell the exact location of the Knights Templar's bank. Then I no longer need that sniveling idiot.*

He reached back for the mobile and switched it off, then stopped at an intersection where he unshouldered the pack and rested it atop a pillar. He swapped his mobile with a prepaid model he had purchased last week in a Paris suburb, then re-shouldered his pack. He powered-on the disposable as began walking.

Off-the-grid. Goddamn nanny state. Return France to the French, and we won't need to track anyone. Send the immigrant terrorists back to their own countries.

14

D arwin and Eyrún turned to face a bright beam of light.

"*Que faites vous ici?* What are you doing here?" said a priest, emerging from behind a beefy gendarme holding the light.

"Step away from the tomb," said the gendarme.

"It was like this when we arrived," said Darwin, shading his eyes.

"Someone called thirty minutes ago about a robbery in the crypt," said the gendarme.

"We can explain," said Darwin.

"Step away now!" commanded the gendarme.

They did, then followed the priest up the crypt stairs as the cop instructed.

"Where's the key," asked the priest, pointing to an empty hook next to the door at the top of the stairs. "We lock the crypt at night." He looked about the floor for a few seconds, then passed through the door. Darwin and Eyrún followed the priest to his office and took the chairs where he directed them to sit. The gendarme moved his imposing frame across the closed door. Southern France was rugby country, and Darwin imagined the fellow locking heads in a weekend scrum.

"Explain yourselves," said the priest.

Darwin moved in his chair so he could see both the priest and the

51

cop. "We're investigating a missing document from the Vatican Archive. We flew from Rome today and, during our flight, learned that someone would try to steal a relic at about four o'clock. But we landed too late. As you saw, the tomb of Roger of Trencavel has been opened."

"And how do we know you did not open it?" asked the gendarme.

"You saw me pulling on it when you got to the crypt. If I had opened it, I would have been pushing it closed."

"Humph," the gendarme said, shrugging.

This isn't going well, thought Darwin. *From the gendarme's perspective, we look guilty as hell: speeding, dangerous driving, and breaking into a crypt.* He was brainstorming what to say next when Eyrún turned toward the priest.

"Did someone from Vatican security call you recently?"

"Why do you ask that?" The priest crossed his arms and tilted his head.

"Two researchers from the Vatican Apostolic Archive visited your cathedral and claimed to be auditing historical church documents. As part of the investigation into the missing document my husband mentioned, a Vatican security officer called to ask about the researchers. You mentioned it was odd that the researchers spent so much time examining the crypts." She watched the priest fold his arms and furrow his eyebrows. She persisted, "Check the airport records. We just arrived on a private jet from Vatican City. The security officer who called you must have left a number. Please call him."

The priest translated for the gendarme and went to his desk, where he scanned the papers and picked up a small pad. He tapped the numbers into his mobile and waited.

"Allô, this is Father Lampard from the Cathédrale Saint-Nazaire et Saint-Celse in Béziers. We spoke the week before last."

The stout stone walls of the office rendered the office impervious to outside sounds. Darwin could hear the gendarme's heavy breathing and a tinny voice through the mobile held at Father Lampard's ear. The two callers exchanged pleasantries before Lampard said, "I have two people here who broke into our crypt just now and who claim to know about our conversation last week."

He listened, then added, "Yes, but how do I know you are not working with them?"

Father Lampard listened a long moment and went to a shelf where he removed the black covered book, then said, "Okay, I have it." He ended the call, paged through the book, and, holding a finger over a spot, lifted the handset from a desk phone and entered a number. He pushed a button that activated the speakerphone.

The phone was answered on the second ring. "*Pronto.* This is Miguel Suarez, director of Vatican Security."

"Director Suarez, it's Father Pascal Lampard; we were just speaking."

"Yes, and thank you, Father Lampard, for trusting the process. I understand you have two people sitting in your office caught breaking into your crypt."

"Yes."

"Darwin Lacroix and Eyrún Stephansdottir are working as contract agents with Vatican security to recover stolen relics. Is anyone else with you?" asked Miguel.

Father Lampard answered in the affirmative and, once Miguel explained this was a confidential church matter, he asked the gendarme to wait outside. The cop protested, but Father Lampard said he would be fine and could wait just outside the door. When it closed, Miguel explained that Darwin and Eyrún were working to recover artifacts related to the Avignon papacy.

"We had a tip today about a break-in at four o'clock. Look at the photo I just texted. Have you seen this man in your cathedral?" asked Miguel.

Father Lampard's mobile made a cricket noise. He tapped the picture and held it so they all could see.

"Yes. He was here this afternoon. Calls himself Philippe," said Father Lampard. He spent another quarter hour describing the man he knew as Philippe. The priest had approached him last month after seeing him visit the cathedral a few times. This afternoon, Father Lampard saw Philippe again but was busy, and he was gone when the confessional time had ended.

15

A fter moving the car to a legal parking spot, Darwin and Eyrún left the cathedral and went to a café in the plaza. Eyrún had found a ticket on the car's windscreen, but it turned out to be a note from the cop saying to keep her speeding to the racetrack. He also attached a donation envelope for the local police charity.

Darwin and raised his glass in a toast. "You were brilliant."

Eyrún clinked her glass against his and sipped. *Nice.* She studied the bottle, a rosé from the Coteaux des Béziers whose lightness and oily minerality suited her palate. As she drank again, Darwin explained that Béziers was part of the same Languedoc region as Limoux, which produced the Blanquettes and Crémants she enjoyed.

She took another mouthful, letting it glide across her tongue, then raised her shoulders and rolled them back and down. Tiny lights dotting the umbrellas' spines softened the shadows, and the wine eased her deeper into the twilight. The evening air moved softly over her skin, and a warmth spread through her that was more than the wine—it was a sense of belonging. She felt at home in this Mediterranean way of living.

My life is so different now. I needed to change. Eyrún reminded herself of the drudgery of overworking. Her always-on ambition was a

54

holdover from being the one who kept her family together after her father died. But, with her sister now graduated and in her medical residency and their mother finding a new partner, Eyrún's job as a provider was done.

Now it's time for me. Darwin turned and smiled, and she corrected herself. *For us.*

"You were truly fantastic in the priest's office," he said. "What made you think of calling Miguel?"

"The priest was never going to believe us, and he wasn't going to believe the story you were making up."

Darwin thrust out his lower lip and ground a knuckle in one eye.

"Oh, stop," she said. "We didn't have time, and I remembered Miguel saying he called the Béziers priest. It was a gamble that worked."

He studied her and, after a brief moment, clinked her glass again. "You're right. I had no idea what to say. We make a great team."

A moment later, the waiter brought two plates. Eyrún chewed a slice of saucisson and followed it with local goat cheese.

"I could like this part of France," she confessed after swallowing and reaching for a piece of baguette.

"You say that about every part of France."

"What do we do now?" She sipped more wine.

"Dunno. Jacques has the second clue, and we have no idea where he's going," he said, picking up his mobile and swiping through to the pictures they took of the tomb.

After the gendarme departed, Father Lampard had gone with them into the crypt where Darwin had removed the tombstone. He took out the helmet, which was turned at an angle. The right eye socket was damaged, and the bone around the ocular cavity was whiter than the rest of the skull.

Before leaving, they promised Father Lampard they would find and return the stolen relic.

Darwin swiped to the photo of the skull and put his mobile on the table where he and Eyrún could study it. "It looks like something was in there," he said.

"Definitely." She shaded the device from the overhead lighting. "Something small. A key, maybe?"

"Could be. The Knights Templar codex said steps but didn't specify what type. Problem with a key, though, is knowing what it fits into."

"How big around would you say the object was?" she asked.

"Maybe a little bigger than my thumb," he said, holding a thumb near the photo. "We were so close." Darwin leaned forward, elbows on the table. He rested his chin on clasped hands and closed his eyes.

Eyrún finished the last of the goat cheese while watching Darwin. *What goes on in that brain? He has brilliant intuition but throws himself into action and forgets his original plan.* She smiled, knowing they had committed to meeting Stevie in Paris before this wild goose chase popped up.

Darwin's eyes opened. "I can't think of what to do," he said.

"You're funny. Remember yesterday? We agreed to meet Stevie in Paris."

"Oh, right. And see her friend Aya at the archaeological crypt."

"I definitely want to see Stevie and Zac, but what are we looking for in the crypt? Jacques took the clues."

"Call it a hunch. I don't think the Knights Templar would have left an important discovery dependent on serial clues. Meaning, if one were lost or destroyed, their secret would be irrecoverable."

"So let's catch a train in the morning. We should find a hotel too," she said, motioning to the waiter for the bill.

"Let's go in the afternoon. I want to check out the other basilica," he said, tapping his credit card on the waiter's handheld device. As Eyrún stood, he asked, "What about your parking ticket?"

She picked up the envelope lying on the table and laughed at the gendarme's note. She dug in her purse and put a thousand euros in the police charity envelope. She dropped it into a yellow La Poste box at the plaza's edge as they walked to their car.

I should start racing again, she thought while opening the driver's door.

16

The next morning Jacques sat up as the TGV reached full speed after an intermediate stop in Valence, two hours into the journey from Béziers to Paris. As a night-owl, he found the half-past-eight start a struggle, but he had slept most of the journey's first half. He pulled the bag containing the lead tube from his pack and put it on the seat-back table in front of him.

He brought the seat back upright and stretched himself from side to side, glad he insisted Franz increase the payments. The first-class carriage's single seats gave him the personal space he craved. He watched the river Rhône glisten in the mid-morning sun. The train leaned as it snaked through the hills lining the river.

A stone watchtower bore witness to a long-ago defeat. So many of these extinct fortifications dotted southern France that he doubted anyone paid much attention to them. Half a millennium had passed since they were inhabited by more than passing shepherds.

He lifted the plastic bag to the window and studied the tube inside. It was the same dimensions as the one he extracted from the floor in Notre-Dame, but something had broken on the soldered endcap. He turned it, trying to see inside, then removed the tube from the bag and held it close, hoping for a better view, but the crack was too small. He resealed the bag and returned it to his pack while thinking back to yesterday afternoon.

Was there moisture in the tomb? It took a half hour to pry open the tomb of Trencavel—or rather, his bones. Jacques had stepped back, expecting a wave of stench, but it was merely dank and moldy, not unlike a pile of rotten leaves.

The Notre-Dame note said the next step was in the "head of the founder." According to the Knights Templar codex, Franz's researchers determined it had to be Trencavel, who founded the bank. Jacques shuddered while studying his next action. *Christ, what if he had been buried headfirst?*

Grasping the helmet in gloved hands, Jacques separated it from the body with ease. He pushed down the urge to vomit and studied the metal-encased skull. A gold florin stamped with a haloed man holding a cross-topped staff had been placed over the right eye. Jacques lifted the coin and revealed the lead tube protruding from the socket beneath.

He pocketed the coin and grasped the tube. It resisted. He grimaced and looked at the vault's ceiling. *Just do it.* He braced the helmet against his midsection, pinched the tube, and twisted. Brittle bone crunched as he turned the tube free, the sharper bones scoring the cylinder. Suddenly, his hand flew upward as the tube broke free, the helmet almost dropping.

Regaining his balance, he replaced the helmeted head and studied the lead in the faint light. The end inside the skull was cracked. He grimaced at the thought of someone pounding the tube in the socket. *What if the corpse was fresh?*

He stashed the tube in a bag, stripped off the gloves, and threw them in the tomb before resetting the stone. Its right side jammed and, after struggling, he left it ajar. *Screw it. Nobody knows who I am.*

Swinging the pack over one shoulder, he brushed the dirt off his hands, pulled the crypt gate closed, and mounted the stairs. He lifted the key from the hook beside the door and locked it from the pulpit side.

On the train, the carriage dimmed as the train entered a long tunnel. He felt drowsy and reclined the seat once more.

17

Heavy rain pelted the office window, and trees lashed the cottage's siding. Jacques stood and stretched from having been hunched over studying the fragments that had spilled from the lead tube. He moved to the window and put a hand on the cold window glass, where a foggy print formed around his fingers.

Dammit! I need that other €50,000. What did Franz say about that firm in Zurich? There must be a way to read the clue. Jacques returned to the desk to search for Franz's emails about the ancient document recovery firm in Switzerland.

The blackened material from the lead cylinder lay in a white porcelain dish—most of it still clung to the inside, and, unfortunately, none of it readable. Instead of a vellum sheet like the contents of the tube he found in Notre-Dame, decayed and broken bits spilled out of this one

A new email had arrived:

```
Jacques, I tried to reach your mobile, but
there is no answer. I found out about the
competition but don't want to put it in
email. Call me.
```

Jacques remembered he had turned off his phone yesterday to prevent Franz from pestering him. Switching on the device, he walked to the kitchen while it booted up to make coffee and warm himself from the dreary weather. While the water heated, he tapped Franz's number.

"*Pronto.*"

"Franz. It's Jacques."

"I know. I know. I needed to get out of my office. Where have you been?"

"I turned my phone off. It's only been a day."

"Where's the next clue?" Franz's voice echoed as if he had stepped into a closet.

Jacques explained the split lead and what he had found inside. The line was silent for a long moment.

"Can you read any of it?"

"No, and most of the vellum is still stuck inside the container. What about that special lab in Zurich?"

"That might work. They do a lot of work for the Archives. I'll set you up with them tomorrow." Franz agreed to text him back a time and suggested he get to Zurich tonight if the meeting had to be early in the day.

"What about the competitors you mentioned?"

"This is more important. Get to Zurich first. I need to make phone calls before their workday ends. Look for my text." Franz ended the call.

Idiot! Jacques took his coffee to the office, where he booked a train to Zurich. The four-hour express would give him time to read, and he could avoid the airport traffic on both ends of the journey.

18

Paris

At midday on Friday, three days after they had rushed to Béziers, Darwin and Eyrún sat at a window table in the St. Regis restaurant on Île St. Louis, just across the bridge from Île de la Cité and Notre-Dame.

"It's quaint," said Eyrún. Dark wood banquettes and wainscotting atop black-and-white marble tiles combined to create a cozy classic atmosphere. The narrow restaurant opened from the street corner; its two aisles squeezed through a dozen tables toward a bar filling the back wall.

Eyrún leaned to look closer at a shiny cake tier containing the desserts of the day as a server lifted the thick glass cover. A buttery caramel aroma wafted her way. *"Bonjour. Pardon. Qu'est-ce que c'est ça? What is that?"* she asked.

"Gâteau moelleux aux prunes. Plum cake," the server said, plating a slice.

"Yum. I want one," she said and had returned to studying the menu when a loud voice rang out.

"Hey, you two," shouted Zac. Most of the restaurant turned to see a well-built man and a small woman with curly auburn hair at the front door.

"Stevie!" said Eyrún, bursting from her chair and embracing her friend.

Darwin and Zac hugged like brothers and then swapped to greet the women. Zac nearly bruised Eyrún's nose as he navigated the double-cheek kiss.

"What's this?" Eyrún asked, running a hand over Zac's face. He had grown a beard and shaved his head since they'd last seen each other.

"Oh, God. Don't get him started," said Stevie. "I hate it."

"You said you liked how it tickled, Babe," Zac said.

As they moved to their table, Zac explained that he had shaved his head off and on but that the beard was new. Darwin teased him about getting old when he put on a pair of black-rimmed glasses to read the menu.

"I don't really need them, but one of the VCs said it makes me look smarter," said Zac.

"You have a Ph.D., isn't that smart enough?" asked Eyrún.

The waiter arrived and took their lunch orders and, a few minutes later, returned with the bottle of Chinon that Darwin had ordered. They toasted to their friendship and caught each other up on news since their last gathering. Eyrún showed pictures of the renovations on the mountain house.

"It's cute," said Stevie, commenting on the granite façade and majestic pine trees framing its entrance. "When can we visit?"

The waiter delivered their meals, and they ate in silence for a few minutes before Zac said through a mouthful, "I gotta hand it to you French. We Americans invented the hamburger, but the five best burgers I've eaten have all been in France." He swallowed and swathed a wad of fries through the juices on his plate.

Darwin grunted and nodded, having just shoved in a substantial slice of his entrecôte steak. Eyrún and Stevie each worked through seafood salads brimming with a combination of braised and smoked fishes. As he began to fill up, Darwin thought about their upcoming meeting at Notre-Dame and asked Stevie about her friend Aya.

"We've known each other since childhood," Stevie said, pausing to dab her mouth with a napkin. "Her father was among the people who discovered Chauvet Pont d'Arc cave. She and I used to explore a lot and even went to university together, where we were biology partners our first year." She continued with an account of Aya's career working on the history of Paris and becoming a director at the Musée Carnavalet before also taking on the role as head of the archaeological crypt under Notre-Dame.

Their server interrupted, and they ordered dessert. Eyrún got her plum cake and Zac, a chocoholic, ordered à mousse. When the man left, Stevie asked Darwin," What will you ask Aya?"

Over the past few days, Darwin had been thinking about Jacques's escape from the blaze and whether Aya might know about secret tunnels under Notre-Dame. It was a crazy long shot, though, so he kept it to himself. Instead, he answered, "I'm not sure. She might know something about the tombs where the man who ran into the fire went. Perhaps there are other Templar relics."

When they had finished haggling over who would pay the bill, Darwin pushed back from the table, saying, "Shall we go?"

As they all approached the bridge linking the islands, Darwin could see the undulating river higher from a surge brought on by the previous day's thunderstorms. The unseasonably warm weather gathered the puddles and drew them back into the heavens. Midspan, he stopped and put an arm around Eyrún's shoulder.

"*Mon Dieu*," he whispered, looking at Notre-Dame de Paris. He had seen pictures and videos of the cathedral, but nothing prepared him for the naked impact. His eyes roamed the scaffolding, trying to fill in the missing roof. Replaying the night of the fire, he imagined a dark sky and flames, tall as buildings, stretching skyward to blood-orange clouds that reflected the savagery below.

Almost as quickly as he envisioned the disaster, his attention returned to the present moment where intricate wooden arches supported the flying buttresses. The planks and beams formed a framework, not unlike those he had seen in drawings depicting the medieval construction. Rows of steel bolts held the wood in place, reminding him of rivets in London's old railway bridges.

Two workers clung like rock climbers to opposite sides of one buttress and tightened the bracing materials. Their safety harnesses ran up to a crane, one of at least a dozen he counted around the cathedral. The neon colors of the machines clashed with the muted taupe stonework.

Built in the 1100s, much of the ancient stone desperately needed repair. A giant scaffold over the cathedral's midsection had been installed before the fire facilitated the work. But now the thousands of steel pipes formed a cruelly blackened and twisted matrix perhaps a dozen meters thick. To Darwin, it looked like a charred bramble where, if you reached in to grab an object, the entire bush would crumble.

"Can they fix it?" asked Eyrún.

"We hope so," said Darwin, echoing a collective desire.

19

They continued and crossed the intersection at Notre-Dame's rear garden. Tourists posed for pictures as locals scurried past, no longer looking up. As they got closer, a tan construction barrier loomed three meters in height, blocking all view of activity on its other side. The ugly steel pressed across Rue du Cloître-Notre-Dame paralleling the cathedral's north side, wedging pedestrians against the stores and forcing them into single streams of opposing traffic.

"*Avancez, s'il vous plaît.* Move, please," said a woman when Zac stopped to look at a hat in a store window.

"These poor shops. How will they make it?" asked Stevie.

"Dunno," said Darwin, who pressed against the wall to let the lady pass. Where once the cafés and souvenir vendors spilled onto a wide sidewalk, they were now shoved into their buildings, and few people stopped, lest they hold up the flow.

At the end of the block, the intersection with Rue d'Arcole next to Notre-Dame's forecourt gave people room to pause and look at the bell towers. A partially opened gate punctuated the corrugated wall, and armed members of the Gendarmerie national eyed the crowd. When Darwin approached the gate, one of them stepped forward, her assault rifle angling downward.

"*Arrêtez. Vous ne pouvez pas entrer ici,* you can't come in here," she said.

Stevie explained that they had an appointment with the chief archaeologist, Aya Raiss. The gendarme called to a colleague standing inside the gateway and explained their request. While this went on, Darwin studied the closest bell tower, which, from his angle, blocked the cathedral's missing roof, making the construction chaos appear more like a tourist inconvenience. He heard an American woman to his left ask how long the repairs would take. *There's an argument for politicians,* he thought, recalling the current fighting over preservation versus modernization.

"*Procédez,*" said the gendarme with the rifle as the gendarme at the gate waved them over.

Stevie ran toward Aya, who had walked up from the inside. They were both petite, but Aya had long, flowing hair, almost black, and a warm complexion from her Amazigh ancestry. They hugged as Darwin watched a forklift with a pallet of stones pass behind them and stop by one of the white tents that filled the forecourt.

"Eyrún, this is my friend Aya Raiss," said Stevie.

"It's nice to meet you," said Aya, kissing Eyrún's cheeks.

They greeted all around, and Aya led them across the forecourt. The first tent began near the cathedral's frontispiece and extended half a football field away. Inside, industrial racks held stones, blocks, and other parts salvaged after the fire. Several pallets of near-identical blocks sat on the ground by one entrance where several workers in hard hats sorted the blocks.

"Those are from the vaults that collapsed when the spire fell," said Aya.

Darwin lifted one. It was not quite square; its sides cut at subtle angles to form the curve when stacked. "Where is the keystone?" he asked a woman who was moving the blocks.

"Over there." She pointed to a locked steel cabinet.

Darwin stood figuring that even with round-the-clock security, it made sense to hide some relics. These pieces from the vaults might fetch a hundred euros, but a keystone from Notre-Dame would be a priceless collectible. He caught up with the others as they turned into a doorway in the rear of the farthest tent. Aya led them into a room where they took chairs around a rectangular table.

She explained the salvage operation: "We've stabilized most of the cathedral's superstructure, and my teams have been removing material for a month now. We 3-D-scanned the interior and are comparing those scans with scans made before the fire. We also took hundreds of high-resolution photos of the collapsed vaults. Think of it as a giant puzzle where it helps to have a picture of what it's supposed to look like."

"Can you put it back together?" asked Eyrún.

"I'm sure we can, even if we have to build new blocks," she said. "The techniques of vault construction are well known, and these big cathedrals have survived worse disasters. Right now, our biggest problem is the damaged scaffolding and the open ceiling. Without the roof, too much stone is exposed to weather."

Aya answered a few more questions before a knock on the door interrupted her. It opened, and the woman whom Darwin met at the block pile announced, "The pompier is here" and retreated as a tall man with dark, wavy hair stepped through the door.

"*Bonjour.* I am Pierre Laporte. You sent for me."

"*Oui. Bonjour.* Nice to meet you. I'm Aya Raiss, chief architect for the restoration. Thank you for coming. Let me introduce my colleagues."

Pierre appeared less imposing than the photographs Darwin saw of him with the water cannon robot during the fire, wearing bulky, protective fire gear. A few seconds later, everyone looked Darwin's way as Aya finished saying that he would explain the reason for the meeting.

"Oh right, sure," Darwin said.

"In French, please, since Pierre's English is limited."

"Tell us about the man who ran into the fire," said Darwin.

Pierre recounted that night as he and Antoine guided the water cannon up the cathedral's central aisle. He described how the man had run around the wooden chairs and up the north aisle to the transept with the collapsed roof trusses and the spire's burning joists.

"Wouldn't he have been burned?" asked Darwin.

"Possibly. It was hot, but he never got closer than five meters to the flames. We turned on the water cannon, so it would have cooled the air."

"Describe what he did in the floor?" asked Darwin.

"I have told the police. Did you not read their report?" Pierre folded his arms and leaned back in the chair.

"My client does not wish to involve the police," said Darwin.

"Who is your client?"

"I'm not at liberty to say."

"Then I don't know if I should tell you about a police matter," said Pierre, who reached for his mobile on the table and pushed back his chair.

A hand squeezed Darwin's thigh, and he turned to see Eyrún nod.

"Wait. Pierre, I apologize for being rude," said Darwin, and the pompier paused. "You are a Catholic?"

"*Oui.*"

"My client is a representative of the church. They think the man you saw removed a relic from beneath the floor," said Darwin.

Pierre remained silent but eased his chair back to the table.

"What I'm about to say can't leave this room." Darwin paused while Pierre and Aya agreed. Then he continued, "Vatican security believes a relic taken from the floor of Notre-Dame contains a vital clue to the recovery of stolen church documents." He let the assertion sink in a few moments, then slid a photo of Jacques taken in Béziers toward Pierre. "You recognize this man?"

"*Oui.* That's him. The man who ran into Notre-Dame," said Pierre.

"This photo was captured from a video camera inside the Cathé-drale Saint-Nazaire in Béziers three days ago. He broke into a crypt and stole another relic. Your photo from September helped identify him," said Darwin.

"What did he take?"

Good. He's talking. Darwin explained that they did not know but alluded to church relics from a period early in Notre-Dame's history. "What did you see in Notre-Dame?" he asked.

"Antoine and I had been ready to enter the cathedral for an hour, but we were held back because the initial heat was too intense after the spire collapsed. Finally, we got in. That man," he pointed at the picture, "entered maybe ten minutes after we engaged Colossus, the water cannon. Antoine was to my front, about where he's sitting." Pierre pointed diagonally across the table to Zac.

"He ran between us and looked at me. I'll never forget the face, bright white in my helmet lamp. But his eyes—wide open, as if he was terrified, or maybe just crazy. I would have grabbed him, but my hands were on the controls. Any wrong movement and the water cannon had enough pressure to damage the cathedral's columns.

"I shouted for Antoine to catch him, but our commander radioed to let him go. If the man wanted to die, so be it. As I told the police, the day was surreal, and the fire was the biggest any of us had ever seen."

"What did he do next?" asked Darwin, eager to get to how the man exited the burning cathedral.

"I didn't see him for a few minutes since I had to focus on Colossus, but Antione pointed to him," said Pierre. "I turned Colossus to bring its lights toward the man. He was in the transept under the north rose window."

Darwin took a folded paper from his jacket pocket and spread a rough map of Notre-Dame's interior on the table. Pierre pulled it toward him.

"I was here," he said, pointing to a spot in the nave about halfway up the aisle to the transept. "The man was here. When I moved the light, he stood and held up his right hand to use my light to study something. Then he shoved it in a pocket and ran to his left and disappeared."

"Could he have gone out the side door, the one in the transept?" asked Darwin.

"*Non*. The teams outside saw no one."

Darwin scanned the map's legend for the names. Pierre put his finger on it. "This one. The Portail du Cloître. I'm part of the fire brigade special detail for Notre-Dame de Paris. I know her better than most people."

Darwin's heart skipped. *Here we go. Maybe he knows something.*

"What about the Porte Rouge?" asked Darwin, pointing to a smaller doorway farther along the same wall that priests and royals used.

"Not a chance. We would have seen it open. My colleagues worked a pump directly outside the door. No one came out," said Pierre.

"Then where did he go?"

"Until I chased him on Île Saint-Louis, I thought he died in the fire."

"You said you know Notre-Dame better than most people. In your training, did anyone ever suggest there might be tunnels under the cathedral?" asked Darwin.

Pierre looked at the map a long moment, then at Aya, before saying, "*Non.*"

They wrapped up the interview when it was clear Pierre had no more to tell them. He offered help in any way he could, and Darwin promised to tell him what they found.

20

After Stevie had filled Zac in on Pierre's story, Darwin turned to Aya and asked, "Why did he look at you that way before he said no?"

"What do you mean?"

"He didn't answer me. He looked at you and tilted his head like he was debating what to answer. As if you two had a differing opinion, and he didn't want to be the one to say anything."

Aya did not answer.

"I know this sounds crazy, but what if this man who knew the exact location of a relic in the floor of Notre-Dame also knew there was access to a secret tunnel," said Darwin.

"Why did he wait until there was a fire?" she asked.

"He probably visited earlier," said Darwin. "But let's first consider the timeline. The Vatican Archive codex was stolen on March twentieth. That's twenty-six days before the fire. It probably took a week to decipher and maybe another five days to get Jacques on board. He no doubt explored the cathedral, but you can't pull a relic out of the floor in broad daylight. I'm guessing he was figuring out a plan when the fire forced his hand."

Eyrún jumped in. "Aya, please help us. The church is afraid of something. This man was willing to die to get at the answer."

Aya looked at Stevie, who said, "I trust these people with my life. You can tell them."

Aya looked down at her hands and sighed. "I've never told this to anyone." She paused before looking up at them. "There's a legend that the Louis kings built a tunnel between the palace near Sainte-Chappelle and Notre-Dame. A few years back, we dug on the far side of the forecourt, beyond the walls created by Haussman during his destructive remodeling of Paris, and found evidence of a tunnel dated to the early seventeen hundreds. But, after twenty meters, it was too badly crushed to follow. However, it lined up with Sainte-Chappelle."

I knew it. Darwin leaned in. "What about the other way?"

"The Paris fire brigade, Pierre's people, denied us permission. They said it was dangerous and could undermine the cathedral."

"Would it?

"Of course not. The foundations are monstrous."

Darwin unfolded his map again and considered locations for a tunnel beneath the cathedral. Dark squares showed where the primary columns shared the structural load with the outer walls and buttresses. There was plenty of space to dig a tunnel. He asked Zac, who, as a US Army Ranger, had experience with tunnels in rooting out insurgents in Iraq and Afghanistan. Zac confirmed that it could be done. Keeping it secret would be the hardest part. Darwin looked up at Aya.

"Why do you think the Sainte-Chappelle tunnel goes under the cathedral?"

"My turn for secrets," she said, looking from face to face as they nodded agreement. When the last of them acknowledged, she continued. "The old caretaker, Didier Dubois, had dropped hints for years about a secret tunnel under the cathedral. He was with the archaeologists who rediscovered the crypt beneath the forecourt in 1966. On the day Didier retired, I met him for drinks. It cost me two very good bottles of Burgundy, but he told me about finding a wooden door that opened into a dark tunnel."

"Did you find it?" asked Darwin.

"Of course—Didier told me its location. But it's sealed behind an exhibit wall, and I'd have to break it down. Impossible with all the alarms."

Zac jumped in. "What it's like under there now? I mean, the damage after the fire."

"The crypt is closed," said Aya. "I've only been in once since the fire because residual water kept setting off the alarms."

"Did you reset them?" asked Zac.

Aya shook her head no. Zac and Darwin looked at each other. Then Darwin looked at Stevie, who grinned, and Eyrún, who nodded. He turned to Aya and asked, "As head of *La Crypte archéologique*, would you like to find out where that wooden door goes?"

21

Five days prior, Jacques had been full of hope when he found the second clue in Trencavel's tomb, before discovering it was useless. The Zurich lab had failed to decipher anything after removing the remaining bits from the cylinder. The molds and bacteria that breeched the crack had consumed the vellum. He had stored tubes from both Notre-Dame and Béziers cathedrals in a box under his desk.

He took the photos of Darwin and Eyrún that lay on his desk beside notes from his conversation with Franz. He glanced back and forth between the pictures. *Wait... I saw them in Béziers. They drove up in a hurry as I left through the side door.*

"They know who you are and have been following you," Franz had said on their phone call an hour ago.

"What the hell game are you people playing?" Jacques had demanded the other €50,000 for fulfilling his end of their agreement.

"Another faction in Vatican City wants to find the Christ papyrus. They've hired Darwin. Look, I worked with Darwin earlier this year in Egypt when he found the lost Library of Alexandria. He has an unmatched sense of intuition. Just turn the tables and follow him."

"And what if there's no treasure to be found?"

"You get the rest of the money. Follow Darwin. He'll either pick up the next step of the Templar's trail or abandon it. He has a short attention span. Either way, you get your money," Franz had said.

Jacques had agreed. He did not like it, but neither did he have another high-paying job prospect. He got a glass of water from the kitchen, then searched for Darwin Lacroix and scrolled through several hits. Most linked to an archaeological breakthrough in Iceland, but a BBC article from August caught his attention. It covered Darwin's work with the new Library of Alexandria and his lead role in examining scrolls found in a previously unknown tomb in Siwa, Egypt. A quote jumped off the page.

"The trouble with academia is its lack of creativity and welcoming of theories that don't fit the well-worn thesis. Instead of thinking like scientists who should seize on data that challenge existing views, academia holds to its dogma in religious fervor. Groundbreaking ideas are buried by rhetoric from institutional redoubts of certainty," said Lacroix.

Interesting guy. He rails against idiots and their rigid adherence to failed ideas.

After reading another of Darwin's articles, Jacques searched Eyrún Stephansdottir and learned she held a Ph.D. in Geothermal Power Generation and was Principal Volcanologist and Advisor at Stjörnu Energy in Iceland. She had met Darwin on their joint discovery of the North Atlantic Tube, a lava tube that connected Iceland and Scotland. Eyrún's company now capitalized on the unusual transport network for its methanol produced from fusing hydrogen and carbon dioxide. The article also mentioned that she and Darwin had a significant stake in a diamond discovery made in the Iceland lava tube.

They don't need money. Why're they after this Knights Templar treasure? The thrill of the hunt?

There was nothing more to learn, so Jacques decided to visit their hotel. *The sooner we solve this, the sooner I get my money. And if there is a treasure, all the better.*

He transcribed the hotel address that Franz had given him into a small notebook and pocketed it on the way to the front door.

22

Later that night, Darwin and Eyrún stood on the Petit Pont between the Saint-Germain Left Bank of the river Seine and Notre-Dame on Île de la Cité. Tourist boats passed beneath them, and Eyrún waved at the people videoing their Paris river tour. "Look!" She pointed across the city at the Eiffel Tower, its strobe lights a twinkling spectacle over the city.

"Right on time," said Darwin, glancing at his watch, reading ten p.m.

"It's so pretty," said Stevie, who fell in next to them along with Zac.

"Nervous?" Darwin asked Zac.

"A little, but not like Afghanistan nervous." Zac had seen two tours of duty in the Middle East with the US Army Rangers.

When they had been kicked out of the conference room two days earlier for another meeting, Aya told them to meet her for drinks. Later at the bar, she confessed to thinking about the wooden door since the fire had shut down normal operations. They formed a plan, and now they waited for her on the bridge nearest to the Archaeological Crypt.

She joined them a few minutes later, and they waited together until 10:20, when she knew the private security company had finished its quarter-past-the-hour check on the crypt doors.

"Let's go," she said.

The group split. Darwin and Eyrún turned and walked toward the island. Stevie and Aya took Zac's arms, like friends out for an evening, and angled across the bridge toward the crypt entrance. Just before reaching the stairs, the women released Zac's arms. In a single motion, he spun, sweeping his right hand from his jacket pocket, and fired a gun at the security camera focused on the crypt's entrance. His first shot went wide, but the second and third splattered the camera lens with orange paint.

"I thought it would be louder," said Aya, commenting on the gun that sounded more like someone spitting loudly. They hurried down the steps where Darwin and Eyrún joined them a few seconds later.

"You said you never missed," Darwin said, chastising Zac.

"Paintballs have crappy ballistics. First shot spun left. I adjusted."

"Get in," hissed Aya after she keyed open the door. "Move straight through the metal detector and stop at the register."

They moved cautiously through the darkened entry, lit only through the glass front doors. Aya locked the door and stepped to the side, pausing to look up the stairs for a full minute to ensure that no one had followed them before joining them at the register.

"I guess we get in free tonight," said Zac.

"Private tour. Follow me and stay close," said Aya.

23

J acques had followed Darwin and Eyrún from their hotel and now
stood overlooking the river Seine. He had been exploring the
hotel's lobby when they had come downstairs and he pursued
them across the city. Dozens of people in small groups strolled the
quayside walkway enjoying the cold clear evening. The traffic surged
in waves, racing along the riverside drive. Another couple and a third
person, a woman, joined Darwin and Eyrún on the bridge from the
Left Bank to the street fronting Notre-Dame. A couple of minutes later,
they pointed toward the Eiffel Tower when it lit up during its hourly
display.

A quarter hour later, they remained at the bridge center. *What are
they doing?* The night air had begun to seep under Jacques's clothing,
and he shivered. He was about to walk around to warm up when the
group on the bridge split up. Darwin and Eyrún walked onto Île de la
Cité. The three who had joined them did the same but crossed the
bridge-top street in the process. Jacques moved slowly across the
bridge, avoiding the streetlights as best he could.

Suddenly, the man with the two women turned and shot at a pole
near *La Crypte archéologique* entrance. Darwin and Eyrún ran to join
them, and all five disappeared down the crypt's steps.

Jacques carefully closed the distance in case they came back up. He moved toward Notre-Dame and stopped near the wall that protected the steps leading into the crypt. He leaned over the wall's edge. No one was on the bottom landing in front of the double glass-door entry. A faint shadow moved on the white marble below as if made by someone inside the crypt.

He waited several minutes, then used his prepaid mobile to call in an anonymous tip that someone had broken into the crypt. He had a sense that this would flush Darwin out. Force him into action.

24

Darwin had been to the crypt once before when he was a boy. His grandfather Emelio had taken him, saying this was the real Paris. The city of the Merovingian kings and before them, the Romans who, in their day, had appropriated the land from the Parisii, the Gaulish tribe who first settled the island.

The crypt's prime exhibits featured stone walls excavated down to their foundations and outlining ancient rooms and workshops. They walked by what must have been a bath. Stacks of twenty or so terra-cotta squares were left standing. The marble floor they supported had long ago been recycled. Hot water pumped into the underfloor space heated the steam rooms above.

They reached the end of the walkway and turned down a staircase that doubled back to the left. More foundations formed an exhibit whose far wall was painted to resemble a wharf on the Seine circa the first century CE.

"We're here. It's behind here," said Aya, pointing to a sidewall. She ran her palms over the wallboard and rapped it with her knuckles until she isolated a hollow sound.

"What if we're caught?" said Stevie.

"Let's hope Darwin's connections at the Vatican are as powerful as he says they are," said Aya. "Give me the wrecking bar." She swung the curved end at the wall, and it bounced off. She waved them back and swung again. A few strikes later, the tool punched through, and she ripped out a chunk of the wall. "This confirms it," she said, holding a piece of plaster embedded with two small wooden slats "Old-school plaster of Paris. No one has been in here since it was originally sealed. Let's get to it."

Zac grabbed the bar and, twenty minutes later, had opened a human-width hole.

"*Mon Dieu*," gasped Aya as she squatted down and thrust a light in the opening. She moved aside as they leaned in to look. About three meters beyond the wall stood a wooden door with a gold-leafed fleur-de-lis on its center.

"Stevie, take photos. I can't have them on my phone. And be sure to capture this symbol." Aya removed a marker from her pack and drew on the wall: two large, inverted Vs with a small letter "m" between their peaks, with two dots like eyes under the "m." She explained it was the symbol of *La Chauve-Souris*, the bat, a notorious urban underground explorer who eluded the Paris police.

Aya then slipped into the hole and went to the ancient door, where she took some tools from her pack. She had it unlocked in less than a minute. When Aya looked back, Stevie raised her eyebrows, and Aya winked.

"What was that?" whispered Zac.

"Aya's *La Chauve-Souris*, but the police don't know it," Stevie whispered back.

"Give me a hand," called Aya, pulling on the large brass doorknob.

"It's swollen shut," said Zac. "And the floor's wet. Darwin, gimme the pry bar. The rest of you stand back."

Zac wedged the bar in the gap below the lock and worked it back and forth to free the door from the jamb.

"Whoa, get back," yelled Zac, pulling Aya with him as the door swung free. Water slashed at their feet and shot up their shins as they tried to back away, but it was over as fast as it started, and the water fanned out across the exhibit floor.

"I'd hate to think… I mean, if it was full," said Zac. They determined that perhaps a bathtub's worth of water had been behind the door.

"What about the rest of the tunnel?" asked Eyrún.

"We're about five meters below the cathedral. Almost at river level. The tunnel will slope up from here, so all the water will have drained," said Aya. "Let's get going."

They followed her up the tunnel. Zac, the tallest of the group, had to stoop. About thirty meters in, the tunnel hit a sharp right bend.

"I counted steps, and we should be about even with the cathedral's north portal. The floor looks wet ahead. Be careful," said Aya.

The floor had sloped upward from the crypt between one and two meters, since they could not see the door when looking back from the bend or the bottom of the tunnel ahead when they entered.

"This feels hard," said Zac, tapping on a rock at the tunnel's bend. The day before, Eyrún, Stevie, and Aya had visited the Musée Carnavalet, the museum of Paris, to research the geology around Notre-Dame. While inconclusive, the documents showed that the cathedral sat on alluvial soil not as dense as the quarries farther west but substantial enough to support tunneling.

"Granite," said Eyrún, wiping away the soil and shining her light up close.

"Good. This is probably the foundation of the north bell tower," said Aya, shining her light toward the cathedral. "Darwin guessed right. The tunnel runs between the main walls of the buttresses."

Water ripples moved away from her boot as she tapped the ground. She turned her light to the wall, which showed a watermark a few fingers' width up the side. She began walking, and her boots made a soft, sucking sound against the muddy bottom. About every two meters, they passed more hard rocks. She paused at one.

"This is part of the earlier Merovingian church. I'm sure of it. Amazing, I must figure out a way to explain why we should explore it," she said.

"I think that hole in the exhibit wall back there kinda gives it away," said Zac.

"I see an opening," said Aya, who quickened her pace.

"Aya, be careful," Stevie said.

Less than ten meters ahead, Aya stopped and shined her light up into a space that swallowed the beam. She stepped back to allow the others to see a stairwell cut in the wall, braced with wood and paved with marble.

Stevie recorded the scene as Aya went up. Darwin followed, one step behind. He counted four steps, then three more that angled as the stairwell turned left ninety degrees. He watched Aya go up six more steps and move into a crouch as they reached a ceiling. They were in a space a little more than a shoulder's width and as long as a human was tall.

The walls gave way to rough-cut marble in a perfect rectangle. The ceiling was of the same marble, but with iron handles mounted in a row at its center point.

"It's a tomb," said Aya, grasping one handle. "Won't budge."

"Let me try," said Darwin, and they squeezed by each other to swap places.

"Don't break anything," said Aya.

The others crammed into the space at the stairway corner as Darwin sat on the uppermost step and pushed up, his head just touching the slab. The slab moved upward, and a faint light poured in.

"Close it! Close it!" Aya said frantically, waving her hands downward.

The light shut out as the marble thumped back down. Darwin grabbed his light and slowly moved it around the top steps.

"What are you looking for?" asked Eyrún.

"Here," said Darwin, tweezing something between thumb and forefinger. "Look, granite chips. And here." He pointed to the tomb edge and slab where pieces had flaked off.

"This is recent," said Aya. "Someone came down these steps. *Zut alors!* We've made a mess."

"*Merde,*" said Darwin, realizing they had rubbed muddy prints over the evidence.

"Doesn't matter, you guys. They didn't go out the way we came in," said Eyrún, backing off the lower step. "The tunnel keeps going this way."

"Wait! Eyrún," said Darwin, but it was too late. Everyone followed her, and he fell in behind. Ten meters ahead, he watched their lights turn one by one to the right. He rounded the corner, and they halted. Pressing in close behind Aya at the back of the line, he saw the tunnel's roof drop precipitously.

"Where do you think it goes?" asked Stevie.

"Aya, how deep is the Seine? I think this goes under it," said Eyrún.

25

Aya shouldered her way to Eyrún and shined her light down a steep staircase. A patch of floor was visible beneath the angled roof, half a dozen meters down. She knelt and surveyed the steps. Each was made from a single granite slab, about the width of an average shoe length.

"See anything?" asked Zac, who leaned in behind Eyrún.

"It's faint, but there are footprints, probably from the mud in the tunnel," said Aya. She stood and looked in the direction they came from, traced her eyes across the ceiling, and closed her eyes as she looked down the stairs. A few seconds later, she opened her eyes and said, "We need to see where this goes. Eyrún's right. It goes under the Seine and probably connects with the *carrières* in the Left Bank."

"The quarries?" asked Darwin. "Are you sure?"

"I've been in underground Paris a lot," she said. "The quarries are much bigger than anyone thinks. Zac, come with me. It's never wise to go alone. Five minutes, no longer."

Darwin, Eyrún, and Stevie watched them go down the stairs and paused at the bottom to say the way was clear. When they had disappeared into the tunnel, Eyrún asked, "Did she mean the Catacombs, that place with all the bones?"

"Partly, but the ossuary is about three kilometers from here," said Stevie. "The quarries are literally that: mines for stone. Most of ancient Paris was built using the limestone and gypsum dug in the settlement's outskirts, which meant most of the Left Bank a thousand years ago. No one documented them, and the massive underground holes were totally forgotten until the eighteen hundreds when buildings collapsed into them.

"Have you been in them?" asked Darwin.

"Sure. Aya and I had some archeology and geology field lectures in the quarries," she said.

"Is that why Aya winked at you?" asked Eyrún.

"Yes. Her bat symbol was no joke. She's a legend and uses her alter ego to explore places the French authorities won't allow. If she says this goes under the Seine, then it does."

"*Mon Dieu*," they heard Aya yell from below. She was halfway up and stopped at the top to catch her breath before continuing. "It's amazing. There's a door. I swear I've seen it from the other side. I knew it. The Louis kings built secret tunnels." She stopped again to breathe from her sprint up the steps.

"Zac?" asked Darwin.

"Iron door. It's a one-way affair. No handles, but someone's been through it recently. The bars that braced it closed on this side are on the floor," said Zac.

"Where—"

"Shhh!" hissed Eyrún, turning in the cathedral's direction. "Turn out your lights."

Darwin put his hand against the wall for balance in the total darkness. A light glowed in the turn from the cathedral, its beam moving up and down as if searching.

"Stay here. I'll be right back," Aya whispered, and her silhouette moved away. When she had nearly reached the corner, she turned and ran back. "Go, go, go. Down the stairs," she commanded. "It's the cataflics."

"Who?" shouted Eyrún, sliding her hands along the wall for balance as her feet danced on the steps.

"The police. Cataflics is slang for the police unit that patrols the quarries," said Stevie, reaching the bottom right behind Eyrún. Zac, Aya, and Darwin helped them through the iron door and pulled it closed.

"Wait!" Eyrún whispered. "We don't know what's down this tunnel. It could be dangerous. Aya, you said we're under the river. What if this comes down?"

"It's safe. We're in solid rock below the water channel," said Aya.

"*Ils sont là-bas*, they're down there," came a muffled voice from the other side of the door.

They looked at one another, eyes wide. Darwin's mouth went dry, and he searched for anything to block the door.

"We can give ourselves up. Tell them it's a misunderstanding," said Eyrún, wincing as if even she did not believe it.

"*C'est la police. Nous sommes armés.* This is the police. We are armed," boomed a voice that sounded closer. Light flashed around the doorjamb.

"No," said Aya. "We need to run. The *Gendarmerie Nationale* will see breaking into Notre-Dame as a terrorist action. They're crazy hungry to blame someone for the fire."

Suddenly Zac reached around the door with the paint pistol and squeezed the trigger. The gun spat as voices on the other side shouted "Gun!"

"*C'est de la peinture*, it's paint," a man yelled.

"Take this," said Zac, handing the paint pistol backward. Darwin grabbed it while Zac pulled a red-paper-wrapped package from his jacket. He ripped the paper and with his other hand sparked a lighter. A fuse fizzed to life, and he tossed it around the door. "Run!"

The women were first up the stairs, and Zac pushed Darwin, who had hesitated a moment. He was half a dozen steps up when the firecrackers burst in rapid staccato. Darwin glanced back at Zac, who was lighting something else.

"Smoke bomb. Get going," said Zac.

At the top of the stairs, Zac lit another smoke bomb. The tunnel ahead went straight and flat. Darwin jogged on the smooth floor but slowed his pace when the lights carried by the women disappeared around a corner. In about twenty more strides, he reached a rough chamber.

"Where are they?" asked Aya.

"Held up a while. They'll have figured out the paintballs and fire-crackers, but the smoke will slow them down," said Zac.

"How did you?" asked Eyrún.

"Urban warfare improvisation. You don't always need lethal force. We went to Chinatown yesterday. Better food than San Francisco, by the way," said Zac, peering down the tunnel. "Smoke's coming this way. We gotta go."

"Zac, give me the pistol and some smoke bombs. I'll lead them away," said Aya.

They turned toward her with alarmed expressions.

"No. No. Don't worry," said Aya. "I've beaten the cataflics for years. Stevie, you know my symbol. Follow it down that tunnel. It intersects with a storm drain. Go left. It empties into the Metro tunnel, then go right. It's less than fifty meters to the Maubert Mutualité station. Take the train any direction for two or three stops, then disappear in the streets."

They turned to go, but Aya grabbed Stevie's shoulder and said to wait. She put a finger to her lips for silence and looked toward the cataflics, then whispered, "They're too close. Here, get in this well. There's a cutout in the bottom where they can't see you. I'll make a noise and lead them away. Go. Now."

Aya lit a smoke bomb and carried it a few steps into the tunnel before dropping it, so the cataflics would know where she went. Darwin was the last over the rough stones into the well. He pressed against the others in the dark corner. Moments later, voices filled the chamber above them, then receded again as one shouted, "*Ils sont allés dans ce tunnel.* They went in this tunnel."

All above turned silent, and Darwin swore he could hear his own heart pounding. *Or maybe it's all of our hearts.* He looked toward Eyrún, felt for her hand, and squeezed her hand. She pulled his hand to her lips. He felt a warmth spread through his body and sighed. He took another breath and imagined his heart slowing down while they waited.

Some minutes later, a hand gently pushed his back. "Time to get out of here," whispered Zac. "It's as safe as it will ever be."

He boosted Darwin, Eyrún, and Stevie up the short wall and climbed out himself using holds where stones had fallen out. He nodded for Eyrún to lead the way and Darwin followed her. They moved slowly at first, then picked up speed. Darwin glanced back to see Stevie and Zac close behind. He turned to follow the tunnel, which was smooth and wide. *We'll be out of here in no time,* he thought.

26

Z ac stopped about thirty paces into the tunnel and pressed himself against the wall. Moments later, a cataflic stepped out of the shadow of the Notre-Dame tunnel and followed them. *Bingo! Just what I would've done.* He turned and hugged the wall as he caught up to Stevie. "Hey Babe, slow down," he said and put a hand to her shoulder as her pace slowed.

"What? Are you hurt?" she asked, running her light over his body.

"No. Keep walking. Don't look back, but someone's following."

"What's up?" asked Eyrún, who had closed the gap.

Zac explained the situation. "It's what my tactical teams did to let bad actors think they escaped. One or two Rangers hid while the rest of us went in different directions. When the bad guys moved, the Rangers followed them."

"What do we do?" asked Darwin.

"Keep moving. Don't look back. We walk in a tight line. Stevie, find a cutout in the wall I can slip into. When you see a place, move to that side. I'll step into it, and you keep going," said Zac.

"What're you going to do?" asked Eyrún.

"Take him out. Stop asking questions and keep moving."

They continued as Stevie scanned ahead with her light. The rough-cut walls protruded at odd angles, but nothing was large enough for Zac. A short distance later, the tunnel ended at an opening that dropped into the storm drain. Bricks from the opening were piled to one side, evidence of the ongoing cat-and-mouse game between the cataphiles' explorations and the cataflics' containment.

The *Chauve-Souris*, Aya's bat symbol, was painted in purple above the hole. Someone had also scratched *Le Métro* with a left-pointed arrow in the brick. Zac peered in. *Perfect. I'll do it here.* He turned back to the others. "Easy, two-meter drop, at most." He slipped through and helped the others land on a smooth concrete floor.

"Ugh, the smell," said Eyrún. "There's more than rainwater in here."

The drain's floor sloped inward to a central channel where a stream flowed toward the Seine. Black slime clung to the walls at the high-water mark, typical for rainstorms. A splattering from the river direction revealed water spilling out of the wall.

"Must be from the street above," said Zac. "Let's get going."

"What about an opening?" asked Stevie.

"I'll go behind that waterfall. He'll look toward the Metro. Wait for me at the Metro tunnel. Whoever's following won't be more than two or three minutes behind."

Zac stepped across the stream, careful not to leave any wet footprints, then jumped back once he passed the cascade. The flow splashed enough that Zac felt the droplets on his pants. *At least it's clean,* he thought while flattening himself against the wall and waiting.

"*... seventy-one, seventy-two,...*" he counted, marking the time. The water prevented him from seeing the hole, but three counted seconds later, he saw a pair of boots toe-hold their way down the wall.

Now! he spun away from the wall and closed the gap as the figure dropped to the floor. Zac slammed the body into the wall. The man gasped as air burst from his lungs. Zac drove his knee into the man's back and wrapped his right arm into a chokehold, using his left hand to compress the arteries in the man's neck. Zac winced as a boot slammed backward into his shin.

The struggle ended in seconds. Zac lowered the man to the floor, laying him on his back. *Shit, the fireman. What's he doing here?* He recognized Pierre, who had met them two days before. Zac pulled a zip tie from his pack and tightened it around Pierre's boots, the pompier already moving his head as the blood flow resumed.

"Sorry, man," said Zac, jumping to his feet and sprinting toward the Metro tunnel. In less than a minute, he reached the others who sat against the wall by the Metro. A train passed, stirring up familiar tar and ozone subway odors, and its brakes squealed as it neared the station.

"Let's go. He's down, but not for long," said Zac as the last carriage went by. "Stay to the wall. Don't go near the rails."

"Who was it?" asked Darwin.

"Pierre, the fireman."

"What!" said Eyrún.

"Talk later. Keep going. Get up that ladder on the platform edge," said Zac as the train rolled away from the station. He looked behind for Pierre, but the tunnel was empty. They mounted the steel rungs used for maintenance work and climbed onto the platform. The station was empty now except for people who had exited the last train and moving to the exit in the opposite direction.

"Good. No one saw us," said Zac, joining them on the platform. Other people trickled in to catch the next train. "Keep walking to the far end."

Two couples dressed for a night out stared at their mud-stained clothing. When they reached the far end of the station, Zac said, "We need to split up. You two catch the next train here and get off in two stations, as Aya said. Stevie and I will cross over and take the train going the other way."

"Okay. We'll meet at your hotel," said Darwin.

Stevie and Eyrún quickly hugged before Zac took Stevie's hand and led her up the stairs to the crossover.

27

Pierre sat up, rubbing his neck. He sucked in deep breaths as his head and vision cleared. He pulled his feet in to stand and felt the zip tie. *"Putain!"* he shouted and felt around for his light. It had rolled against the wall, beam still on. He grabbed it on hearing a train pass and shined it up the tunnel where human shapes ran in after the train.

He pulled out a pocketknife from a cargo pocket on his thigh. Seconds later, the cut zip tie on the floor, he was running toward the Metro tunnel. *How did they know which way to go?* In addition to his job on the Paris Fire Brigade, Pierre was a part-time cataflic who aided in search and rescue. He had responded to tonight's request when he saw it involved the Notre-Dame crypt.

He turned into the Metro tunnel but saw an approaching train's lights, backed out while it passed, and immediately followed it to the platform. The last carriage stopped too tight against the platform to get around it, so he jumped on its rear coupling and clambered to its edge to look down the platform. Thankfully, the station was on a straightaway.

Where are they? His eyes sorted through the bodies streaming in and out of the doors. As he searched, a train on the opposite track pulled into the station. Pierre felt a heat wave surround him.

There! They were at the far end of the station. He swung back and looked in the carriage window. It was the newest model with opened-ended couplings that allowed a view through the whole train. In the farthest car, he could see people standing apart from two people with mud all over their clothing.

A loud hiss foretold the adjacent train's departure, and a moment later, his train also began moving. *Merde!* He jumped down, carefully avoiding the tracks, as both trains sped out of the station. He turned to the platform edge, opened the maintenance call box, and keyed in the emergency code.

28

D arwin and Eyrún stood back from the platform's edge as the train stopped. They waited as passengers disembarked and looked up and down the platform for any police. Once the last new passengers were aboard, they jumped in just as the doors closed. The passenger traffic was moderate, and people moved away from them.

"Do we smell?" asked Eyrún.

Darwin raised a sleeve to his nose. "Not really, but we look a sight," he said, brushing his pants and raising a small dirt cloud.

"Where does this line go?" she asked.

"Through the sixth and seventh toward the Eiffel Tower. Right now, we're under Boulevard Saint-Germain," he said, looking at the line map above the door. "Next stop is Cluny La Sorbonne. We'll get off at Odéon, the second stop. Big crowds there will let us disappear easily."

"That was crazy," she said. "Do you think Aya got away?"

"Dunno. Hopefully. I don't know what I expected, but it was cool. No one's been under Notre-Dame like that for centuries."

"Except for Jacques," she said.

"Right, except him."

"I was scared when the police cornered us."

He pulled her close, and they rocked in the train's motion, one of the carriage support poles between them. He vacantly stared at the carriage window, his blank expression and wild hair reflected back. One side of his collar was up, and he fixed it with his free hand.

"So was I," he said. "Are you okay now?"

The train slowed to a stop, and the doors opened. They turned to the doors and nervously scanned the platform and train. Only one person got in their car and a few more, farther down the train. The doors re-closed, and the train rolled forward.

"Yes. I'm better now," she said. "Next stop, right?"

"Yes," he said, bending to kiss her. She leaned into his shoulder as he stroked her thick, dark hair. A minute later, the train slowed for the Odéon station, and they turned to face the door.

"Oh, no," Eyrún cried out as they rolled past a group of gendarmes. When the train halted, three gendarmes entered the doors on each side of them.

Darwin slowly moved his hands out wide in surrender.

29

Zac shut off the shower and grabbed a towel from the hook. He threw it over his head and held it against his face as the memory of Pierre at the emergency call box played again.

Stevie had desperately tried to call Eyrún's mobile to warn her about the police, but Paris did not relay cellular signals in the Metro. One stop later, they had exited the train at Cardinal Lemoine station and ran for the street level. She barged through the metal barriers but slowed inside the station, looking around.

They had cautiously emerged on Rue Monge, stepping back against a boulangerie to survey the street. Stevie tried Eyrún again. No answer. Zac asked which way to go, and she took his arm and led the way up Rue Monge, opposite the river. She called Eyrún again with her free hand: voicemail. She swore and pocketed her mobile.

"We need to find a taxi and get back to the hotel," Zac had said, feeling Stevie stiffen. Looking left at the street, he knew why: a police car rolled by much slower than the speed limit.

"In here." She pulled his arm. They entered a wide space between the buildings that opened into a small park. Benches and potted plants created a neighborhood meeting place. It took Zac a few strides to see the steps going up the park's rear wall that doubled back to an upper level about two stories above.

They sprinted in double steps up the left side. At the top, the landing gave way to Rue Rollin, a narrow pedestrian-only street. They moved at a fast clip through pools of light cast by street lamps.

"What if they circle around the other side?" he asked.

She started running, and he followed. They passed a few people: a couple kissing in one doorway and a man placing a recycle bin for collection. In half a minute, they reached the far end, where people spilled into the street around a walk-up pub. Zac and Stevie slowed to blend in.

"This way," she said, once through the crowd. They went right, down a short block, then left on Rue Clovis. "The Pantheon is ahead. There're always taxis."

Stevie tried Eyrún again twice during the taxi ride back to their hotel, but no answer. Zac kept watch out the back to determine they were not followed.

Coming back to the present, Zac sighed out a long breath. The chase dredged up memories of his time in Afghanistan, where mortal threats lurked in every alley and doorway. He hung up the towel and walked into the bedroom, where Stevie lay on the bed, messaging someone. He sat and ran a hand over her back.

"Who are you texting?"

"Aya. She got out near Jardin du Luxembourg. Said it took all that distance to lose them. She's almost here, so get dressed."

―――――――――

J ust under a quarter hour later, a knock brought Stevie to the door and, looking through the security hole to confirm it was Aya, she opened it.

"You made it," Stevie said, closing the door.

Aya moved quickly into the room's center. She grabbed a water bottle and chugged half before rummaging through the minibar and, finding a tiny bottle of tequila, ripping off its top and downing it. She coughed on the back of her hand and gulped more water.

"Putain! That was close. They almost cornered me in Ursiline's church. I had to use an old telegraph tunnel and got stuck for a while," she said, pouring a glass of wine from an opened bottle. She tossed back the burgundy and poured another glass before plopping down in the desk chair. She sighed heavily. "I'm getting too old for this." She sipped more wine and asked, "What about your friends?"

Stevie explained their escape, Zac taking out Pierre, but Pierre reappearing on the train platform. "Eyrún isn't answering her phone," she said. "Our plan was to meet here."

"It's been over an hour, Babe. We need to check," said Zac. He keyed open the room safe and removed Darwin's mobile, powering it on as he walked back to the desk. Their backup plan included leaving Darwin's phone in their room and Zac's mobile in Darwin's and Eyrún's hotel room. He tapped Darwin's passcode. Stevie and Aya stood next to him while he swiped to the find-a-person app and tapped Eyrún's photo.

Seconds later, a map of Paris filled the screen, overlaid with a small picture of Eyrún. Zac zoomed in, spreading the image with thumb and forefinger. Her picture remained directly on top of the préfecture de police in the middle of Île de la Cité.

"Damn it, Pierre!" Zac pounded on the desk.

30

Darwin and Eyrún sat in a brightly lit, three-meter-square room. The police had removed their handcuffs when they were brought into the room an hour before. Darwin squinted against the bright white overhead lighting and searched for movement beyond a large window in the wall to his left, but horizontal blinds on its outside blocked any view.

Before the police converged on them in the Metro, he had told Eyrún not to say anything except to give her name, age, and address when asked.

"I've never been arrested before," she whispered.

"Don't worry," he said. "Don't answer anything else. We'll stall them by asking for lawyers. You are not French, so ask for the Icelandic embassy."

Once reaching the préfecture de police, they gave only their personal details when asked by a junior detective. Eyrún then requested they contact the Icelandic embassy, since she was not a fluent French speaker. Darwin gave them the name of a Paris lawyer whose firm had advised him on the diamond royalty agreements with Iceland and Scotland. He knew the firm had attorneys who dealt in criminal law.

Thirty minutes passed before the door opened again, and a woman deposited two paper cups of water on the table and left. Another half hour went by before the junior detective returned. He placed Eyrún's mobile, sealed in an evidence bag, on the table.

"Where is your mobile?" he asked Darwin.

"I lost it in the tunnel," Darwin said.

The detective snorted and stared at Darwin for a long moment before saying, "I called her embassy, and no one is available until the morning." He waited for Darwin to translate, then added, "Also, your lawyer did not answer."

Darwin did not respond.

"It will help your case if you tell us why you were under Notre-Dame."

"We were exploring the quarries with friends when the cataflics began chasing us," said Darwin.

"Why did you run?"

No answer.

The junior detective pressed on. "The catacomb police say you broke into the Crypt Archaeological. They discovered a smashed wall that led to a tunnel under Notre-Dame. When they followed the tunnel, they found your party." He paused, then added, "Running away from Notre-Dame."

Again, Darwin remained silent, partly because no question had been asked, but also because he now knew the police were talking about serious charges, perhaps even terrorism. He turned and translated what the detective had said to keep up the illusion of Eyrún's poor French.

At that moment, Eyrún's mobile vibrated on the table. The caller ID showed "Stevie."

"Who's that?" asked the detective.

"A friend," said Darwin.

"Why were you in the Crypt Archaeological?" asked the detective.

"We will wait for our lawyers," Darwin said.

The detective swept up the bag with Eyrún's mobile and left the room. A short time later, he returned and said they would speak again in the morning when their lawyers and embassy responded. They were led to a holding cell where a large guard pulled a heavy sliding door across the opening. He looked at them through the small window in the door before also closing it.

Darwin and Eyrún surveyed the cell. Its off-white cinder-block walls were interrupted by a concrete bench along the back wall. Above them, a bright white light beat down, and a ceiling vent softly whistled. A seatless aluminum toilet thrust out of the front wall next to the door. Darwin was tempted to make a rude gesture at the camera mounted in the corner above the toilet.

"Zac must've turned on your phone by now. I hope you're right about Richard's help," she asked.

"If not, it might be a rough few days. I guess we should have ordered extra pillows," said Darwin, sitting on the rock-hard bench.

"At least you don't have to sit." Eyrún stood, hands on hips, looking down at the pewter-colored toilet.

D arwin awoke hours later with a sore neck. He slowly moved his head back and forth to ease the stiffness. Eyrún's head lay on his lap, her body pulled up in a fetal position across the bench. His ass was numb, and he squeezed his butt cheeks to get the blood flowing. Unfortunately, his movement awoke Eyrún.

"Ow, this damn bench," she said, sitting up. Then she stood, limping on her right side while rubbing her hip. "What time is it?"

"Dunno," said Darwin, walking to the toilet and peeing.

Eyrún followed, flushed, and then washed her hands in the tiny sink. She rubbed water over her face. "Oh, that feels nice," she said, shaking off the remaining drops as best she could.

They did bodyweight exercises and yoga to wake up and pass the time. As they worked up a sweat, the sound of a door bolt pulling back drew their attention. A slot opened, and a food tray appeared with two cups of black coffee, a plate of scrambled eggs, and two croissants and butter.

"What time is it?" Darwin yelled through the opening. No reply. He was not surprised.

Eyrún moved the tray to the bench. "I'm starved," she said, ripping off a piece of the croissant and awkwardly spreading butter with the plastic spoon.

Darwin took one coffee cup and sipped it while standing. He looked out the opening again but could see nothing but cinder blocks in the hallway. He finished the coffee and shared the eggs with Eyrún. They split the other croissant.

In what seemed hours later, someone banged on the door and slid open the window. A guard looked in, then opened the door. Stepping back and pointing, he said, "Follow him."

They were led back to the same interview room and offered coffee. Eyrún declined, but Darwin said yes. Minutes later, a besuited man with a neck like a rugby forward entered carrying two coffee cups. He placed one in front of Darwin and the other in front of himself.

"Madame, can I get you anything?" he asked Eyrún.

"No, thank you," she said.

"I am Charles Laporte, detective inspector with the Police Nationale," he said, looking at a document in an open folder on the table.

"Er-in Stephansdottir. Did I pronounce it right?"

"It's pronounced Eh-rune," she said.

"Eyrún," he said. "It's a lovely name. And Darwin Lacroix. It seems you had a little fun last night that got out of hand. The Icelandic embassy said they can send someone later this morning and, Darwin, your lawyer's office called to say someone is on the way over."

Charles closed the folder and sipped his coffee before continuing, "You are charged with breaking and entering a French national monument, and the prosecutor is considering it a potential terrorist action. Last night cannot have been comfortable and, given the charges, we could keep you in that cell for almost a week. Now, is there anything you want to tell me before your people get here?"

"No," said Darwin.

"As you wish," said inspector Laporte and left the room.

31

About an hour and a half later, their interrogation continued, as a translator from the Icelandic embassy and Darwin's lawyer had arrived. After the introductions, inspector Laporte asked if the lawyer would represent both parties, as the embassy official was not an attorney.

"Yes," said Eyrún.

"Fine. Let's begin. Tell me about what you were doing on the tracks of the Metro Line last night?"

"Climbing back on the platform. We got lost after becoming separated from our guide," said Darwin.

"Who was your guide?"

"Someone named *La Chauve-Souris*. She told us that cataphiles don't use actual names."

"But it was a woman?"

"As best we could tell."

"If I may interrupt with a question?" asked the lawyer, Christine Rèdmond. When the inspector nodded, she continued, "While it is illegal to enter the quarries, it is a minor offense that includes a fine. How did the police make the determination that my clients committed a 'potential terrorist action?'"

"They were seen in a tunnel that crosses under the river Seine to Notre-Dame, by a member of the mines police who was investigating a break-in at *La Crypte archéologique*," said Laporte.

"And did this officer actually see them in the crypt or in the tunnel under Notre-Dame?" asked Rèdmond.

"We have a video of a suspect shooting a security camera with a paintball."

"Is either of my clients in it?"

"No," said Laporte.

Darwin suppressed a smile. *She's good*, he thought. *But stay cool. We're a long way from being let go.*

"Do you know this man?" asked Laporte, sliding a photo of Jacques Bourbon across the table.

Darwin leaned in. It was the photo that Miguel had shown them at the Vatican. He sat up and studied the inspector. *Laporte. The same name as the pompier, Pierre Laporte. Miguel said the fireman who took the photo sent it to his police detective brother. What are the odds?* Deciding to gamble, he said, "No. We don't know him, but we have seen this photo."

"How?" said the inspector, eyes wide in surprise.

"We were told the man in it was seen running into Notre-Dame during the fire and was assumed dead until this photo was taken."

"Who told you?"

"Your brother, Pierre," said Darwin.

Inspector Laporte crossed his arms and cocked his head in disbelief. Rèdmond turned to study Darwin, who continued, "We're after the same man. He stole a codex from our client, which contained a step to find a relic in Notre-Dame, a relic valuable enough for this man, Jacques, to risk his life. We think he exited the cathedral through a secret tunnel in one of the tombs, likely Christophe de Beaumont's," said Darwin.

Laporte stared at him a moment, then burst out laughing. "And I thought my brother was crazy."

Darwin reflexively chuckled, and the others smiled. Then Laporte resumed a straight face and said, "You're saying this man ran into the raging inferno, stole a relic, and escaped through a tomb, in a tunnel that no one knew about."

"*Oui.*"

"Let's put that aside for a moment. Who is your client?"

"We are not at liberty to say," said Darwin.

"Fine. How are you so sure about this tomb?"

"We've seen the underside of it."

"Monsieur Lacroix," Rèdmond interjected. "I advise you to stop there." She turned to Laporte and continued, "I need to speak with my clients, privately."

The inspector left the room, saying he also needed to confer with his colleagues. Rèdmond turned to Darwin and Eyrún and, speaking in English, said, "You're incriminating yourselves. Do you realize the severity of the charges?"

"Yes, we do," said Eyrún.

"Then tell me what is going on, so I can help you."

Eyrún politely excused the translator, as both her husband and their attorney would translate for her. And, when the woman left, Darwin gave a brief account concerning the theft of the Knights Templar codex and the relics in both Notre-Dame and Béziers cathedrals.

"Your client is the Vatican?" asked Rèdmond.

"Yes," they answered in unison.

At that moment, Laporte burst through the door, closing it firmly behind him. He sat and leaned in, arms on the table. "Who the hell do you know?"

"What?" Rèdmond said, holding up a hand to silence Darwin and Eyrún.

"Your clients," he said, red-faced, with an artery pulsing in his temple. He took a breath and started over.

"I'm in the hallway outside talking with my staff, asking them to get detectives over to Notre-Dame to check out this secret tomb entrance, when the director-general of the national police walks up asking for a private talk." He paused again while studying their faces.

"A man I've met only once in my entire career tells me to drop all charges. I asked why, realizing it may be a career-limiting move, to which he replied that the President of France received a call early this morning from a sovereign leader, asking that the French Republic help you two in any way it can." He finished and sat down, shaking his head.

32

An hour after Christine Rèdmond dropped them off at their hotel, Darwin was sitting on the bed browsing a map of Paris, when Eyrún stepped out of the bath, a wave of steam billowing behind her.

"I had mud everywhere and the smell—something stank in that sewer. I put our clothes in the plastic laundry bag," she said, twisting a towel around her hair and sitting next to him. "What's that?"

"Mmm. You smell good," he said and kissed her bare shoulder. "It's the Neuilly-sur-Seine neighborhood where Jacques lives." He pinched the map outward to give a broader view of Paris. "It's northwest of here, across the Périphérique, the main road around Paris, and next to the Bois de Boulogne."

"That's the big park with the cute restaurant on the island."

"Right, that one," he said, zooming back onto Jacques's house on Rue Perronet.

Darwin rotated the image around a four-story main house on Rue Perronet. A guest house occupied the rear corner of the lot with a large lawn between the two. Wide driveways separated the property from the neighbors, which left plenty of space for anyone to come and go unnoticed. The cottage's front door opened at the end of a pathway along the property's rear fence. Its upper floor had tall, sloped windows that peaked into a terra-cotta roof.

E arlier that morning, after settling down from orders to let them go free, the inspector had listened to their tale of finding the tomb beneath Notre-Dame and the tunnel under the Seine. They left out Stevie, Zac, and Aya.

Laporte had confessed that his brother, Pierre, was obsessed with finding who had started the fire. It was plausible that Jacques did it, though, he admitted, there was scant evidence. Darwin suggested that they were working to the same end—justice for France—and proposed a collaboration. At that point, their lawyer, Christine Rèdmond, excused herself, saying that she could not listen in on a potentially illegal operation.

"What do you have in mind?" Laporte had asked when she was gone.

"We need to see Jacques's research. We don't know what he found in Béziers," said Darwin.

Laporte agreed to bring Jacques in for another round of questioning about the video of him in Béziers cathedral, and the new discovery in Notre-Dame. They then took Darwin and Eyrún to a more comfortable office, where Laporte brought them coffees and left a fat manila folder labeled "Jacques Bourbon." At first, they were surprised at the amount of content but soon realized the police had been following him for some years. The reasons became evident as they read his family background.

Jacques Bourbon was seven years old when his parents were killed, allegedly by Carlos the Jackal, in 1974. He was raised by his father's sister, who owned the property on Rue Perronet. The notes described her as "ultra-right-wing and monarchist." Her husband, thirteen years her senior, was a hero of the Resistance in World War II and an executive at a French arms manufacturer. They shuttled Jacques off to boarding schools from an early age, and he was a model student. He excelled at school and passed his *bac littéraire* with a rare *félicitations du jury* mention.

"What's that?" Eyrún had asked when Darwin whistled. He explained that the *baccalauréat littéraire* was an exit exam from French high school and weighed heavily on entrance to the best universities. It meant Jacques was uncommonly bright. This was evident in his attending the Sorbonne and receiving multiple degrees in political science and philosophy.

His Ph.D. dissertation on the French system of government proposed the return of a constitutional monarchy as a way of uniting political factions. He went on to a teaching career moving up the ladder but failed to achieve a full professorship or tenure. After a decade, he moved between increasingly lesser universities. The reason seemed to be Jacques publishing of ever-more-radical papers on a monarchy and a string of arrests in protests that had turned violent.

Jacques's aunt died in 2005, leaving him the house and a comfortable inheritance. Tax returns showed he had backed far-right-wing political candidates with mixed success, and bank records showed he had mortgaged the house in 2007 and again in 2015. He rented the big house to a German executive, but the income barely covered the mortgages. He currently taught basic political science at community colleges, but only part-time. In short, with his inheritance used up and a floundering career, Jacques needed cash.

When Charles Laporte returned to the office an hour later, Darwin and Eyrún had a good idea why Jacques was lured by the Knights Templar treasure. Eyrún took a photo of the page with Jacques's address, and Laporte provided them the opportunity when he said the justice department agreed to his request to detain Jacques for questioning. "You'll have about a six-hour window before his lawyers get him out. I'll text you when," Laporte told them.

Now they waited in their hotel for Laporte's message.

"What do you think?" asked Eyrún as Darwin zoomed in as close on the small house as the resolution allowed.

"I think we should arrive shortly after the police pick him up," said Darwin, putting the iPad on the bed.

Eyrún looked down and crossed one leg over the other to examine a bruise on her shin. "I don't remember hitting anything," she said, leaning forward to rub it. As she did, the knot holding her towel slipped undone, collapsing the towel around her torso.

Darwin knelt down and kissed the bruise. After a moment, he stood and let the towel fall from his waist, then gently lowered her backward. She scootched up the bed, and he followed, lowering his bare chest on hers. Their lips met in a series of kisses before he moved to her neck. Her hips arched, and she made a deep-throated hum as Darwin burrowed—a sharp knock at the door announced that room service had arrived.

"*Merde!*" Darwin jumped up and grabbed a towel.

Eyrún giggled and rolled under the covers.

33

The next morning at a quarter past nine, Darwin was working with a strength trainer at a gym near their hotel when his watch vibrated. He racked the bar after the last rep and tapped the message.

Arrive 13:00. You have until 15:00. Read email for details.

Plenty of time, he thought and applied his attention to the next set.

Following a post-workout massage, he showered and got a table at a café across the street from the gym. He waited for Eyrún as the late-morning sun angled down the road, casting enough warmth for him to be comfortable in short sleeves, but cool enough in October to be refreshing after a hard hour with the trainer.

He ordered a cold brew coffee and a breakfast roll with eggs, bacon, avocado, and chili jam. Halfway through the coffee, his food arrived, and he bit into the roll, the French equivalent of an American breakfast burrito. By the third bite, his stomach had ratcheted into top gear, and he reduced the roll to a single remaining piece when Eyrún crossed the street.

"Hungry? You look a sight," she said, laughing and pointing at his napkin and making a wipe-your-chin motion.

While Darwin had been taught good manners, when hungry he tended to forget them.

"Sorry," he said, shoving in the last bite and wiping his face.

She ordered, and he went through a second coffee and a pain au chocolat by the time her food arrived. He told her about the text, between mouthfuls and an email from an anonymous encrypted source telling them a warrant had been secured and to enter the house with the forensic team.

"Last night was fun," she said, referring to their dinner with Stevie and Zac at Le Jules Verne restaurant atop the Eiffel Tower. Zac had insisted they have a touristy evening together and, later, they boarded a disco bus and danced their way around the city's main monuments. The evening's champagne had caused a slow start to Darwin's workout.

"It was. How's your head?" he asked.

"Better after the sauna and massage."

"They're a nice couple."

"Yes, but Stevie has a wild spirit. I love her, but she disappears for months on her adventures," said Eyrún.

"Hmm," he said, knowing Zac had privately complained about it once. Zac was also deeply passionate about his start-up company and had distractions of his own. But for now, they were together and traveling to the south of France, where Stevie had promised to show Zac some caves with early human art. *They're good together, but we shall see.*

34

Neuilly-sur-Seine

A few minutes before one o'clock that afternoon, Darwin's and
Eyrún's rideshare stopped two blocks from Rue Perronet, in the
commune of Neuilly-sur-Seine on the edge of Paris. They walked the
remaining distance to Jacques's house. A police van rolled by them,
and they found it a minute later parked in the driveway. The junior
detective who had interviewed them the night of their arrest intercepted them as they approached.

"*Bonjour,*" he said.

"*Bonjour,*" they said in unison.

"The team has gone inside. You can enter after their initial sweep.
Follow me," he said, directing them inside the van, where they put on
shoe coverings and gloves. He handed them a clipboard with a document. Darwin translated it for Eyrún, and they signed the release
agreeing to work as specialist consultants to the Police Nationale. They
waited in the van until the junior detective's radio alerted them it was
safe to go in, then he led the way to the front door into a brief entry
with a narrow honey-colored table, its surface scored from years of
use. Darwin ran a hand across the grain, his fingertips slowed by the

slight stickiness of natural wax. A coat rack mounted above the table held a single coat, a puffer jacket probably taken out of storage for the cooler evenings of late.

Darwin's stomach growled in response to the aroma of roasted chicken, the rosemary and thyme bouquet melded with earthy celery and carrots, all bound by butter and chicken fat. An opening to the kitchen on his left was the source of Jacques's interrupted lunch.

"You have two hours. Take nothing and put all objects back in their place. I am to monitor you," said the junior detective.

Darwin paused at a stairwell where a brighter light shone down. *Likely from the tall windows upstairs,* he thought.

"The rest of the house is off-limits to you," chided the detective as he led them through the front room.

"Oh my," said Eyrún, stepping onto the parquet flooring that creaked as they moved across its well-worn surface. The entry's modest hominess gave way to an eighteenth-century French sitting room replete with pastel blue walls and gold filigree. An ornate chandelier resembling a balloonist floated over the sitting area.

A man's portrait dominated the far wall. His quasi-military dress featured a large medal over his left breast and another suspended from a broad red ribbon around his neck. The youthful round face had a neutral expression, but his dark eyes bored into the viewer. Darwin guessed the style as the mid-1700s. The subject's curly white hair gathered in the back rather than the cascading mountains of hair in fashion the century before. He whistled low. *If it's real, that's bank.*

Eyrún lightly grazed the fabric of one cushioned chair atop an elegant hand-woven carpet. A large, elaborately carved and gold-leafed mirror opposite the painting gave the space a wider dimension. France was full of antiques, but Darwin sensed these also had strong provenance.

"Let's go," said the junior detective, leading them down a short hallway lined with dozens of photos. Most people were dressed formally, and, judging from the dresses and hairstyles, the gatherings ranged over decades. They turned into a well-lit room where two fluorescent ceiling fixtures cast the room in a commercial-office white.

Two modern office work tables lined the wall opposite the door. A

PC under one table connected to two high-resolution monitors, its wireless keyboard and mouse resting in a tray below the desktop. On the other table, Jacques had arrayed research papers in straight rows. Twin printers, both laser and color inkjet, rested on a shelf below.

"It's just like my office," joked Darwin, whose research spaces mimicked a shoreline full of flotsam and jetsam. He turned to the opposite wall where Eyrún was reviewing floor-to-ceiling bookshelves. He knew some of the titles, having studied philosophy for two years before switching to archaeology.

"This guy's a monarchist throwback," said Darwin.

"How so?" asked Eyrún, stepping beside him.

"These titles," he said, translating them for her. *"The Bourbon Restoration. In Search of a Conservative Interest in Post-Revolutionary France. French Foreign Policy of the First Restoration.* And this more modern stuff, Fascist Ideology of France and an entire row of Action Française publications."

"What does that mean?"

"He's deeply committed to far-right politics."

Darwin returned to the research on the table above the printers. Most titles were on Notre-Dame, the Nazare cathedral in Béziers, and the Knights Templar. One article from the *European Journal of Human Genetics* caught his attention, and he picked it up. Dated October 2013, its abstract reviewed how Y-chromosomal DNA analysis of three living descendants of Louis XIV disproved that blood on a handkerchief in a macabre display case was that of the beheaded Louis XVI.

Weird, he thought, paging through the document. He stopped on the Bourbon family tree, beginning with Henry IV, King of France, who died in 1610. Rectangles with the names, titles, and dates were arrayed in four columns. The leftmost column contained Henry's descendants, ending with Louis XVI in 1793. The three other columns branched sons in Henry's line who were not in line for the throne. Columns two and three were Bourbons, while the fourth, right-hand column was the Orléans. Each of columns two, three, and four ended with one of the DNA study's living descendants.

Jacques had drawn a red circle around "Louis Dauphin of France" in the left column. Unfortunately for the heir apparent Dauphin, he died before his father, and the crown passed to his son Louis XVI, the beheaded king.

An arrow from the circle pointed to a notation: "Anne Marie 3x great-grandmother. Affair with Dauphin," then another arrow with a box around the name Jean-Michel Bourbon.

Darwin put the article back in its place and picked up the one below it titled: *Avec les jeunes royalistes français*. The article was part gossip and part fact, with large color photos of a handsome man in a blue suit and other well-dressed people posing with him for selfies.

Eyrún had walked over and asked, "What's it say?"

"With the young French royalists," he said and summarized the article for her. "It's about a gathering last summer near Pont Neuf, that's the bridge over Île de la Cité, to celebrate this guy's homecoming. He's Louis Alphonse, Duke of Anjou, who claims he should be king of France."

"That's crazy," she said.

"I know, huh? Wait—" he grabbed the DNA article again and turned to the genealogy chart. "Look, he's this guy here. A direct descendent of Philip V, King of Spain, who was himself a son of Louis, the Grand Dauphin."

They studied the chart and the people in the *Vice* magazine article.

"But what does this circle and note about three X great-grandmother mean?" asked Eyrún.

Darwin's eye traveled upward to two framed photos on the wall. While the main room and stairwell featured dozens of photos, the office was sparse. The first photo was of a man and woman in faded color. A small boy, likely Jacques by his blond hair, sat between them on a park bench. The second photo was of the man with long hair besuited in the wide lapels and tie worn in the early 1970s.

A third frame contained a yellowed newspaper article. As Darwin read it, a void opened as he thought back to the drowning of a family friend. "Aw, jeez," he said, looking down and placing his palms on the table.

"What's it say?" she asked.

"His—" He swallowed hard and started again. "His parents, Jean-

Michel and Amelie Bourbon were killed in a terrorist attack by Carlos the Jackal in 1974. Jacques was seven years old."

"Oh, my God," said Eyrún, putting a hand to her mouth.

"I think it explains a lot of what we read in his profile yesterday. His right-wing immigrant-hating rhetoric is fueled by a combination of his parents' murder and his aunt's politics. But this is the most interesting, by far," Darwin said, picking up the document with the family tree and pointing to the red-penned note about the three-times great-grandmother's affair and Jean-Michel Bourbon. "I think Jacques Bourbon is claiming he could be a contender for king of France."

"What!" said Eyrún. "No one in France can seriously think it will come back. I mean, the monarchy ended in 1789. Les Misérables and the guillotines."

"You'd be surprised," he said. "The battles between the revolutionists and the monarchists lasted for years, and *Le Mis* is about a revolution in the eighteen-thirties."

They stepped toward the door, where a meter-square map of France filled much of the wall. City maps of Paris and Béziers tacked along the sides of the big map provided detailed views. Jacques had connected locations by strings pinned between the main map and city maps and written commentary on Post-it notes. Darwin studied the maps and mentally went through the codex steps as he followed the strings.

Jacques gets the clue from Notre-Dame. The first step is to go to Notre-Dame and look beneath the tiles. He finds an object in the floor that sends him to Béziers, where he gets the third step out of a crypt. Wait...does the codex say step three? He dug his iPhone out of a pocket and tapped to a photo of the decrypted Knights Templar codex, and scrolled down its bottom section:

We encased the papyrus in lead and stored it in a special vault within the Reserve Bank. This is the True treasure.
I care not about the gold and suggest you disperse it in a manner that benefits His kingdom on Earth. Would that we could distribute it to the poor... But we must answer to our fate.

Three steps lead to the Reserve Bank, each one reveals the next.

First, go to Notre-Dame de Paris and stand in the transept beneath the boss. Traverse the black tiles northward until directly under the north transept vault.
Step two lies beneath your feet.

When you align the clues, you will find the cave.

May God guide you.

What the hell? Thought Darwin. *There's no step three.*

35

Darwin glanced back and forth between his iPhone and the map. *Step one is Notre-Dame. Step two is under the floor tile in Notre-Dame that we guess pointed Jacques to Béziers. Why else would he go there?* He ran a hand through his hair and bit the inside of one cheek. *But it doesn't say step three. It just says, "align the clues."*

As if hearing his thought, Eyrún asked, "Why is Jacques hanging around Paris? Why did he come back here from Béziers?" She noticed the junior inspector had drifted into the other room for a phone call and, motioning Darwin to stay by the door, whispered, "There's a magnifying headset by the monitors. Pierre said Jacques found a small object in Notre-Dame, and we think the Béziers clue is thumb-sized. Right?"

"That's right," said Darwin.

"Maybe he's got it hidden. I'll take a closer look at what's under the desk while the inspector's out of the room. Keep an eye on him."

Darwin focused on the junior inspector's voice when, moments later, Eyrún snapped her fingers. He moved to her side of the room, where she was peering into a small fireproof lockbox, its lid open. "The box was under there," she said, pointing below the table.

Inside lay four plastic bags: two contained thumb-width lead tubes, one cut open cleanly, the other one also cut, but its end cap had been crushed. One ziplocks protected a vellum document, but the other contained just blackened flakes. Darwin snapped a photo of each.

"He's coming," she said and closed the box, returning it to its space under the table. They pretended to scan the books again as the junior inspector returned.

"Did you find anything yet?" he asked.

"No," said Darwin.

The junior detective sat in the desk chair, put in earbuds, and played some music. They used his disinterest to carry on a conversation while Darwin scrolled through the photos he had just taken.

"What's it say?" asked Eyrún, pointing to the vellum.

"It's hard to read through the plastic, but this word is clearly *Béziers*. I'll bet it's the clue from Notre-Dame."

"Show me one of the entire box," she said. He thumbed to it, and she continued, "Look, the vellum is next to the clean-cut tube. We see what a neat-freak he is, so these must be in order." She swiped to the photo of the broken tube and zoomed in on its cut end.

"See, it's cut clear here between the cap and the rest of the tube, but the cap—" she forced the zoom with her fingers and held it "—it's cracked. See all this black material. I wish we could look at it again."

"Doesn't matter," he said, swiping to the photo of the bag containing the blackened flakes. "It's destroyed. Vellum is an animal tissue. I'm guessing the tube was punctured when it was driven into the eye socket. Even if the body was long dead, molds and bacteria would have entered the tube and destroyed the vellum. It's been in there, what, seven hundred years."

"Then he doesn't know the next step any more than we do. Damn it," she said. "Show me that Knights Templar codex again. Maybe we overlooked something."

He did, and they stood together, reading and rereading the text. After a moment, Darwin turned his attention to the map on the front wall. He handed Eyrún the device and went to the map, where he studied the notes again. He cut a piece of string from a spool on the desk and pinned it between Paris and Béziers.

"Why did you do that?" she asked.

"Dunno. It feels like there's a connection, or maybe the connection is just they're the only two locations." He stepped back and photographed the map again. They made another slow pass around the room, avoiding the junior inspector, who was now thumbing his way through a game.

"Can you think of anything else we should look for?" he asked when they converged again near the map.

"No," she said.

Darwin tapped the junior inspector's shoulder and said they were ready to leave. The inspector paused the game and led them back through the house. Darwin stopped in the front room, taking it in.

"What is it?" Eyrún asked.

"There's more to this guy than being a treasure hunter," said Darwin. His eyes settled on the portrait for a long moment, then he googled "Louis Dauphin France" on his mobile.

"You said he needs the money," she said.

"Yeah, but look at this room. These pieces would fetch thousands at auction and—" he looked at the search results "—I knew it. That painting is the Dauphin of France, father of Louis the fourteenth. He's the guy on the genealogy chart who Jacques circled and had an affair with Jacques's three-time great-grandmother."

"So Jacques is really descended from the French kings?"

"Looks like it and depending on the artist and provenance of that painting, it could be worth more than all the houses on this block," he said.

"Then he could sell these things," she said.

"I don't think so. These things, this room, is his legacy. Selling that painting or the furniture would be like cutting off an arm. No, Jacques's quest is more than personal. He truly wants to see a French monarch," he said.

"He wants to be king?"

Darwin shrugged.

"Let's go," said the junior detective.

They followed him and doffed the gloves and booties in the van, then thanked him for helping. As they reached the sidewalk and turned onto Rue Perronet, Eyrún took Darwin's hand. A breeze lifted some leaves, tumbling them on the concrete before dropping them in the street. She gathered her scarf against the coolness.

"What if we can't figure out the missing clue?" she asked.

"Then the treasure's lost," he said.

36

Deep twilight covered Jacques's yard when he returned home and keyed open its front door. He switched on the light and surveyed the room. Nothing seemed out of place. Then he strode into the office, flicked on its light, and went to the lockbox under the desk. He turned the key and lifted the lid. The bags looked as he had left them. Everything else on the desk looked untouched.

But they were here. With that guy Darwin. I know it. Why else would they have held me all afternoon, asking the same questions over and over? He seethed at the violation perpetrated by the police. *The bastards cower us into submission with bullshit anti-terrorism laws while the nation is diluted by the terror of immigration.*

The police had shown Jacques a still photo from CCTV of him entering and exiting the crypt in Béziers and a photo of the iron door across the tunnel under the Seine. They repeatedly asked about the door and a desecrated tomb in Notre-Dame, but there was no evidence he had opened either.

He had explained the Béziers visit as research for a paper on the Cathar suppression. On Notre-Dame, he maintained the alibi of being at a political rally, knowing his *gilet jaune*, yellow vest, friends would continue backing him up. They had even more animosity toward the police.

When Jacques demanded release after two hours, the lead detective showed him the judicial order allowing a search of his home. At that point, he requested a lawyer. Two hours later, a lawyer who had represented many in the National Rally party ripped through the police's weak charges, and Jacques was released.

They abused the law to get into my house. His arms were shaking, and he looked at his clenched fists, knuckles white from the compression. He uncurled his fingers and released the upper body tension.

He moved to the map. *Something's different.* His eyes roved the map of France, running between it and the detailed city maps until his vision came to rest on the new string pinned between Paris and Béziers. "I knew it!" he yelled and ripped at the string, its pins flying across the room. He tore the maps from the wall until he stood panting before the blank blue wall punctuated by small white divots where the pins had torn the wallboard.

He collapsed in the office chair, its back creaking as he reclined. After a minute, he went to the kitchen and filled a glass from a half-full bottle of wine. He had purchased a mixed case of high-vintage Bordeaux with the money Franz had wired. This third bottle was, so far, the best. He gulped twice, topped up the glass, and returned to the office.

A lighter head soon followed the warmth in his gut and helped unravel the knot behind his eyes. He brought the glass to his nose. The wine had muted overnight but still bore its quality. He tipped it back and let the 2009 Bordeaux from Château Palmer, Margaux, roll over his tongue.

His intellect, now freed from the overpowering emotions, began to work the problem. *What did he want? The clues, of course,* came the answer. *He must have looked in the box and knows the second clue is useless... Now he's stuck, just like me.*

He looked at the mess on the floor. *You need to control your anger, Jacques,* came a voice from his past. He gulped the remaining wine to drown out his ex-wife's regular caution. *Leave me alone!* He pounded the table to drive out the memory and returned his focus to the map. He remembered Franz saying the guy had brilliant intuition.

Why put a string between Paris and Béziers? What did you see, Darwin?

Jacques got up and spent the next quarter hour replacing the maps, notes, and strings, finally putting back the string that Darwin had added.

The treasure's not lost. It's somewhere here, away from Paris, but likely at some crossroad for easy access. He traced a finger along the string. The Knights Templar had hidden it from the corrupt Philip and his puppet Pope. *But de Molay would want the surviving brothers to find it. He wanted them to create a new republic, with a true king, not some greedy bastard.*

Jacques agreed with Philip's secular separation of France from the Pope's rule, but his appreciation ended there. The corrupt regime exceeded its fiduciary right to rule when Philip murdered the Templars.

The Grand Master wrote it's in a cave... Darwin's an archaeologist... He would know about caves...

Jacques rushed to the chair, wheeled in front of the monitors, and tapped the keyboard. He consulted a notebook while the screens woke up and typed three words—Darwin, Lacroix, and Cave—in the search bar. He scanned the results and clicked on one he had remembered reading when Franz first told him about Darwin.

His eyes swept back and forth on a magazine interview where Darwin talked about his theory about the Roman military using cave networks in Gaul. *He must know something!* Jacques spun to look at the map. *Why else would he have put the string there?*

Jacques printed the article and grabbed his notebook. He paused, tallying what to bring, and decided on the DSLR camera with a 300 mm zoom lens. Then he ordered a taxi from his mobile, checked a weather app, and put a down vest in his pack. Before leaving the house, he grabbed a leather fedora to shade his face from the increasingly intrusive Eurozone surveillance.

37

Darwin ordered charcuterie and cheese plates back at the hotel, and, soon afterward, the aroma of freshly baked baguette filled their suite. He tore off a point of the rustic bread and bit down on his favorite part of the loaf. He then cut a chunk from a saucisson, soon clearing a wide swath across the platter.

"Oh, cute. Look at this photo of Stevie and Zac," said Eyrún. "They're kayaking near Vallon-Pont-d'Arc."

She sat next to Darwin, holding her mobile as he wiped his hands on a napkin. Then she put down the device and spread goat cheese on a piece of baguette. She stood and walked to the window. After a bit, she turned and said, "I've been thinking about what you said outside Jacques's house. That the treasure would be lost. I think there's no way de Molay and the other guy, er..."

"Geoffroi de Charny," said Darwin.

"Right, de Charny. There's no way they'd let that happen. A document written by Christ would be valuable beyond measure. There's no way they'd risk having it lost forever."

"Okay," said Darwin.

"They needed their heirs to find it when it's safe, but they couldn't know if that would be in a decade or a hundred years. When did the codex get back to the Vatican?"

"Thirteen-eighty-seven."

"So, two generations after they wrote the codex," she said. Darwin spread cheese on another piece of baguette and handed it to her. "Thanks," she said, taking time to chew and swallow, then asked, "Did the Knights Templar continue on after the purge?"

"Well, The Order of Christ in Portugal absorbed any Templars that survived the massacre, but there can't have been many," he said.

"Still, if you were de Molay and de Charny, you'd want the treasure to survive even a catastrophic collapse. You'd have to make sure any brother could recover the treasure. I guess what I'm trying to say is, they wouldn't leave only serial clues," she said.

Darwin stood up suddenly and began pacing the room. "I think I get it," he said, turning around at the window and stopping. "You're suggesting that if the clues depended solely on being found in sequence and one was destroyed—like the one from Béziers—the treasure would be lost."

"Exactly! They'd never allow that. They protected the papyrus, used it for leverage, whatever, for hundreds of years before the purge. They'd have left multiple ways for someone to find it as a backup," she said.

Darwin switched on the TV with the remote and grabbed his mobile. Then he used a screencast feature on his mobile to project de Molay's codex onto the flat screen.

Eyrún touched the TV. "This sentence."

When you align the clues, you will find the cave.

"What does he mean, align the clues? How does the clue in Paris align with the clue in Béziers?"

"Wait. What? Say that again."

"How do the clues in Paris and Béziers align?"

"Exactly!" He tapped rapidly on his mobile and switched the TV projection to the photo he took of the map in Jacques's office. He studied it up close. "What if it literally means 'a line'? Here's Paris."

He put a finger on the French capital and moved his finger along the string in the photo. "And here's Béziers."

"Uh-huh," said Eyrún.

"Literally, a...LINE between the two clues." He walked back to her, and they both sat on the bed, looking at the map. *It's there. I can feel it.* His heels drummed on the hardwood floor. He switched the TV view back to the codex.

Eyrún read from the screen. "When you align the clues... you will find the cave."

"The cave. The cave," repeated Darwin.

"Stevie says there're caves all over the south of France," she said.

"Hundreds—wait." He switched back to the map photo. "What kind of cave—think large underground chamber—would allow the Knights Templar complete control of access?"

"A lava chamber?" she asked.

"Precisely! Clermont-Ferrand!" he said, tapping his finger on a point between Paris and Béziers. "It's got to be the Puy de Dôme volcano."

"But is Clermont-Ferrand in a direct line?" she asked.

"It's close," he said, following the string. "Maybe ten kilometers off, but back in the Templars' day, that was close enough to a straight line. I need to study my old notes."

Eyrún's watch chimed. "I've got my board call in five minutes. Should take about an hour and a half."

"No problem. I'm good here," said Darwin.

Eyrún went to the suite's bedroom side to take a board of directors call with Stjörnu Energy. While she took a few months of leave from her day-to-day responsibilities, her role as chief scientist and principal required her to participate in strategic and financial discussions.

She watched him a few moments before closing the door. Darwin's sense of wonder was infectious, but she still clung to her own sense of professional achievement. A month back, she had begun journaling at

Stevie's recommendation. It was more a list of what made her happy and not than a compilation of feelings. Not surprisingly, she learned that exploration fueled her desire to get up in the morning, but she had a fear of taking significant risks. When she considered Darwin, he was almost the opposite.

He's crazy-creative and plunges into things. Well, sometimes with the wrong people. She rolled her eyes at his adventure in Siwa Oasis with a psychopathic archaeologist. But she felt his runaway intuition was the perfect pairing to her methodical, engineer-like approach. *I've always been good at making things work, getting out of trouble.*

The videoconference activated, and, as the business started, she recalled what Stevie had once said: "You're a fixer, Eyrún. Darwin's a great finder. You need each other."

38

A short while later, the door closed, and Darwin listened to Eyrún's animated voice greeting her colleagues. *She's so good with people and knows how to deal with all that corporate bullshit.* He had heard her frustrated talk over the antics by this or that executive during many of their dinners. With no patience for politics, he was again thankful for the windfall he got from the diamonds in Iceland.

He had dreaded returning to his associate professorship at the University of California, Berkeley. He enjoyed researching and publishing, but not the constant gossip and sucking up to department heads. No wonder his grandfather had left academia. *How the hell do my parents stand it? Merde, I promised to call them.* He popped in earbuds and called.

"Hey, Dad," he said when his father, Olivier, answered.

"Darwin! What's up? We're at Marie's. It's Chloe's fifth birthday. Here—I'll hold the phone for her."

Darwin sang a birthday song for his niece and imagined the family at his sister Marie's house in Lyon. Chloe told him about her cake and launched into a story about a friend. He smiled, imagining her hands waving while she chattered. *She could filibuster the American Congress.*

He tapped on his iPad as he listened, navigating to research on lava chambers and tubes kept in a secure cloud folder. "Hey, Mom," Darwin said when Chloe handed off the phone and gave his mother a brief update on what he and Eyrún were doing as he swiped through the scrolls. When his mom passed the phone back to his dad, he started reading a document.

"What? Uh…sorry, Dad. Say that again."

"That's okay. We're ready for the cake here, and it sounds like you're busy with something," said Olivier.

They ended the call with Darwin promising to visit them in London before the holidays. He tossed the mobile onto a chair and continued reading, but flipping back and forth between documents proved a challenge. *I need printouts.*

A quarter hour later, Darwin stood over a printer in the hotel's business office. He needed to see these scans of Roman scrolls laid out side by side to follow their details. The fragile papyri had been dug up in Herculaneum by his three-times great-grandfather Pasquale Lacroix. The scrolls had been saved by a fireproof box buried in the eruption of Mount Vesuvius in 79 CE.

Darwin pulled the first page from the printer, a letter found on top of all the box's contents when it was opened over two hundred years ago:

> *My time is at an end. I cannot flee the eruption, and I fear burial with the town is my fate. Take the contents of this box to my son-in-law Agrippa Cicero in Rome. There is gold to compensate for your journey.*
>
> *May the gods guard your safety,*
>
> *Martinus Saturninus*

Darwin read this three years prior when he first opened the box with his grandfather Emelio. The scrolls, mainly written by a Roman named Agrippa Cicero, detailed Roman military movements across

Europa using lava tubes. Unfortunately, no physical evidence remained, so the writings were deemed a hoax.

However, Emelio was undeterred and compromised a promising academic career by chasing proof. And, against his father, Olivier's, strident advice, Darwin took up the family quest that had been dubbed the Lacroix curse. But whereas generations before him had failed, Darwin got a lucky break when a lava tube in Iceland revealed evidence of Roman artifacts.

The printer finished, and he gathered the warm paper, put his iPad on top, and returned to the suite.

A s he climbed the stairs, he thought about his hunch. Agrippa Cicero had documented lava tubes around Herculaneum and across other parts of Europa. In particular, Agrippa wrote about Augustonemetum, the ancient Roman city that became modern-day Clermont-Ferrand and lay in the shadow of an ancient volcano, Puy de Dôme.

This Templar's cave is connected. I feel it.

He opened the suite and heard Eyrún talking. A glance at a clock showed her call would go on another forty-five minutes. He had spread the papers across the sofa, table, and chairs in the sitting room. Then he scanned letters between Agrippa and Nero, the Roman Emperor. Judging from the familiar tone, Darwin guessed the two had a shared past, as Nero referred to their adventures in one letter. As the timeline progressed from 57 to 59 CE, Agrippa explored the Roman, now Italian, peninsula, and southern Gaul.

A second scroll from 60 to 63 CE documented discoveries across Gaul and into Britannia. The third, and last, large scroll contained the exhaustive detail of mining in excursions to Britannia and Germania. It ranged from 63 to 68 CE. Darwin knew from a personal diary left in the box that Agrippa's family left Rome after Nero's murder, but nothing else. Vesuvius erupted in 79 and buried the box.

Darwin focused on the second scroll. Three years earlier, he had followed a resurfaced lead in Clermont-Ferrand that led to him finding a lava tube deep under the city's cathedral. He found evidence of the Christian Crusaders in the tunnel complex and suspected there was much more, but the Catholic Church controlled access and prevented him from exploring farther.

Not a day had gone by when he had not thought about those tunnels. The Knights Templar were formed in the years of the early Crusades. *If my hunch is right, then Trencavel would've known about the tunnels. If there was a large chamber, he would've found it.*

He brought steepled fingers to his nose and eyes closed, visualizing his one visit beneath the cathedral. Access was tight, through an old grate deep in the crypt. It fit. Trencavel, as a Catholic knight, could have controlled the aboveground entrance to the tunnels. Darwin paged through the transcript for the second scroll.

Something's not right. He looked at the first and third scrolls. *These have much more detail. The second is more of…. Emelio!* He reached for the phone and tapped the number.

Emelio answered on the fourth ring. "Darwin, my boy, how are you?"

"Great. How about you?"

"I'm an old man, every day lived is wonderful. Did you see the Pope? What did he want?"

Darwin caught him up on his visit with the Pope, realizing it was only five days since they were in Corsica.

"Emelio, what can you tell me about Agrippa's second scroll. The one that Dad sold?"

"What do you want to know?"

This was a sore spot in the family, as Olivier had sold it during a fit of teenage rage. Emelio had tried to recover it and failed, but told Darwin that he had made a full transcript. But from his reading of it a few minutes back, Darwin knew it was written from memory.

"It doesn't have the same detail as the others. Are you sure the transcript is right?"

Emelio was silent, but Darwin could hear breathing.

"Grand-père?"

"I'm sorry. I wrote the transcript from my notes. I lied to you. I didn't scan them all until after your father sold the second one," said Emelio.

"It's okay, *grand-père*."

"No. No. I should have told you. I...," he trailed off.

"Emelio. It's okay. We made a brilliant discovery in Iceland from your work. I think we have a chance to do it again."

"Really?"

Darwin explained the clues found and how they might line up to Clermont-Ferrand, but said he needed to see the details.

"I need that second scroll. We have enough money to get it back, whatever the cost. Do you know if Robert still has it?"

"I don't know. He's dead."

39

Jacques exited the taxi two blocks behind Musée d'Orsay, in a neighborhood of galleries and antique dealers. He preferred approaching the hotel on foot. He knew the street, having worked with some dealers on appraisals of the big house's furnishings. Jacques had consolidated the most valuable pieces when he moved into the cottage. One dealer enthusiastically offered her services should he ever want to sell the painting of the Dauphin.

Jacques would sooner part with a lung. His ex-wife had once commented, "You have the same eyes." But he never mentioned its provenance. His great-great-great-grandmother Anne Marie and the Dauphin of France were lovers and had a son. The royal family disavowed it, but upon Louis's premature death, they gave Anne Marie the painting to buy her silence.

He turned on Rue de Verneuil and two buildings down entered the lobby of Darwin's and Eyrún's boutique hotel. He paused, gathered his bearings, and walked to a small corner table in the hotel's lounge. He ordered a cocktail and relaxed into the low chair. While watching the bartender measure the ingredients into a beaker and fill it with ice, he mentally organized what to do next. The cocktail spoon twirled rapidly as the condensation clouded the glass.

Jacques could see the front door and the short corridor to the lift. His drink arrived, the ice sphere knocking against the crystal sides as the barkeep set it down. Asked if he needed anything else, Jacques said, "*Non. Merci.*" He sipped the Vieux Carré, his favorite from *Nouveau Orleans* in America. He shuddered at the incompetence that lost what rightfully should have remained in the Kingdom of France.

He called Darwin's and Eyrún's room from a lobby phone and, getting no answer, figured they had gone out. He ordered a bottle of still water and an appetizer as he scrolled news articles on his mobile. Several minutes later, he heard laughter and looked up to see Eyrún and Darwin passing through the lobby to the lift. Jacques picked up the camera, switching it on as he aimed. If asked, he would claim to work as a freelance photographer. He zoomed in to fill the frame with Eyrún's face. Her pale, clear, Nordic complexion featured round cheekbones pushed up by a dazzling smile. Jacques snapped a photo when she turned slightly in the camera's direction, the viewfinder winking as it captured her eyes. Her long, dark hair occluded her face as she turned into the lift, laughing again at something Darwin said.

She reached for the lift buttons, and Jacques zoomed in full on the mirror on its back wall. He squeezed off a series of shots as the doors closed. He then reviewed the photos through the camera's rear display until a clear image showed Eyrún's finger depress number six. The next one confirmed that button six was lit. Jacques put down the camera and sipped his drink, now mainly flavored water.

He gathered his notebook and left a fifty-euro note in the leather folder the barkeep had placed on the table. Being cheap in this hotel would draw more attention from the staff than would being generous. He rode the lift to the second floor, where mahogany-paneled walls reflected a warm light and smelled of beeswax. The deep-pile blue carpet absorbed his footfalls like a well-tended lawn.

Only four rooms opened on each side, and he pushed through the last door on the left labeled *Sortie,* exit. He let the door close quietly and tested it. *Unlocked. Good.* He could move between floors unnoticed.

He climbed to the sixth floor and peered out. Seeing it empty, he stepped out and crossed to the other end. There were only two doors on this floor—one in front and the other to its rear. The front side door opened, and Jacques put the mobile to his ear and turned to a small table. He mimicked a call as he used the glass in a painting to see who came out–four people, including two children. He turned slowly to confirm it was not Darwin and Eyrún, then retreated to the stairs, noting their room number, 603.

40

Jacques returned to the lounge, gambling on the idea that Darwin and Eyrún would go out for dinner. A little after 8 p.m., he was rewarded when they left the hotel. Darwin's sports jacket and Eyrún's dress led him to deduce they were headed to a nicer restaurant. When he was sure they would not rush back for a forgotten mobile or something similar, he gathered his things.

His heart quickened as he furtively looked around. The lobby had at least two cameras, but he had not seen any on the sixth floor. This time he passed the lift to the stairwell and descended to the basement. The small gym and a conference room were empty, and the housekeeping office had one of its scuffed double doors propped open.

He paused, listening for voices. If anyone came out, he would ask directions for the toilet. They organized the space for capacity, with supplies crammed in among towels and linens. The well-heeled guests above paid for space, and the laborers below got what was left over. A metaphor for many things, he thought, and moved to the desk. A printout on a clipboard showed which rooms needed servicing.

His timing was right. The staff was upstairs on its turndown service run. Scanning the desk, he did not see what he needed, the master room keycard. *Not something they'd leave around, or they're all with the staff. But what about a spare?* He opened the desk drawer. *There!* He removed a blank, white, plastic card that leaned against the drawer's side and retreated from the office.

Jacques tested the keycard on the gym's door and heard the familiar chunk of the lock mechanism being released. *Good!* He tried the door and continued upstairs. On the sixth floor, he paused, letting his heart rate settle, and continued to the entrance of 603.

Looking left and right, he keyed the door and pushed in. He turned and let the door close quietly before straining for sounds of anyone still in the room. "Room service," he called out, keeping a hand on the door in case of a reply.

Nothing.

He moved into the suite and found few signs of occupation. Darwin and Eyrún each had a small case on stands in the bedroom, but there was little in the bathroom. *They travel light or had planned on a brief trip,* he thought. As he walked into the sitting room, he saw the open cabinet door and the small safe, its LED lights showing LOCKED. His shoulders slumped. *There's nothing here.* He had counted on Darwin, leaving at least something. *Relax. Focus. Look around,* he coached himself and massaged his temples to release tension.

The suite's doorbell rang, and a moment later, the lock clacked open. "*Service de préparation à la nuit,* turndown service," said a female voice.

Jacques started for the bathroom but froze, knowing she would go there. He pirouetted to the bedroom armoire, but just before opening it, he saw some paper sheets in the trash bin. One looked like a handwritten note. He grabbed the folded sheets out of the bin and then squeezed into the armoire, bumping his head on the clothes bar. He winced and rubbed the spot.

His heart thrummed like a scooter on full throttle. *What if she opens the door?* Fixing one eye to the slit between the doors, he saw her move from one side of the bed to the other as she rolled back the covers and left chocolates on the pillows. The sound of running water meant she had moved into the bath. Then all went quiet.

He thought he heard the front door close and waited a bit longer before he risked coming out. She had set the bedroom lights into evening mode and left small lamps on in the sitting room. He peered around the bedroom door. She had gone. He made one more pass around the room and found a pad on a table near the sitting room's rear window.

CDG > Johannesburg
AF 990 11:35 > 11:20 Thursday

What the hell? He snapped a photo, then exited the suite.

41

"I need to go to Johannesburg," said Darwin after the server picked up their appetizer plates and poured the decanted red wine.

"What!" said Eyrún. "You can't be serious."

Never good at conflict, Darwin looked into his wine as he drank.

Eyrún continued. "What's in...oh, no. This has got to be about Ian."

Their main courses arrived, and they sat back as the plates were centered, and the servers retreated.

"I talked to Emelio this afternoon while you were on your call. He confessed that he did not scan the second scroll before my dad sold it to Robert Van Rooyen," he said.

"But Robert's in prison in Marseilles. Isn't he?"

"Was. He passed away."

Darwin explained the lack of clarity in the second scroll and that Agrippa had probably written as much detail in it as he had in the other two scrolls. When Emelio learned of Robert's death, he contacted the estate's attorney. And when Emelio had asked about a Roman scroll, the lawyer referred him to Ian, who was the estate's executor.

"Did you call him?"

"I thought it best, given our history, to meet him in person. He'd be—"

"Likely to punch you or worse—*given our history*," she said.

Ian Walls had gone with them in the expedition through the Iceland lava tube. A key investor on the project, Robert Van Rooyen, had backed Ian over Darwin, whom he deemed too inexperienced. At the time, Eyrún agreed with Van Rooyen's assessment but changed her opinion of Darwin during the journey when one of Ian's men rigged an explosion, nearly killing them all. Ian was exonerated of wrongdoing, but Darwin had not spoken to him in the three years since they parted company.

"I looked him up. His company seems to do well," said Darwin.

"And you think that means he'll forgive and forget? Why do you need this scroll so badly?"

"I need to know what Agrippa found. His scroll on Brittania is precise, listing the tube connections into the lead and silver mines. And my gut tells me there is more under Puy de Dôme. The Crusaders left graffiti in the tunnels under the Cathedral, so the Templars must have known it," he said.

She tore off a piece of bread and mopped up some of the sauce in her chicken tarragon dish. "The geology's right for caves. I'll give you that," she said, leaning to put the bread in her mouth. She wiped her chin and added, "We'll both go. He might not react well to you, so I'll call. Tell him we're on holiday and would like to get together with him and his fiancée. He's probably married by now."

"Thanks," he said.

"Don't thank me. The sooner we get this over with, the sooner we can get back to Corsica. I want to finish the house before winter."

42

Jacques paused in the stairwell and looked at the photo to make sure he read it right. *What're they up to?* His hand went to his jacket pocket, where he had put the papers from the bin. *I can't read these here. I need to get to a safer place.* He ran down the stairs, the balls of his feet flying off each carpeted step. Slowing to a moderate walk when reaching the lobby, he left the hotel and, three blocks later, ducked into a Starbucks.

He took a barstool seat at a sidewall and began reading the pages. Four were descriptions of tunnels and an account of the metals in each. He figured this is why they went into the bin. The fifth was a letter written in 1943 that was both enlightening and perplexing:

My dearest Amelie,

I miss your friendship tremendously and I can only hope your new life in Paris is as fulfilling as you expect. My job as a junior priest is more administrative than I imagined, but it led me to an exciting discovery.

While cleaning the Bishop's office, I found an old book of accounts. Most of it concerns procurement for the cathedral, but I happened upon some entries for the mid-1800s that detailed supplies and labor to seal up tunnels in the newly discovered crypt.

There are payments to your grandfather for his services to explore and document the tunnels. There is a letter inserted in the pages written by a Bishop Féron and signed by Giraud, swearing him to secrecy about the tunnels.

I had to put the book away as the senior priest Piguet returned. He questioned me and said to leave the old books undisturbed.

When you return, I will show you the book. It has notes about the sarcophagus that hides the opening to the deep tunnel. We'll find what your grandfather kept secret.

Yours in Christ,
Marcel

Did Darwin throw this away by mistake? A deep tunnel. Which cathedral? He flipped over the page. *Blank.* He shuffled through the other pages again. *Unrelated. Dammit. And Johannesburg. Is this Amelie or Marcel there? A descendent, maybe?*

Some mental arithmetic estimated the ages of the parties in the letter over ninety years old. He searched on names and various combinations, but the results were too broad. He could not even be sure what connected the flight to South Africa and this letter. He leaned forward, elbows on the counter, and massaged his forehead.

I have to follow them. Darwin's onto something, something he saw on my map. He could think of no other explanation for Darwin's burst of activity today. *Fine, Darwin. Now I'm stalking you.*

He sat up and looked at the time—half-past nine. *Go home. Look up Thursday's flights to Johannesburg.*

43

The taxi deposited Jacques the next day just after 7 p.m. Last night, when he had checked Johannesburg flights matching those times, he learned it took off Wednesday night at 11:35 p.m. and landed Thursday morning at 11:20 a.m. He paid the driver and walked to a black Renault Espace parked half a block from the hotel. He tapped on the window, and the driver clicked open the locks.

"*Bonjour*, Guy. See them yet?" asked Jacques.

"*Bonjour*. No one's come out of the hotel since I arrived about six," said Guy.

"Thanks for coming out on your day off." Jacques handed Guy four folded fifty-euro notes.

"That's too much," Guy protested.

"Take it. You need it with your son going to university. I'm getting paid for this, and so should you."

Guy grunted and stuffed the bills in his pocket, then excused himself to use the hotel's toilet. Jacques rechecked the flight on the Air France app. It was on time and still had available seats. The coach price held, the same as this morning, at €2,307. He was loath to burn down the cash from Franz but stayed focused on the end payout.

An hour later, Guy followed Darwin's and Eyrún's limo across the

Seine in thick traffic. Jacques and Guy talked about the new starting eleven for the Paris-St. Germain football club and then argued about a new leader in the Assemblée nationale who had backtracked on major reform legislation.

"Bums. They say anything to get elected, then change their tune. They're all bums," said Guy, kneading the steering wheel like stubborn dough.

Jacques fell silent as they whisked by the suburbs. Forty minutes later, traffic slowed in Roissy as they neared Europe's largest airport. They funneled into the terminal road, and Guy took a parking pass from the machine at Terminal 2E. Darwin's limo, two cars ahead of them, pulled into a spot. Guy drove past and took a spot farther down. "Good luck," he said as Jacques removed his small wheeled case from the back seat.

Darwin and Eyrún entered the terminal and joined the business-class queue. Jacques followed them inside but went to the coach check-in. Its line wrapped halfway around the terminal with travelers going to every corner of the French-speaking world. Children played tag around the carts piled high with cases and boxes wrapped in plastic. He knew the customs and security delay, even leaving the country, would take nearly the entire two and a half hours until takeoff.

He sighed and went to the concierge, where he told a sad story that his uncle in Johannesburg had suddenly passed away. The woman at the desk expressed her sympathy and walked him to the first open agent at the queue's front.

Following an uneventful transition through customs and security, Jacques wandered the airport shops to avoid being seen by Darwin and Eyrún. He waited until everyone had boarded before approaching the departure gate. But he had not seen them since separating at the check-in counters and now scanned the boarding area again. *Where are they?*

"*Monsieur, l'embarquement est sur le point de fermer,* the boarding is about to close," said the gate agent.

"I'm looking for my friends," he said. "I don't want to go without them."

"Everyone has checked in, sir."

At that moment, the stairs below the jet-bridge lit up as a black Mercedes-Benz S class sedan rolled to a stop. The driver opened the doors for three passengers, a woman with a small dog and Darwin and Eyrún. They mounted the steps as Jacques hurried to the gate.

"I found them. They're on the plane." Jacques realized they must have been upgraded to first class, which meant a special boarding privilege.

He apologized for the delay, and they said it was no problem but to hurry, as they were about to close the doors. He hurried down the ramp where a flight attendant checked his boarding pass, and Jacques walked what felt like halfway back to Paris to find his seat in the last row on the aisle. Several families with toddlers and lap infants occupied the surrounding rows and, with no room in the overhead bin for his case, he shoved it under the seat, filling what little leg room there was.

Wrinkling his nose at the toilet adjacent to his seat, he squeezed closed his eyelids and sighed, steeling himself against the next eleven hours. The seatback video screens lit up with the safety announcements, and he tapped the recline button.

"*Putain!*" he muttered, realizing the last row did not go back. He massaged his temples, wondering if it could get any worse.

"Monsieur Bourbon?" said a man's voice.

Jacques opened his eyes to see a flight attendant with the purser's badge squatting next to him.

"Please come with me and bring your case," said the purser.

44

Johannesburg, South Africa

Twelve hours later, the jet touched down in Johannesburg, with Jacques having slept a good seven hours. His only problem with the upgrade to business class was encountering Darwin or Eyrún if they walked around the cabin for exercise. He had slept facing the wall and, during the breakfast service, had worn sunglasses and a hat. But, as best he could tell, they had remained in the first-class cabin the whole flight.

For the last forty minutes during the descent, Jacques had fretted about how he would follow them after landing. He worked on multiple plans, but each had gaps. If they exited the plane to a car service as in Paris, he had no idea how to catch up with them.

The plane jerked to a stop. At the sound of the bell, everyone sprang from their seats, like racehorses. He stayed sitting but could see Eyrún moving about beyond the now-opened curtains that had separated the cabins. They were across from each another in the four-seat premier cabin. Passengers bunched in the aisle next to Jacques, and the door finally opened.

Eyrún and Darwin talked with the purser for a few moments.

Darwin waved his hand in polite decline, and they began walking down Jacques's aisle. He quickly leaned down to rummage in his pack as they walked past.

"I'm done with that damn dog," said Eyrún. "It was cute the first hour, but that lady has no control over her animal. She even insisted I share my breakfast with it. Besides, I need to walk."

Jacques let half a dozen people from the back of the plane go before falling in behind them and walking up the jetway into the labyrinth of corridors that led to customs. The priority pass given to him by the Paris agent allowed him to stay with Darwin and Eyrún as they entered the customs hall.

A quarter hour later, he followed them to the taxi stand, where he let two couples he recognized from the flight move between him and Darwin and Eyrún. The spring temperature felt identical to Paris, right down to the breeze swirling in the shaded arrivals area.

As they got into a taxi, Jacques saw only one other cab behind it. When the people in front of him moved to take it, Jacques burst forth and shouldered his way in. They yelled, and the driver protested until Jacques put 200 euros near the gearshift. A left hand picked up the cash, and the car pulled away.

Jacques had no other plan than to stalk their hotel and follow them. He had no clue why the sudden diversion to Johannesburg, but it must have something to do with the papers that Darwin had printed. He stared out the window as light-industrial buildings gave way to suburban houses.

He connected to the local telecom provider and opened a bookmark on his mobile to a saved article on Darwin's Iceland discoveries. The story had a photo of Darwin, Eyrún, and others at the Edinburgh University Hospital visiting an injured group member. *There!* The last paragraph mentioned that one of the group had been detained by the Scottish national police as a person of interest: Ian Walls from Johannesburg, South Africa.

Searching Ian Walls returned over three pages of names. It would be difficult to narrow it down without more context. *Why did Darwin have to visit in person? He could have called.* The taxi entered the driveway of The Westcliff hotel and paused for steel gates to open. Jacques had seen these kinds of luxury compounds before in France's former colonies.

"Stop there, please." Jacques pointed to a spot outside the portico. The driver pointed to the entry. "No, no. There, please," Jacques insisted. He converted the meter reading in South African rand to euros and added fifty percent to cover any tip and currency exchange.

"Thank you very much, sir," said the driver.

Darwin and Eyrún entered the lobby as Jacques held back, pretending to take in the view.

Ian must have something Darwin needs.

45

"This is lovely." Eyrún stepped out the double doors onto the terrace overlooking Johannesburg. Bright sun warmed the porcelain tiling, but a cool dry breeze, and thin gray clouds, warranted a light jacket. She grasped the wrought-iron railing and took in the wooded neighborhoods whose hills rolled away from them toward the distant plain where their flight had landed. Despite the overnight travel, they were wide awake from sleeping almost the usual number of hours and waking up in the same time zone as Paris. They ordered room service lunch, and each took a quick shower and changed into fresh clothing.

Their server set up lunch on the patio, and, when she learned it was their first visit, gave them a verbal tour of the grounds. "You must visit the spa. Dial two-one-two," she said and confirmed that everything was as ordered before leaving.

Darwin tore into a plate of biltong, a cured meat. The menu had promised a riot of flavor, and the mixture of savory coriander and tangy cloves did not disappoint. He forked more meat onto a flatbread and spooned on chakalaka, a spicy vegetable chutney.

"Ian's office is about twenty kilometers from here. We should call him after lunch, right?" asked Eyrún.

"Yeah," Darwin said through a mouthful. "Like we worked out on the flight. We're here for a short visit and wondered if he would consider having a drink with us."

"What if he declines?"

"We move to plan B. Tell him we want Robert's scroll and will pay for it."

46

Jacques's modest ground-floor room looked out on a garden. He showered and put on a clean shirt, then prepped his small pack for an extended day tailing Darwin and Eyrún. He stopped in the gift shop on the way to the restaurant and bought a South Africa Rugby cap.

Over lunch, he read more search results for Ian Walls while also keeping watch on the lobby area. By the end of the meal, he was no closer to figuring out which Ian, nor had he seen the Lacroix and guessed they ordered lunch in their room. An hour later, when his head nodded against the lobby chair, he got up to get coffee. A thought hit him halfway through a second cup, and he dialed the hotel operator on the lobby phone and asked for Darwin Lacroix's room.

"Hello," Eyrún answered.

"Good afternoon, Ms. Lacroix. This is housekeeping. Would you like us to refresh your room before dinner?"

"No, thanks, but we're going out at five. You can do it then."

"We will do it then. Goodbye," said Jacques and hung up.

That made it easy. He could use the downtime and retreated to his room.

At half-past four, Jacques's alarm sounded. He had drifted into a dream for a while but had been awake when the reminder went off. After gathering what he needed, he headed to the lobby and waited for Darwin and Eyrún. A few minutes before five, they appeared. Jacques watched them from a chair behind a generous plant.

As they entered their car, Jacques hurried into the entry and requested a taxi. Twenty-three minutes later, his driver pulled up at the restaurant behind Darwin's and Eyrún's car, and Jacques stayed in the cab until they went inside.

47

"Hey, you guys!" Ian boomed as they reached a standup table with stools. Darwin extended a hand. Ian took it and pulled him into a hard hug. Then he kissed Eyrún's cheeks and stood back and said, "This is my wife, Katie."

They greeted all around and chatted a few moments before their server checked in to take their drink order.

"This is your turf, Ian. What do you recommend?" Darwin asked, having eyed rows of argon gas-tapped wine bottles for tasting by the glass in one of the world's great wine regions.

"You probably know our South African whites, so I'm going off the beaten path. There's a new generation of winemakers. It might be a while before we rival France, but let's give it a go, eh?"

The server returned with twelve glasses and three bottles. She talked through each wine's vintage and pedigree while filling the glasses, each with two fingers of red wine. The first, a Cinsault, was described as enjoying a revival in South Africa. The second, a Pinotage, was followed by a Shiraz blended with a whisper of Cinsault.

Ian led a toast, "To friends. We started rough and finished proud."

"To friends!" they joined.

Darwin sniffed the glass and sipped a mouthful. Flavors of red berries and cherries complicated by wild herbs cascaded across his taste buds.

"I've only had Cinsault as a blend in a rosé. This is super." He sipped again, seeing the bottom of his glass arrive far too soon. The Pinotage had a curious coffee-bean flavor on top of a classic Pinot Noir structure, and the Shiraz was as bold as one should be.

Ian ordered a second flight and continued describing how his business had expanded in the last three years. He and Katie had married the previous summer and honeymooned in Tokyo.

"World Cup?" asked Darwin, referring to the Rugby World Cup that had taken place the previous autumn in Japan.

"Oh, yes! It was epic," said Katie. "Our boys did us proud. And the shopping was fantastic. I'm glad it's spring so I can wear this again."

"It's cute," Eyrún said, admiring Katie's dress and listening to her go on about the Tokyo designers.

Ian described their great seats at the thrilling match over Wales and how they trounced England in the final. Then he cut to the chase: "So, what brings you to Joburg? You know I got a call from your grandfather a few months back."

"Best not to beat around the bush. It's about the scroll Robert left you," said Darwin." We'd like to get it back into our collection."

"What makes you think I want to give it up?"

Darwin blinked. No words came to mind.

"I'm kidding," said Ian, swatting his shoulder. "I don't give a shit about it or anything that bastard Robert left me. It's in a box at my office. Come around tomorrow and get it. We'll go to lunch."

They ordered dinner, and Darwin got a bottle of the Cinsault. His fears of an awkward meeting had gone away by the time the second tasting flight arrived. They now fell in as the best of friends but avoided talk of their "rough" beginning, as Ian called it. Darwin had always felt a bond with Ian, despite the tension during their first encounter. He excused himself for the toilet.

When he came out, he found Ian waiting for him. "Hey, Darwin. I wanted to catch you alone. Thanks for what you did. It meant a lot. To both of us, me and Katie. That money got us started."

"No problem. You deserved it."

"I didn't want to say in front of Eyrún in case she didn't know."

"I tell her everything. She said I should have given you more."

"No, kidding," said Ian.

"Do you need it?"

"No. We're good. See you back at the table." He pushed into the toilet.

Darwin stared at the closed door for a moment. During negotiations for royalties from their diamond discovery, he had insisted on giving Ian a share. The others objected, and, in the end, Darwin gave up a quarter of his share for Ian. Deep down, he knew the expedition could have gone much worse, and they owed Ian their lives.

When he got back to the table, Eyrún and Katie were laughing like old friends. *I did the right thing,* he thought.

48

After waiting outside for five more minutes, Jacques cautiously entered the restaurant and saw them on its far side at a table with another couple, laughing and chatting. He found an inconspicuous seat at the bar where he could see them.

At one point, Ian followed Darwin to the toilet, and they both seemed to take a little longer than usual, but unless they exchanged an item small enough to fit in a pocket, Jacques was stumped. He went back to articles about Ian and Darwin in Iceland and Edinburgh. His fingers drummed on the bar as he thumbed through the stories. He was still drawing a blank about why Darwin needed to see Ian in person. *Dammit, Darwin. Why're you here?*

"Got stood up?" asked the bartender.

"What?" said Jacques, taking a moment to register the question. "Er, no. Problem at work. Another one of these, please." He tapped the wine glass. The bartender refilled it and moved on to other patrons. Jacques sipped his wine and put the mobile face down on the bar.

He caught a break an hour later when they left the restaurant. Jacques moved toward the front door, careful to keep his face buried in his mobile when he heard Ian say, "come over around ten." *That's it.*

Darwin and Eyrún left in a car, and Ian and his partner walked to a car farther out in the car park.

Jacques returned to his bar seat and pulled up his mapping app. Ian's office was a half hour's drive from the hotel. *Whatever's happening is tomorrow.* He finished his second glass of wine and called a taxi.

49

Midmorning the next day, one of Ian's security drivers picked up Darwin at the hotel. The clear sky reminded him of California. He missed its climate but knew their Corsican mountain house was much like a professor's summer cabin he had visited in California's Sierra Nevada forest.

While aimlessly staring out the passenger window, he drifted into thinking Eyrún was right. *We need to finish the remodel before winter. This scroll probably has what I need to finish writing. But what if it holds vital information about what's under the cathedral in Clermont-Ferrand? How do I convince Eyrún to keep going?* Darwin knew if he could find evidence of a lava tube network, not just isolated locations like Iceland, Rome, and London, then he could publish proof that Romans knew about and used these secret tunnels.

An idea struck him. *What if the Knights Templar found the Roman lava tube network? It's plausible. It—*

"Here we are, sir," said the driver, breaking Darwin's speculations and parking in front of a nondescript row of commercial offices. Ian met Darwin briefly and, saying he had a client meeting, left him with the box of Robert's things. They would go to lunch once Ian returned.

Darwin opened the box: *Robert Van Rooyen's violent, manipulative past distilled down to this. You couldn't manipulate death.* He shook his head at the losses in the man's wake and focused on the contents, going straight for two cylinders containing scrolls.

The first label read "Various Roman military operations in Gaul." The second label was simply "Lacroix". *Couldn't be more obvious than that*, he thought and unscrewed its cap. He pulled at the wrapping and slid the contents onto a table. Ian had said he did not open it. Grabbing scissors from the desk, Darwin cut the tape. With the plastic wrapping material aside, he inspected the cross section. A coil of thick acid-free paper surrounded the papyrus.

He put on cotton gloves and unrolled the scroll until seeing Agrippa's familiar hand:

Written by the hand of Agrippa Cicero in the 4th year of Imperator Caesar Vespasianus Augustus, this scroll documents the period of the 6th through 8th years of Nero Claudius Caesar Augustus Germanicus.

He checked notes on his mobile to confirm the dates. Vespasian became Emperor in 69 CE, which meant Agrippa wrote this in 73 CE, six years before Mount Vesuvius erupted. The scroll's timeframe covered 60 to 62 CE of Nero's reign. Agrippa opened the scroll with his arrival in Augustonemetum in the spring, having traveled three days from Lugdunum, modern-day Lyon.

Yes! His arms thrust out in victory. *We got it back, Emelio.*

He wanted to open it farther right then but stopped, knowing that if the papyrus was in poor shape, it could crack or tear. *Best to wait until I have a better facility where I can adequately scan it.* He re-rolled the scroll, sealed the plastic wrapper, and replaced the tube's end cap. He opened the second tube and found three scrolls squeezed in. He decided not to take them out and replaced the lid.

Several folders contained letters between Robert and collectors. Treasure hunters? Thieves? Darwin could not tell, but given Robert's past, these people were probably the latter. He paused on one letter. A tight hand wrote in stilted English as if the writer were translating from a dictionary. Its author offered a Roman scroll for sale.

Merde. It's my father. Darwin paused, imagining his father as an angry seventeen-year-old. He almost crumpled the note but stopped. They might need it later to prove the scroll's provenance. The letter would explain its location in the last half-century. He continued looking through the contents.

"Find anything?" asked Ian a few minutes later.

"Letters between my dad and Robert. The rest of the stuff, dunno. Can you ship it to me?"

"Sure. Let's get lunch. I'm starved. Bring the scroll. I've got meetings all afternoon, so I'll drop you back at your hotel after we eat."

Darwin took the Lacroix scroll and a folder with his father's and Robert's correspondence and walked with Ian to the car. Ian drove a circuitous route to give Darwin a small tour of Johannesburg. There was not much to see in the suburbs, but Ian pointed out the distant ridge and talked about the parks and game preserves to the north. Darwin found himself agreeing to visit again for a more extended stay.

Halfway through lunch, Ian said, "Tell me more about this scroll. You could've asked me to ship it to you. Why's it so important?"

Darwin explained the Knights Templar codes and his idea about the cathedral in Clermont-Ferrand.

"You mean the one where those Crusaders left their names," said Ian.

"I didn't say which one, but good guess," said Darwin. During their Iceland adventure, he had shown Ian photos of the lava tube under Clermont-Ferrand as an example of what they could find in Iceland.

Ian whistled. "And you think the Knights Templar left a load of gold in there."

Darwin nodded.

"Who else is interested?"

"There was a guy in France who got the jump on us. Someone with a Vatican connection."

"Is that the same guy who followed us here?"

50

Jacques got a ham sandwich from a takeaway place and sat on a bench while monitoring the restaurant. At least the weather was pleasant. He shuddered at the thought of tailing someone in the Paris rain.

Earlier, Darwin had carried a plastic tube from the office of the security company he visited and kept it on his person while in the restaurant. Jacques knew it was the reason Darwin had flown to South Africa. Though why Ian had it perplexed him. *Doesn't matter. I just need to get it.*

He assumed Darwin and Eyrún would head back to Paris straight-away. *Or maybe not,* he thought, realizing the scroll could take them anywhere along that line Darwin made between Paris and Béziers. *But where?*

51

"**S**it down, bruh," said Ian, grabbing Darwin's arm. "Right now, the advantage's shifted. He doesn't know that you know. Keep it that way."

Darwin ground his teeth and breathed heavily through his nose. *Fucking Jacques.* He pressed his fists into his thighs, imagining them pummeling Jacques. He stopped when his leg muscles protested in pain.

"Is this the guy?"

Ian showed Darwin a picture of Jacques on his mobile that an employee had taken a few minutes before when he drove by the restaurant.

"Yeah, that's the guy from Paris."

"I remember seeing him last night, thinking he took too much interest in our table. At first, I thought it was Eyrún and Katie, but then your driver reported being followed to the office this morning. My roundabout drive to the restaurant allowed me to confirm the tail. What's he want?" said Ian.

"The scroll, but how does he know about it?"

"Maybe he doesn't. You said he lost the trail of the Templar's treasure. He's probably following you, hoping you lead him to it."

Darwin told Ian he just wanted to look and walked to a restaurant front window. Standing behind a plant, he could just make out Jacques sitting on a bench about thirty meters away. His blond hair fell under a ball cap.

"How the hell did he follow us?" asked Darwin back at the table with Ian.

"You're a decent man, Darwin, but Eyrún was right in Iceland. You need to trust people less. Gold has a way of luring treasure hunters—dangerous treasure hunters."

"We can lose him on the way back to Paris," said Darwin.

"That's what I mean," said Ian. "You didn't even know he followed you here. Don't put yourself and Eyrún in danger. I have a better idea."

A half hour later, Ian dropped Darwin at the hotel, and they embraced. Ian said he was serious about them coming back. "The gals get along. Eyrún said she wanted to see lions in the wild. I've got connections. You take care," he said, then added, "I'm going to have two of my guys shadow you until your flight. You'll only see them if this guy, Jacques, causes trouble. You stay cool and don't provoke him."

They embraced again, and Ian drove away. Darwin waited a few minutes inside the lobby, but in a place where he could see a car stopped a little way from the entry. Its passenger, Jacques, exited.

"Bastard," Darwin muttered, turned, and carried the tube back to his room.

E yrún arrived about twenty minutes later, gushing about how much fun she had with Katie. She kissed him, the lunchtime wine lingering on her breath. She tossed two large bags on the bed and pulled out a dress to show Darwin.

"What do you think?" She held it against her chest.

"Nice. I like it. Compliments your eyes," he said.

"God, I miss spending time with a girlfriend. We should come back for a longer visit."

He agreed, saying Ian invited them on a safari.

"Oh, let's," she said, kicking off her sandals. "Did you get your scroll?"

He pointed to the gray plastic tube on the bed.

"Is it the right one?"

He told her that he had read Agrippa's first words but then decided it best to open the scroll in a safer environment. He suggested they take it to Emelio's house in Ajaccio, where they could scan it and leave it with the other scrolls.

"What do you want to do until we go to Corsica?" she asked, stepping close and thrusting her hands in his pockets.

"I booked us a couples' massage. Starts in an hour."

"Oh, God, I need one." She hugged him.

"It's nice to see you relaxed," he said. "You were overworking yourself."

52

Jacques sat in the lobby with a sparkling water and, when Eyrún returned, discreetly followed her back to their room. With no need to stay longer in Johannesburg, they could leave anytime. He put an ear to their door and could not believe his luck when he heard Darwin mention a spa reservation.

He knew the tube was too large for the room safe, and Darwin would leave it in the room. *Unless he gives it to the front desk. Shit.* His fingers tingled, and nervous energy coursed through him, knowing he had to break in again. He backed away down the hall and waited for them to leave.

In less than five minutes, he heard their voices in the hall and watched them retreat to somewhere deeper in the resort. He went to the housekeeping office hoping to get the master keycard as in Paris but found three staffers joking in the office. *Damn.* They looked to be taking a break or likely had no work to do until turndown time. *Too long!*

He headed back toward their room. He stopped. *What if I can get Darwin's key during the massage?* Jacques backtracked and went to the spa. The men's side had twelve lockers. There was one attendant, but he busied himself with cleaning the equipment in the weight room.

Jacques tested the handles on the lockers and found only two in use. Each had a keypad with numbers in three rows of three beginning at one. The last row was a star, zero, and a hash sign.

Wait! Lucien installs these. He tapped his friend Lucien's number. *C'mon. C'mon.* Finally, Lucien picked up on the seventh ring.

"Jacques! Sorry it took a while. I'm in the middle of a job," said Lucien.

Jacques explained what he needed. Lucien laughed.

"Happens all the time. I'm in a health club right now opening a locker for some executive." He gave Jacques three possible master codes used by the primary lock makers. When Jacques asked why he didn't provide the code to the health club, Lucien replied he got paid €150 to open it in person.

The first code opened the locker, but it was the wrong one. Pack of cigarettes and the clothes reeked of smoke. He went to the next locker, opened it, and removed the keycard from Darwin's jeans. He closed it without locking it and walked to the suite. He opened the door and hurried through the two rooms before seeing the tube on the bed. He slid it from between the bags and twisted off the end cap. He grasped the plastic and pulled the scroll out.

I need to put something back. At least to delay suspicion. He looked about and saw the thin paperboard from a garment in the trash bin. He put some tissue from Eyrún's bags with the paper and rolled it. Sliding it in the tube, it uncoiled against its side, and Jacques tamped it down. Then he put the tube back between the bags and exited the suite. He detoured to his room and deposited the scroll before replacing the keycard in Darwin's pants.

Ten minutes later, he opened a bottled water in his room and chugged most of it, then went to the bath to splash water on his face. He dropped the towel on the sink and went to look at the plastic-wrapped scroll on the bed. He pushed away from the temptation to open it.

I have to get out of here. Stay at another hotel. If Darwin opens his tube, the police will get involved. He looked at the time: 15:36. *When's that Air France flight?* He recalled that one went out tonight when he had looked during lunch. He opened the mobile app. There was just enough time to catch it. He tapped through the ticket purchase and winced at the cost. Then, after packing his case, he scooped up the scroll and headed to the lobby for a taxi. If the traffic went smoothly, he figured on having enough time to find a sturdier tube at the airport. If not, he would put the contents of his case in a cheap bag and use the case for the scroll.

The taxi pulled away just shy of 4 p.m. He asked the driver if there was enough time to make a 7:50 p.m. flight and was told: "No problem, sir."

53

Neuilly-sur-Seine

J acques awoke to the sound of a leaf blower from his neighbor's back garden. He imagined shooting the infernal machine and rolled over. When sleep would not return, he looked at the clock and slowly sat up. He had got five hours' sleep after arriving home at eight and needed to get on with his day. He rocked side to side to loosen stiffness.

The full flight and no upgrade meant he spent the night in a middle row next to a woman who laughed nonstop through movies and a man who drooled on his blanket. He stood in the shower until the water cooled.

He dressed, made a pot of coffee, and drank it black while flipping through the newspaper. Same Paris corruption. Same wet weather. At 3 p.m., he left to meet a colleague in Paris city center who taught Roman political science at the Sorbonne.

He smiled, wishing he could see Darwin's face when he opened the tube.

Paris

Light rain was falling when Jacques exited the Metro at the Alésia station in the fourteenth arrondissement across the city. People finished their Saturday shopping as the open-air market vendors were packing up their stalls and the dark cloud cover gave a later feel to the afternoon.

He walked up the gentle slope toward his destination. The tourists craved the trendier fifth and sixth arrondissements with their shopping and restaurants. Here, in the fourteenth, students and professors favored the cheaper living and an eclectic food scene.

Jacques reached a Moroccan café and, collapsing his umbrella, put it in the stand. He found his colleague sitting beside a stack of papers at a back table. Her pen whisked across the surface of one paper and then scrawled comments down the side of the student's work.

"*Bonjour*, Inés. Another weak argument?" asked Jacques.

"*Bonjour*, Jacques." She stood, and they kissed cheeks.

Jacques took in the musky combination of perfume, body, and cigarette that was Inés. For a moment, he was back in her bed but released the memory. An exquisite lover, she was also unpredictable and fought like a demon at the slightest provocation.

"The students get worse. Lazy, pathetic arguments. They ignore the historical perspective. They write like their education came from Twitter," said Inés.

"It probably did," he said.

They discussed the current semester and the goings-on at Sorbonne. Inés railed against budget cuts and the current nationalist government's focus on French education and abandoning their global influence. Jacques knew it best to allow her torrent to expend itself and did not interrupt.

A server brought tea. Mint leaves sprouted from the edges of the elegantly scrolled pot, whose dents betrayed its busy life. He set down the tray containing two glass cups and tiny plates of almonds and pine nuts. He filled the cups and departed.

Inés had continued her diatribe during the tea service. Now she seized one cup and inhaled the minty steam. They drank in silence a minute. Jacques sucked air over his tongue to ease the sting of the near-boiling water.

"What did you bring me?" she asked. "You said it was Roman."

Jacques grasped the cylinder leaning against his chair. He had found an old fishing rod case in his garage and shortened it with a saw. The rain would have ruined the DHL cardboard tube he had gotten at the airport in Johannesburg.

"Let's use this table," said Inés, sliding along the banquette to an empty table next to them.

Jacques wiped the table, even though it appeared clean. He twisted off the end cap and tapped the tube until the plastic rolled scroll slid out. Inés wiped her hands on a cloth napkin and brought her attention to the yellowed papyrus on the table.

"Where did you get it?" she asked—more in a tone of curiosity than wonder. Roman scrolls were not rare.

"I bought it as part of an estate auction. I don't think the owners knew it. Young kids selling off their *grand-mère's* junk."

She gave him a sideways glance. He shrugged. He knew she did not care but wanted to avoid a fight.

"Let's see. Hold the edges down," She directed Jacques to use the plastic to keep the scroll flat. Her finger ran over the text. It took a minute for her to reach the bottom.

"It's authentic," she said, touching a corner of the papyrus. "It might bring a thousand euros at auction."

"What's it say?" Jacques leaned in.

"It's more or less an inventory of military stores."

"Are you sure?"

"I'm older, Jacques, not senile," she said, glaring at him. "Of course I'm sure. Here—" She pointed to the text as she translated. "The Roman legion under centurion Suetonius has three hundred eleven men, seventy-three horses, thirteen wagons, thirty-seven slaves… You want me to keep going?" She looked up.

"*Putain!*" Jacques let go of the scroll and stood. A hand went to his forehead and squeezed as he walked in a circle. *God damn you, Darwin. How did you know?* His hand smoothed over his hair and rubbed his neck. He went over his movements in Johannesburg. *Darwin carried the scroll to lunch. He returned with it to the hotel. It was on the bed under shopping bags. No. He couldn't have. This has to be the scroll.*

"Read it to me again."

He listened, eyes closed. It was an inventory, but it mentioned a campaign through Gaul into Germania. *What am I missing?* He asked her to reread it while he transcribed it onto a notepad, and forty minutes later had finished.

She studied him. "What's this about, Jacques? You didn't find this at an auction, did you?"

"*Non.*"

"Where did you find it?"

"I stole it."

"Ah, Jacques," she said with a smiled. "Still chasing your old dream. Let it go. It's given you nothing but heartache and destroyed your career. We'll never go back to the monarchy."

He decided it was best not to let her know what he hoped the scroll was about and shifted the conversation to their other colleagues and the courses they taught. She followed his lead, and they talked through another cup of tea. When their conversation stalled, she paused. Her lips curled in the devious way Jacques knew well.

"Do you want to have sex?" she asked.

Neuilly-sur-Seine

Hours later, Jacques returned home. He leaned the tube against the bookshelf and sat at the computer table. He spread out his translation and read it again. He put his elbows on the desktop and leaned on fisted hands: the scroll listed Roman garrison cities, but nothing about caves.

He smelled Inés on his clothes and smiled at a memory of earlier times. The fire in their arguments as each prepared lectures. *Where did it go?* He knew. She leaned farther left, building a unified Europe. He ran opposite, seeing the corruption and dilution of their Republic. They fell apart as a couple but were still drawn together by physical needs. A pleasant soreness in his groin told of today's war in the bed. *How long until the next skirmish?* He wondered briefly, then refocused on the paper.

The words were a jumbled mass, yielding nothing. His stomach growled, and he went to the kitchen. He poured a glass of wine and reheated the chicken he roasted before South Africa. As he stirred the dish, a memory surfaced. While he waited in the restaurant's car park where Darwin and Ian had lunch, a car had driven by. It had the same security logo as the car Ian drove.

It was one of Ian's people. Darwin set me up! I knew it!

He got his mobile from the office and called Franz.

"*Pronto,*" Franz answered.

"Franz, it's Jacques."

"*Un momento,*" said Franz. Jacques heard loud voices recede. "I can talk now."

"Where's Darwin?"

"How should I know? I'm at a family dinner. It's Saturday night."

"He deceived us," said Jacques, and explained the trip to Johannesburg and the scroll. "He knows the third step. I need to find him before he gets to it."

"Okay, okay. Let me ask, but it may not be until tomorrow," said Franz.

Jacques went back to his dinner and wine. After eating, he showered and put on long cotton pajamas. He turned on the gas fire, a modern convenience in the otherwise eighteenth-century room, and sat on the small sofa opposite the Dauphin painting and continued reading a novel on the Carolingian dynasty.

Sometime later, his mobile vibrated with Franz's answer:

Darwin en route to Corsica

54

Ajaccio, Corsica

"There's our house," said Eyrún, looking out the left side of the small jet. Darwin slid in next to her and followed the T20 road along the ridge. A moment later, the window tipped skyward as the Embraer Praetor 600 banked into its approach to the Ajaccio Napoléon Bonaparte Airport. The craft plunged through the crystal-clear sky and leveled off. Darwin watched the cars on the T20, now on the coastal plain, grow larger as the jet descended the valley toward the harbor.

He had called Emelio a few hours earlier from Baku, Azerbaijan, where they had spent the night. The side adventure had done them good by extending the fun they had with Ian and Katie in Johannesburg. Darwin had asked the concierge at the Four Seasons to find flights to Corsica but was discouraged with the two-stop options.

After their massage Friday afternoon, Darwin had found a note under their door from the concierge, inviting them to an experience. Embraer, the Brazilian aircraft maker, was selling a new plane to one of the hotel's guests, and the company offered to fly them to Ajaccio. The only catch was an overnight stay in Baku, as the aircrew required a mandatory break after the long haul from Johannesburg. The concierge had also arranged their stay at the Four Seasons in Baku and said they would reach Ajaccio by noon the day after. They jumped at the chance.

The oil-rich couple from Baku who were considering purchasing the jet turned out to be thoroughly enjoyable. Eyrún had a long discussion on the Caucasus region with the husband, a petroleum geologist who was fascinated with her work at Stjörnu Energy. The wife, who was managing director of the Azerbaijan State Museum of Art, spoke with Darwin about the Silk Road's evolution and its impact on Baku as a regional center. At one point, he asked her if she knew of a recent discovery in the Imisli region where silver drachmas minted by Alexander of Macedonia were found. She said yes, and when the jet reached Baku in the late afternoon, Darwin jumped at her offer to visit the museum to see the coins found in the necropolis.

After they checked into the hotel, Eyrún had asked what was so interesting about the coins. He explained that the Alexander scroll taken from him in Egypt had mentioned Azerbaijan and that he wanted to explore a connection. Unfortunately, it turned out the nine drachma coins, while beautiful, did not tell him much. Without detail on their provenance and context within a scroll he no longer had access to, he had nothing further to explore.

That evening, Eyrún wore one of her new dresses to dinner, and afterward they strolled along the yacht harbor. They stopped at one point to watch a ferry lumber into port. Darwin pointed out to sea when it docked and said, "Tehran is five hundred kilometers that way."

They departed Baku a little after ten in the morning and had a beautiful day flying over the Black Sea and the Balkans before whisking across Italy and down through Corsica. The pilot brought the nose up, and the jet's tires chirped as it touched the runway. She reversed the thrust and braked to make the first turn toward the terminal. As they reached a private aviation area, Darwin ran a hand over the wide leather seat and breathed in the new-plane smell one more time. He could understand the addiction to flying in this manner. The Embraer representative, Dominique, thanked them for listening to her pitch and said she understood they needed to think about it. In the meantime, she gave them a business card for a company that specialized in clients who needed occasional private-jet service.

The pilot shut down the engines, and the door opened, letting in the Ajaccio harbor air. Darwin and Eyrún thanked the flight crew and collected their bags as a French customs agent met them on the tarmac. Once they were cleared, a driver met them at the small office, saying the Embraer representative had arranged it.

"She's got your number," said Eyrún.

"And we have hers. You have to admit, that's flying."

The car dropped them at the Lacroix mansion on Rue des Orangers, where Emelio met them in the driveway, his green eyes twinkling with excitement. A gust swept his unruly hair across his face, and he swept the full gray locks back in place. The three-story building featured a stone facade on its lowest floor and straw-gold-colored stucco on its upper floors. The roof was terra-cotta, like every other house in the harbor.

"Eyrún!" said Emelio, kissing her and then hugging Darwin.

"Here it is, *Grand-père*." Darwin held a white plastic tube, offering it palms up.

"Oh my. I thought I would never see it again. Did you…"

"Yes, I opened it, but only far enough to confirm it was Agrippa."

"Come inside," said Emelio, carrying the scroll.

Darwin and Eyrún put their packs in their favorite upstairs bedroom, which overlooked a large backyard. Eyrún opened the windows to let in the fresh air and stood a moment watching the neighbor, Mateo, tend his enormous rose garden.

"Let's go. You promised lunch," she said.

They met Emelio in the formal dining room, where he had laid an acid-free paper on the dark polished-oak table. The scroll lay to one side. He made a face when learning they would not open it straightaway. "Sorry, *Grand-père*, but I promised Eyrún some lunch. Besides, it will be good to celebrate the occasion," said Darwin. He thought of Jacques and grinned before turning away from the scroll.

"What's that for?" asked Emelio as he grabbed a hat from the rack.

"I was imagining Jacques's mood when he opened the tube he stole from us in South Africa," said Darwin.

"I would imagine he's plenty pissed off. But he deserves it for breaking into our room," said Eyrún.

Warmth radiated from the sidewalk, and they soon crossed Cours Napoléon and the old railway before reaching the quay-side shops. They walked through the mini-mall to the Côté Port restaurant, its dockside tables nearly spilling onto the yachts berthed stern side in. Emelio asked the owner for a champagne bottle worthy of a grand celebration and was rewarded with a Mailly L'Intemporelle Rosé Grand Cru.

As the server filled their glasses, Eyrún eyed two couples sitting on one yacht's rear deck. "I've always wanted a boat," she said.

55

The shadows had lengthened across the Maison Lacroix portico when they returned from lunch. Emelio went to the kitchen to put on coffee while Eyrún and Darwin headed to the basement to get the Box. "I love this place," said Eyrún, walking around shelves containing old appliances and knickknacks. She opened a trunk of old clothes. "These look like they're from Napoléon's day."

"Probably are. We built the house in 1783," said Darwin as casually as if all families lived in 300-year-old houses. He opened a cabinet housing the metal-clad box that contained the Roman scrolls discovered by Darwin's forebear Pasquale. The scroll they got from Ian belonged to this collection and had been missing since 1974, when Darwin's father, Olivier, sold it to Robert Van Rooyen. Darwin surmised the bounce in Emelio's step after lunch to have been for the return of the prodigal son, so to speak.

These scrolls and the box that saved them had taken on special meaning in Darwin's family. Pasquale succumbed to searching for the lava tubes mentioned in the scrolls until the family forced him back into the shipping empire. Every second generation of Lacroix had a member lured by its siren's call, followed by a generation that spurned it.

Olivier had been one of the latter, from witnessing his father, Emelio, drive the family crazy with empty adventures across Europe. Olivier had sold the scroll in a fit of rage. While Emelio had admitted his folly, he was excited to see Darwin pick up the quest. He had often regaled Darwin with the stories it could tell, which was why they had personified it as the Box. With the finding of the lava tube in Iceland, Emelio had celebrated as hard as anyone. Darwin had placed a hand on the Box when Eyrún distracted him.

"OMG, Siggy would be in heaven," said Eyrún, holding up a green satin dress "She constantly played dress-up with my grandmother's clothes."

Darwin turned and laughed at the visual of Eyrún and her little sister, Siggy, playing down here. Then he flushed, imagining Eyrún as a bikini-clad teenager and himself driving their boat out of the harbor toward an isolated cove.

"What?" she asked.

He turned away and grabbed the Box. "Get the door for me. This is heavy."

Eyrún pulled open the basement door and followed him upstairs. "Coffee's ready in two minutes," Emelio called out from the kitchen as Darwin laid the Box on the dining table. "I have to pee," said Darwin, exiting toward the downstairs toilet.

56

Eyrún found herself alone in the enormous dining room. She remembered Darwin describing the Lacroix family as eclectic and could see it arrayed before her. At the room's far end, a bow window reminded her of a ship's stern with its lead-framed rhombus-patterned glass and adjacent brass lamps. An elaborate captain's chair, its back to the window, headed a long table that easily sat more than the twelve chairs currently set—the long wall opposite her incorporated a massive fireplace set in a carved marble mantle. A playful touch had been added from two adjoining elephant statues, their trunks curled upward.

The wall nearest her featured two credenzas: one with elaborate Arabic scrolling and the other, she guessed, Italian from its ornate wooden inlays. Paintings covered the room's deep green walls, mostly portraits, but some ships. She paused on a picture of Pasquale Lacroix on the end wall opposite the bow window. He posed in the captain's chair with one arm resting on the Box, and, judging by the graying hair, it had been commissioned in his later years. She did a double take on Pasquale's face. Abundant hair fell across his forehead, shading one of his bright green eyes. *It's Darwin.* She laughed to herself, visualizing

Pasquale raking back his hair in the same sweeping gesture as her husband.

She turned to the Box on the table, glancing back once at the painting. The artist had captured its essence well. She ran a hand over its rough, pitted black-and-gray surface, imagining its fiery ordeal. When the ash column erupting from Vesuvius collapsed, it jetted a wave of super-heated plasma across the coastal cities of Herculaneum and Pompeii, burying them for more than a thousand years. Ash and grit fused with the dense hammered bronze to create an effect not unlike raku pottery.

It's amazing, she thought, realizing it was not some sterile piece in a museum display. She recalled Darwin saying that Pasquale had found a carbonized skeleton wrapped around the Box. And, she remembered the note placed inside by the dead man Martinus: "Take this box to Agrippa in Rome."

As if in a trance, she grazed the top of the Box with her fingers and continued down one side of two men's magnum opus. She shuddered at the man's fear; she had seen the destruction wrought by volcanoes. Martinus's last desperate act was to save his work, and she suddenly realized: *He was preserving it for future generations. For volcanologists like me. He recorded data long before we coined the scientific method. And its provenance connects Martinus and Agrippa directly to the Lacroix family. This is precious.*

"It's spellbinding. No?" Emelio said softly. She turned as he walked in and set a coffee service on the Arabic credenza. "Few objects communicated more across the ages than this box." He patted its top. "Let's open it together." They grasped its sides and lifted the lid.

57

When Darwin returned, they poured coffee, and while they drank, Emelio recounted a story of the forebear who had built the mountain house. His painting over the credenza showed a surly man surrounded by dogs and guns. They finished their coffees and left the cups on the credenza.

"Well, let's get to it," said Darwin, removing the end cap of the newly returned scroll and sliding out the plastic-wrapped papyrus. The twenty-centimeter-tall scroll wrapped around a dowel affixed with round knobs at each end. Emelio handed out cotton gloves. Darwin pressed down the stiff leather wrapper, and Emelio placed acid-free paper and a book to keep the leather flat. Darwin continued unrolling as Emelio placed heavy silver candlesticks on the edges.

"It looks good. Robert must've taken care of it," said Emelio. He winced at a crackling sound.

"It's fine," said Darwin, smoothing the unrolled surface with a gloved hand. "Eyrún, help with this. Run your hand slowly up and down. I need two hands on the scroll."

He reached the end of the scroll. Emelio ran around his other side and placed more candlesticks on top of the protective paper. They straightened up when finished, and Darwin massaged his low back.

Emelio was first to lean back in. The text was written in fifteen-centimeter-wide columns in pagelike rectangles.

"I just can't get over how these look like books. I mean, except for cutting and binding, it looks like anything I'd pull off the shelf," said Eyrún.

"Vellum, better inks, printing press, digital readers. It all changes and remains the same," said Emelio.

Darwin used a scanner app to capture each page of the scroll and uploaded the files to a secure cloud folder. Emelio opened a binder to the transcription he had made years earlier to compare it to the real thing. "I should have photographed it all before your father..." he said, voice trailing off with the fatigue of remembering a long-surrendered topic.

"Never mind, *Grand-père*," said Eyrún. She draped an arm around his shoulder. "We let it all go in Scotland, remember?"

"I'm not that old, young lady. Of course I remember," he said, grinning. "But thanks for reminding me. Forgiveness is a recurring act, especially for oneself."

Darwin read from the scroll:

We returned to Augustonemetum in the 6th year of Nero Claudius Caesar Augustus Germanicus five days before the festival of Mercuralia. We traveled via the tube from Lugdunum, the last known opening. Nero agreed to increase our funding to expand the lava tube network farther north into Gaul.

The local Celtic people know about the lava tunnel. They use the site above the opening for sacrifices. Hiding underground gives the priests their illusion of magic. They do not go far in the tube out of fear of evil spirits. We negotiated permission to come and go through the above-ground opening, in no small part due to Nero's gold.

Lucius led the first exploration party. He returned six hours later with a wild tale of a massive cavern. He did not go in, as their light was not sufficient.

The next day, Lucius led all of us on a journey of one and a half miles. We stopped at the opening so far it consumed our light before reflecting. The floor dropped six feet. I leaned and slipped, falling to its bottom. My lamp rolled away, spilling oil that caught fire. The flames illuminated a chamber half as large as one of our theaters.

Lucius handed me a lamp and I walked across a floor like the bottom of a bowl, higher on its sides with a perfect curve to its center. The floor was a spiderweb of cracks. The cavern was a massive version of three others we had documented. Lava tubes connected to this chamber. I theorize the lava flowing in the tubes drained back into the earth at this point. The top layer cooled, leaving the floor hard.

At one point, the floor creaked. I hammered with a rock. It sounded hollow below. I poured water from a skin, and it disappeared through the cracks. From that point forward, we stayed to the edges of the chamber and avoided standing close.

"This is it, *Grand-père*. The lava tube complex that will prove your idea," said Darwin.

"This is Eyrún's quest now too. She's family. Besides history, this is a volcanologist's dream."

Eyrún leaned on the table. "Their knowledge of volcano structures is astounding for the time," she said. "What else does it say?"

Darwin read the scroll aloud and summarized it by section. Agrippa's party had surveyed the chamber over two days and documented four large lava tubes that penetrated the cavern. Three were as large as the one they traveled from Augustonemetum and one "tall enough for a short man, but too narrow for a cart."

The massive tube to the left of the Augustonemetum tunnel was blocked at 153 *passi*. Darwin recounted Roman distances where the smallest unit was the *pes* or foot, a *passus* or pace was equivalent to a meter, and a thousand *passi* was a Roman mile. To the right of the Augustonemetum, the narrow tube continued to Germania, and, to its left and almost straight across from the Augustonemetum, a wide tube continued to Lutetia and Londinium.

"He must've written these scrolls after the fact," said Eyrún. "There's no way they could determine where these went in two days."

"Agreed," said Darwin.

Darwin rolled the scroll, returned it to the Box, and closed the lid. The bronze-clad black walnut top fit tightly over the bottom section. While the scrolls and coins protected by the Box had little mass, the hardwood and thick, hammered-metal covering weighed just over twenty kilos. He pushed down slowly on the fire-scarred metal, allowing the air to squeeze out the sides.

The papyrus had survived in the Box for two millennia, and, with the modern addition of desiccant and chemicals to kill any papyrus-eating insects, he figured the contents would remain safe. He still worried about Emelio keeping it in a basement cabinet, but his grandfather treasured the family heirloom above all else and wanted to keep it close.

"I'm going to the toilet," said Emelio and left the room.

The wooden stairway behind the dining-room wall creaked as Emelio ascended. Darwin moved to return the Box to its cabinet.

"Put it down," said a male voice.

58

Jacques stood in the dining room's double-doorframe between two large men who looked like Rugby forwards. Their necks and thighs seemed thicker than Darwin's waist. Each had a shaved head and sported a thick beard, one black and one copper.

Black Beard's arms were sleeved in multi-colored tattoos, with red the prominent shade. Copper Beard had tattoos covering his neck; they looked like green bruises in the low light. Both carried police batons, the polished black glinting under the ceiling lights.

"What do you want?" asked Darwin.

"The scroll or, better yet, the clue," said Jacques.

"What are you talking about?" said Eyrún.

"Oh, you know. You broke into my house. I saw the string, Darwin. Did you think I wouldn't, or were you careless?"

Black Beard moved to the Box. Eyrún blocked him, arms reaching backward to protect it.

"Eyrún stop. It's not worth getting hurt over." Darwin took a step toward Jacques. "Leave her alone. That Box is old research." He stalled for time. *We can't lose the Box. Emelio's bound to hear us and call the police.*

"We won't hurt you. Unless you resist. Now, step aside," said Jacques.

"No, you son of a bitch," said Eyrún. "You followed us to Johannesburg and broke into our room."

"You violated my home!"

"You violated Notre-Dame and stole a relic belonging to the church," she shouted.

"Ah, interesting. You're working for *them*," said Jacques, stressing "them" like the evil empire.

Eyrún's eyes burned into Jacques. Darwin scanned past the doorway, looking for Emelio. He had to be coming back soon. *Maybe he went to the back of the house to avoid being heard while calling the police.* Darwin refocused on Jacques and said, "When the Béziers clue amounted to nothing, you followed us. Who told you we were in Paris?"

"It was you!" said Eyrún, her hands pushing hard on the dining table behind her. "You saw us go into the crypt. The police said someone called them. You asshole."

Darwin turned, hoping to catch her eyes. *She needs to chill.*

"And then *you* turned them on me. Clever," said Jacques, his lips twisted in a wry smile. He spun toward Darwin. "Who are you working for? Who told you about the tunnel under Notre-Dame?"

Darwin did not answer.

"Never mind. Let's get this over with. Grab the box."

Black Beard moved at Eyrún, who stood her ground against the table. He pushed the baton into her belly.

She screamed.

"Don't harm her!"

"I'm not fucking around this time."

Eyrún screamed again. Darwin turned to see Black Beard's baton press harder.

"Okay, okay. It's in the Box. I'll open it," said Darwin.

"We'll just take the whole thing," said Black Beard, shoving Eyrún aside and picking up the box.

A metallic click came from the door. "Step away from her," came Emelio's voice. The long double barrel of a shotgun emerged from the shadow.

Copper Beard moved. Emelio pulled back the second hammer.

"I've got two barrels. Which of you wants to volunteer?" He moved into the room for a better firing angle. Eyrún ran to Darwin, and they both moved behind the shotgun.

"Call the police," said Emelio.

A long moment passed. "There's no signal," said Darwin.

Jacques held out a cellular jamming device.

Emelio turned to Darwin and said in Corsu, *"Viaghjà à Mateo. Hà una fila di terra."*

"But—"

"No buts. Go. I'll be fine here. As long as they are sensible, I won't have to mess up your *grand-mère*'s dining room."

Darwin took Eyrún's hand and led her out of the room. They turned toward the kitchen as she whispered, "What did he say?"

"Take the secret route through the basement to Mateo's house. The guy behind us with the rose garden. He's still got a landline."

"What about the front?"

"Too far."

They sped downstairs. Darwin went to a chest of drawers and pulled its left corner. It ground against the dirt on the concrete floor. Eyrún helped swing it free from the wall. Darwin slid a metal panel aside and pushed open a wooden door about desk height.

"Follow me," said Darwin, dropping on all fours and scurrying into the hole. Eyrún joined him and in a few meters could get up in a crouched run. Lights came on from a wall switch Darwin activated. A large room with bunk beds and a makeshift kitchen opened up.

"Bomb shelter," he explained and began running. In roughly thirty meters, they reached a junction and turned left. "That goes to a culvert outside. This tunnel is also a safety escape. Someday I'll tell you the family pirate stories."

Less than a minute later, they reached a short set of steps. Darwin mounted them and pushed open a storm cellar door, where they emerged in an overgrown side yard. Darwin swept their way through brambles to the rear of the house. Looking back, they could see the Lacroix mansion looming above the rose garden.

Darwin pounded on the door. "Mateo! Mateo!"

Thirty seconds later, an old man peered around the drape on the door's window, then opened it.

"Darwin?"

"Mateo, we need your phone," said Darwin, pushing past him.

"Sure. What's wrong? It's in the hall."

Darwin was already dialing from the spot where the phone had been for decades.

"What…" said Mateo, confused at the intrusion.

"Mateo. I'm Eyrún, Darwin's wife," she said. "Someone broke into Emelio's house. He's got a shotgun on them. But we need the police."

59

"Let's go. The police are on the way," yelled Darwin. "Sorry, Mateo. Thanks for the phone."

"I'll follow you," they heard Mateo say as they ran out the front door and down the block to Montée Saint-Jean. They ran left downslope thirty meters and went left again onto Rue des Orangers. Police sirens wailed from the harbor direction and followed them into the narrow lane. Neighbors had spilled into the cul de sac.

"I heard a gunshot," said an older man.

Darwin kicked into a sprint.

"Wait." Eyrún caught him, and they stopped at the house as two police cars wheeled to a stop

"*Ritorna. Ritorna.* Get back," yelled the officers, spilling out of the cars, weapons ready.

They fell behind one car, where an officer waved them.

"Emelio! Oh, God, Eyrún." Darwin's body shook.

The police covered each other as they advanced on the front door.

"My *grand-père* Emelio's in there," Darwin shouted.

"Emelio!" yelled one officer, shoulder on the opened front doorframe. "Emelio! *S'ferite?* Are you hurt?"

The officer spun gun forward. A second officer folded behind. They disappeared inside. Seconds later, a burst came from the car radios, *"Omu a terra. Chjamate l'ambulanza.* Man down. Call the ambulance."

"Emelio!" Darwin burst from behind the car, Eyrún following. He flew through the front door and into the dining room. Two guns leveled at his face. His hands flew up. A voice shouted through the radios that the civilians had run inside. After a moment, they lowered the weapons.

Emelio writhed on the floor, the side of his face bloody.

F ifteen minutes later, Emelio pulled the oxygen mask from his mouth.

"They took the Box. They took the Box," he moaned as the paramedic tried to get the mask back on. Finally, Emelio yanked it hard enough to snap the elastic bands.

"Get them. It's our life's work. They can't take it," he pleaded.

"You're hurt, Emelio," said Eyrún, trying to settle him down.

"It's nothing. Damn shotgun hit me. Forgot what a kick the bastard has."

Darwin asked the paramedic about his *grand-père's* condition and learned it was a knock on the head and a flesh wound, nothing more. He turned, trying to make sense of the room. Both barrels had discharged into the opposite wall and ceiling, showering the room in lath and plaster. Emelio said one thug threw something at him, and the gun went off. Then they grabbed the Box and ran. Looking at the gaping hole, Darwin thanked God the gun went there. *This isn't worth killing over.*

"Mateo! Is the Citroën running?" Emelio asked his friend. The old man had joined the group after following Darwin and Eyrún around the block.

"Oui."

"Darwin, get our car. Stop them at the airport," Emelio said in English to keep the police out of it. As Eyrún protested, he said, "No. No. You must do this. They can't take our Box."

She grabbed her purse from a dining room chair and retreated from the room. While Emelio described the intruders to the police, Darwin collected his pack and then casually joined Eyrún. Once around the corner, they headed for the kitchen and back into the basement.

"What're we doing?" Eyrún asked.

"Going after Jacques. We have to get the Box before they board a plane." He reopened the secret tunnel door. "Mateo's got a car. Let's go."

She followed, and minutes later they emerged from the storm door at Mateo's house. This time, Darwin ran to the opposite side of the house and opened a side door into a stand-alone garage. He yanked a canvas from a car and pulled open the garage front door.

"This?" asked Eyrún, looking at a lemon-yellow Citroën 2CV.

"Yeah, runs great. I learned to drive in it."

She climbed in the driver's seat while Darwin got in the passenger side. Eyrún looked around the steering column, feeling for the keys. "Here," he pushed an ignition button, and the engine started.

Eyrún tested the clutch and felt for the gears. Edging onto the street, she went left and left again on Montée Saint-Jean.

"Which way now?" she asked as they approached the harbor.

"Left here on Cours Napoléon. It goes to the airport."

"Hang on," she said. The car shot through oncoming traffic, horns bellowing. She shifted on engine speed. Traffic was light as they rounded the harbor, but slowly moving. She gunned it to pass someone out for a Sunday drive.

"Easy," said Darwin as the engine revved.

60

"Is there a problem?" asked an airport police officer. Her partner stood by, assault rifle strapped across his chest.

"No. Not at all," said Jacques, backing down. He had been arguing with the Air France agent.

The metal-clad Box could not go through the x-ray machine, and he had opened it to show the contents were not dangerous. But he refused to let the agent reach in the Box, saying its contents were ancient papyrus and fragile. When he was asked for the antiquities export documents, Jacques engaged in a heated argument that Corsica was part of France. He was not exporting anything. The agent had been telling him of Corsican law, especially for antiquities, when the police arrived.

"Fine. I'll get the documentation," said Jacques.

"What now?" asked Black Beard, carrying the Box.

"Let me think."

Back in the car, Copper Beard asked what happened. Black Beard explained as Jacques peered out the back passenger window.

"What about the ferry?" Copper Beard suggested. "I saw one docked when we arrived."

"Drive there. I'll look up the timetable," said Jacques.

Two minutes later, he discovered the next ferry departed at 7 p.m. —four hours later. Then overnight to Marseilles and still a full day's drive to Paris. Black Beard said it would be another thousand euros because of a gig they would lose for the upcoming week.

Putain! Jacques snorted.

61

Darwin looked at his watch. Just under an hour since Jacques and the beards got away with the Box. They flowed with traffic and once around the main harbor picked up speed to fifty kilometers per hour.

"How far?" Eyrún shifted from second to third as they moved out of a roundabout.

"Maybe three kilometers."

They watched a helicopter approach the private air terminal, and two minutes later, Eyrún braked for a buildup at another roundabout.

"C'mon." Her palm thumped the steering wheel as she leaned left to get a better view.

"There they are!" Darwin pointed, almost hitting Eyrún's nose.

A white sedan came through the roundabout, heading the other way—the unmistakable Copper Beard in the driver's seat and Black Beard on the passenger side. Jacques sat in the back. The Citroën's engine screamed as Eyrún turned onto the dirt meridian, its wheels bucking over the uneven ground.

"What're you doing?" Darwin grasped the shoulder belt two-handed to keep from banging against the side window.

The right front tire screeched and spun as the car fought its way onto the blacktop. Eyrún backed off, ground a gear, and edged back onto the road. "Where are they?" She raced through the gears, getting back to speed.

"Third car ahead," he said.

"Did they see us?"

"Dunno, but they wouldn't know we're in a Citroën."

They followed the white Peugeot back around the harbor. When they neared Emelio's house, Eyrún asked, "Are they going back?"

Darwin started to call Emelio when the Peugeot passed Montée Saint-Jean, and two hundred meters farther turned quayside. "They're going to the ferry," said Darwin. "Back off a little. They'll have to park in that big lot, lined up with the other cars."

Eyrún slowed and made the turn. She pulled under a tree where they watched the Peugeot enter the array of vehicles on the empty dock. "What time does it get here?" she asked.

Darwin tapped on his mobile. "Here," he held it toward her. "Seven p.m. is the next ferry to Marseilles. Prolly arrives by six."

"How do we know that's the one?"

"Only one that makes sense if they're going to Paris."

"What're they going to do for four hours?"

They watched the thugs while discussing what to do. Darwin surmised they must have had a problem getting the Box on a flight. They debated calling the police, but Darwin said Corsica had strict antiquities laws, and the Italians could also claim heritage to the Box and its contents.

"We can't risk it," he said. "It's been in our family since eighteen sixty-seven. It's our only heritage from the Lacroix shipping empire."

Eyrún studied him. Her mind replayed Emelio lying on the floor, carrying on as if a family member had been kidnapped; and her experience just a hour ago studying the painting of Pasquale, one arm embracing the Box like a child. "Those bastards!" She pounded the steering wheel and turned to Darwin. "They can't take it from us!"

"Exactly!" he said, eyebrows shooting up as if hearing a student finally grasp a difficult concept.

"I'm with you. My life was all work before we met. I like this part better." She smiled, then knitted her brows. "What's our plan?""

"Er..." Darwin looked up at the Citroën's headliner as if thinking, and Eyrún turned dockside. All three men had exited the Peugeot and walked to the water for cigarettes. The smoke drifted along with the breeze.

"They left the car," she said.

Darwin was out the door before Eyrún could ask what he was doing. She followed, and he explained as they approached the Peugeot. "We'll steal it back."

"How?"

Darwin found a rusted wire and fashioned its end into a hook to slide between the glass and outer door to trip the lock. They reached the Peugeot. Only five other vehicles were in line, and their passengers were also out walking about.

"There it is," Eyrún whispered. The Box lay on the rear seat.

Darwin forced the wire past the rubber seal and felt around for the lock mechanism. The wire bent. He pulled it out. Made adjustments and pushed it back in.

"Those people are looking at us," said Eyrún. "Under the tree over there."

A man stood and began walking toward them. "Shit," Eyrún muttered. She looked about, saw a piece of broken curbstone, and used it to smash the rear window.

"Hey," yelled the man.

Eyrún opened the door. Swept the glass off the Box, pulled it from the car, and thrust it in Darwin's arms. "Run!"

Darwin ran alongside her to the Citroën, some fifty meters distant. He set the twenty-kilo box on the rear seat, then jumped in the passenger seat as Eyrún fired up the engine. The thugs, alerted to the theft, were getting in the Peugeot. Darwin gasped, hands on the dash, sucking in air. Eyrún U-turned out of the lot and down a side street, nearly taking out a curbside shop display.

"Sorry," she said to the rearview mirror, turning right on Cours Napoléon. "Where do we go?"

"Not to Emelio's," he said, recovering enough to speak. "Keep going."

"I don't know Corsica."

They flew past Emelio's street.

"Get to the airport. The police will stop the beards. We're not leaving the country, so they won't care about the Box."

She rounded the harbor, looking back through the side mirrors. "They're right behind us," she said, approaching the slow traffic turning into the airport.

The Peugeot rolled up behind, then bumped them hard. "They're trying to block us in." Eyrún saw Black Beard get out of the car and accelerated into the left lane. A horn blared, the driver gesturing out the window. Eyrún pulled away on the inside lane of the roundabout.

The Peugeot also pulled out but was now stuck three cars back. Eyrún passed more vehicles as the road arced around the runway. She knew this road—the approaching roundabout funneled left to their mountain house. The other direction continued around the airport on a divided highway with no turns for three kilometers. She had made that mistake once.

She swept to the inside of a truck as they entered the roundabout. The Peugeot had closed the gap and moved to follow. The Citroën howled as she pushed it past the truck. "Hang on!"

Darwin's body thrust against the door as Eyrún swerved in front of the truck. The Citroën's tires squealed across the pavement, just clearing the truck's bumper. Darwin pulled up his feet as they hit dirt between lanes. The Citroën's back end came around. Eyrún steered into the skid and guided them back onto the pavement, then turned hard right to exit the circle up the mountain road.

"Did they make it?" she yelled.

Darwin whipped around to look. "No. They're on the T40."

He turned back and let out a huge breath. "Christ, Eyrún, you could've killed us."

"Doubt it. I've heard these things are impossible to roll. Woefully underpowered, but stable."

62

"**P***utain!* Turn around," yelled Jacques as the Citroën disappeared behind a dust cloud going almost the opposite direction.

Copper Beard had braked hard to avoid an incident with the truck. Now the traffic forced them along behind it as the road bent around the far side of the runway.

"Get around him," Jacques shouted, still looking out the rear window as Eyrún and Darwin passed from view.

"I can't," said Copper Beard. A barrier separated the lanes. He tried the shoulder, but it sloped into a swampy run-off between road and runway.

Jacques zoomed into the map. "There's a roundabout ahead."

"How far?"

"I don't know. Two, three kilometers. Just take it." Jacques focused on the road Eyrún took. The T20 went up the southern mountain ridge. *Where could he be going?* Then he recalled something Franz had said about them moving to Corsica: a house in the mountains.

The Peugeot reached the turnaround, swung counterclockwise in the roundabout, and Copper Beard punched the accelerator.

"How soon before we catch them?" Jacques had to yell over the wind howling in the broken window. He had already lowered his side window to offset the reverberating pressure wave.

"Not long. That's an old two-banger. Can't do over forty."

Jacques calculated the distance to likely houses. Franz had said it took the Vatican emissary less than an hour to get back to Ajaccio. He wondered if they could make it back to the ferry after catching Darwin and Eyrún at their mountain house. The last boat was at 10:30 p.m. *Probably.*

63

Eyrún eased the Citroën over 100 kilometers per hour, feeling what it could deliver without blowing the engine. "What's the story on this car? I'd read they were crap for speed. This one's got something else under there," she nodded toward the windscreen.

"Upgraded to a flat-four in the nineties. Mateo and Emelio were always tinkering," said Darwin.

"I knew it!" She stomped on the accelerator.

He shook his head, laughing. This was a different Eyrún: a window-smashing, rally-driving demon. *Something happened back there in the harbor.* He relived the moment, studying her face as she deftly passed a slow driver. It radiated joy. A fire in his core spread through his chest, racing into fingertips. He squeezed her thigh. She smiled and shifted in the seat.

She gets the quest. Damn.

After a pause to savor the moment, he launched into the story of how Emelio and his best friend Mateo bought the car in the early 1950s to drive tourists around the island. It turned out they were three decades too early for the tourism boom, but Emelio used the vibrant yellow car to woo a young woman who had been dragged to Corsica by her father, a government minister. "My *grand-mère*," he added.

"Emelio wooing. I'll bet he was a terror." She laughed, then went quiet, refocusing on their getaway, before saying a minute later, "You know they're coming after us."

She looked at the dash: 140 km/h. *It'll drift lower on the mountain.* The Citroën's speedometer was its only instrument, so she focused on the engine, knowing its tone and vibration would tell if trouble was coming.

"As long as she holds, we're good." She patted the gear shift.

"How much time? I mean from when they could turn around."

Eyrún curled her fingers one at a time, thinking through the increments, then said, "Figure we've got twenty kilometers' head start with their wrong turn. They have to catch up. The Peugeot's got twenty kilometers an hour over us. They'll close the gap in— " she wrinkled her lips "— an hour. Maybe less."

"It's thirty kilometers to the house from here."

"I know. Maybe that storm will help." She leaned forward, looking up at a gray, thickening sky.

64

"The house is near Bocagnano, about ten kilometers." Jacques read from the message just back from Franz. "Why haven't we caught them? Go faster."

"It's floored. Unless I get rid of you two, this piece of shit's maxed out," said Copper Beard. "They mod'ed that Citroën and the woman knows how to drive."

"There they are!" Black Beard pointed across a chasm where the road doubled back. "Definitely a rebuild. They're going nearly as fast as we are."

Ten minutes later, they reached the commune of Bocagnano, such as it was. A restaurant on the edge of a roundabout. They entered the circle, and Copper Beard yelled, "which way," as a road by the diner went downhill.

"Up! Up!" yelled Jacques. "He said it's on a ridge overlooking the commune."

They continued up. Roadside homes whisked by as a granite wall rose steeply on their left. The route blackened as they entered a tunnel and popped out seconds later. Two more curves and they reached a ridgetop.

"Stop!" Yelled Jacques, bracing against Black Beard's seat, the brakes shuddering.

"Back there. They turned."

As the Peugeot U-turned, they could see a dust cloud waft away from an opening between two trees. Copper Beard turned into the narrow lane, the forest undergrowth brushing the sides of the car, as the single-track road opened onto a plateau that dropped into a gorge below the granite wall. A low stone-and-pine house spread across the lot with the Citroën parked by its front door and beside it, a blue Porsche Macan GTS.

"Stop," said Jacques. "Someone else must be here."

"What if they have weapons?" asked Copper Beard.

"Best to surprise them," said Jacques.

They walked to the front door. Only two small windows faced the front, both higher in the walls. Jacques went to the door and turned the handle. It opened. Holding the door, he turned, "You go around the left. You to the right."

He waited while the beards surrounded the house, then slowly pushed the door. Massive beams supported an open ceiling over wide glass doors along the back walls. He brought up a hand against the glare coming from the stone patio and closed the door. He listened. Nothing.

The floor creaked on his first step, and he moved closer to the wall where the planks protested less. A boar's head projected from one wall, its tusks like daggers. *Hunters.* He had read about Corsican mountain people. Perspiration beaded on his forehead. *Best not to walk into another shotgun. The old man nearly took off my head.*

"Darwin? Eyrún? We just want the Box."

Nothing.

He walked down steps to the lower area where large leather chairs surrounded a table. A fireplace dominated the far wall, its left side stacked with wood, and a stairway opened on the opposite wall. He followed it down to where three open doors flooded natural light into a hallway.

"Darwin? There's three of us." *That sounds stupid. If they have a gun, we're screwed. Best to shut up.*

Each of the bedrooms was empty. He saw Black Beard on the patio outside. His head shook negative: no one out here. One closed door remained at the hall's end.

Jacques twisted the knob, thrust it open, and stepped back. Someone had left a desk lamp on in a windowless room with books lining the walls. He stepped closer—old books. *Mon Dieu!* These were first editions from the early days of the Republic. He reached for one.

The light went out.

65

Four minutes earlier, Eyrún had skidded the Citröen to a stop. Darwin jumped out and grabbed the Box as Eyrún keyed open the electronic house lock. She closed the front door behind them.

"Leave it unlocked."

"I did," she said, following him to the main level and then to the bedrooms.

Darwin set the Box on the library desk, switched on the light, and turned to the bookshelf behind the desk. He pulled latches behind books on high and low shelves and swung out a section. He then pulled a heavy metal door and pushed the Box inside.

"No time to show you around," he said, shutting the door and resetting the bookshelf.

"You never told me about that."

"No reason to, before now. It's from rougher days in Corsica. Now for the tricky part. You got the keys?"

She wiggled her silver key ring. "Never thought I'd need an auto-start feature."

They hid in a locked closet near the front door. Darwin turned the lock from the inside in case the thugs tried it. They squeezed against gun racks and listened to the creaking planks as someone crept across the room. They waited another minute. Darwin opened the door and looked out. "It's clear."

Eyrún followed, looking back across the living area and patio windows as she exited the closet. She shoved Darwin in the back. "Go. The red-bearded guy just saw us. He's running around."

Darwin yanked open the front door and slapped the security panic button, shutting off all lights. An alarm shrieked as the front door slammed. Eyrún squeezed the key fob. The Porsche growled to life as she leaped into the seat. She punched reverse, knocking Darwin against the dash.

"Sorry," she yelled, shifting into Drive as he slammed his door. Copper Beard had rounded the side yard and pounded the back window as the Macan's meaty tires sprayed gravel. He receded in the rearview mirror as they sped between the trees. Once on the road, she gunned it, paddle-shifting through the turns. Darwin kept looking back.

"They're not catching us," she said, rubber squealing as the Macan tore through a sharp curve.

Darwin gripped the handhold above the passenger door as Eyrún summited the ridge over one shoulder of Monte D'Oro and raced down its other side. She eased their speed through Venaco and Casanova, then accelerated on the downslope into Corte, where they had to slow to fit the usual traffic.

"Better check on flights again," she said. "We'll be there in a half hour."

An hour before, on the drive up in the Citröen, they figured a flight out of Bastia Poretta on Corsica's northeastern side was their best option. But after finding no commercial flights scheduled tonight for mainland France, Darwin called the private jet service. The concierge had perked up when Darwin name-dropped Dominique and found a small jet that could make the hop over to Bastia after dropping a client in Livorno, Italy.

"*Allô.* It's Darwin Lacroix confirming our plane's arrival."

Eyrún scanned the mirrors as they moved through the city. The sun had set behind the Corsican spine. The island, geographically similar to California, had a massive granite range running north–south down its center.

"All good," said Darwin. "The jet's on its final approach and needs to refuel. But they're committed to wheels-up within the hour."

Eyrún blew out through puffed cheeks. "I need a drink after this."

Darwin looked at pedestrians milling about town on their Sunday evening. He marveled how his life had changed in the last two years: international fame, albeit brief, from his Iceland discovery, marrying Eyrún, meeting the Pope—twice—and booking an €8,000 short-hop private jet as if he were buying a concert ticket.

He smiled. "I'm going to tell Miguel about our next move." But as he tapped in the number, Eyrún said, "Stop!"

Darwin canceled the call.

"Let's think about this. Every time we've called Miguel, Jacques manages to show up soon after. Paris, Johannesburg, and now here."

"You think there's a leak?"

"Gotta be. Nobody's that smart," she said.

"Huh." A surprised Darwin sat back and recounted their movements. He had told Miguel about going to the beginning of the trail in Paris, then needing to visit a source in South Africa. Yesterday morning he had messaged Miguel that they were en route to Ajaccio. *Merde.*

"It's true. I updated Miguel, and Jacques found us soon after," he said.

"There's a leak in the Vatican. Franz found out, somehow."

"Who?"

"Could be anyone. Even the Pope," she said.

"Not a chance."

"I've seen it, Darwin. The two-faced dealings in Iceland over the lava tube make me sick. People playing multiple parties off each other to jump on the winning side at the last moment. Someone's screwing us here. I can feel it!" Her white knuckles strangled the padded leather steering wheel.

Dammit! Can we not trust even the Pope? Richard's voice slipped into his brain. *We need you to find this Christ codex. There's a vile undercurrent in the Vatican. His Holiness is bringing the church into the modern age, but not all agree with him.* Darwin dismissed the idea of distrusting the Pope. *Richard's never led me wrong.*

He pictured Black Beard poking Eyrún with the baton. A sudden urge to kick the glovebox threatened to overtake him. He pushed it down. Another vision appeared, this time of Abbas, the head of Egyptian antiquities, taking a scroll that was his, a gift from Eyrún. He was infuriated and had vowed to get it back. *Someone's doing it again. How did I not see this?* Face to the side window, he grew reticent.

"Darwin?" Eyrún's voice came from a million kilometers away.

He turned toward her.

"What's wrong, Love?" The Macan slowed.

"These bastards are not taking it from us."

She slowed during a straight section, checking rear mirrors for headlamps. None. "Are you okay?"

"Yeah. I'm okay. You're right, I'm too honest sometimes, but I'm learning to see the bullshit and deceit. This is, my—no, our—legacy. Whatever's in the tube under Clermont-Ferrand, it's ours."

She reached over the center console and took his hand. "It's ours," she said, squeezing hard. A moment later, she sped up and refocused on the road. "I have an idea. Tell Miguel we're heading back to Paris."

"That's excellent." Darwin agreed and called Miguel as they left the town limits. The Macan's headlamps carved through the winding woodland. A couple of minutes later, Darwin ended the call.

"Sounds like he bought it. I'm texting Richard that we need help with the new Bishop at Clermont-Ferrand."

"Good," she said. "It's a milk run from here to the airport. So, tell me why Lacroix houses have secret escape tunnels. I mean, since I'm now a full-fledged member of this quest."

66

Bastia, Corsica

Night was setting in when Jacques and the beards reached the Bastia Poretta airport. An hour earlier, he had groped his way out of the library, wrestling with the electronic lock on the front door before getting outside. The Porsche had a least a five minutes' head start, and he knew they would never catch it.

Copper Beard confirmed that it turned right, which meant destinations on the island's north side. A quick look at the map told Jacques it had to be the airport in Bastia, and they slowed to normal speed across the mountain. An hour later, Copper Beard stopped curbside while Jacques entered the deserted terminal and found a single agent open at Easy Jet.

"*Bonjour*, can you tell me what flights went out to France in the last hour?"

"*Bonjour, monsieur.* Our last flight went to Rome. Air France's last flight was three p.m.," she said.

"That's it?"

"It's Sunday. We have an arrival at nine-thirty, and it overnights here for a seven a.m. departure."

"Thanks." He peeled away from the desk but turned back after a step. "Is there a private terminal?"

They followed the signs to the Aéroclub Bastia-Poretta, where a security guard worked the desk. Jacques asked about outbound private flights but was told that kind of request was not possible.

"Please, sir. Do not insult me," said the guard when Jacques hinted at a bribe.

"There might be another way," said Black Beard, nodding toward a maintenance hangar where a technician was working around a brightly lit business jet. "It will take a few minutes."

"Okay."

"Alone," said Black Beard when Jacques started following. "You look like a professor."

"Fine." He turned to Copper Beard. "Let's swap this car. The window's killing me. There's an Avis office at the terminal."

Twenty-five minutes later, they were back, and Black Beard, after seeing them, wandered over.

"I used to work at Charles de Gaulle," he said. "Talked shop for a while. Made like I was looking for work—"

"And?" said Jacques.

"He refueled a jet about forty-five minutes ago. Bound for Clermont-Ferrand."

"Were they on it?"

"He only saw a woman. She paid him five hundred euros to park her car in the hangar and drive it up the mountain later. Blue Macan GTS."

T hree hours later, Jacques poured the last of the wine, pausing as it dripped. His hand wavered and spilled the last drops on the table. *Putain!* He set down the bottle and picked up the glass. Lights flickered off the harbor as a light breeze broke its surface into a million mirrors. The salt and sardine smell of the quay blended oddly with the terroir of the fermented grapes, and laughter from a couple sitting on a dockside bench across the boardwalk was amplified in his hotel balcony.

He lifted the glass in a mock toast as the couple kissed and melded into a passionate tangle. He pictured Inés. His crotch warmed at the memory of her riding him the other night. He stood, shaking it off. The bedside clock showed 10:33. They had booked an 8:30 a.m. flight to Lyon, where they would catch the TGV to Clermont-Ferrand, arriving mid-afternoon. The cost set him back another three grand.

During dinner, Black Beard balked at continuing this "fool's errand," and Copper agreed. He said it was not about the money, and he despised chasing people for no purpose. The idiots had grown a conscience.

Jacques had met them during the *gilet jaune*, yellow vest, protests. As far as he knew, they had nothing to protest and joined merely to wreak havoc on the streets of Paris. Turned out Black Beard studied philosophy at the University of Western Brittany and Copper Beard was a sculptor. Both worked menial jobs on the outskirts of Paris— close to the life of plenty, yet far out of reach.

Jacques preferred working alone. He had not wanted to join them for dinner, but he still needed their muscle. Before he had entirely rationalized it, he made them a proposition: go back to Paris or continue on to Clermont-Ferrand and get rich. After their laughter died down, Black Beard stared at Jacques's stoic face and said, "You're serious."

At that point, Jacques related the Templar's bank hypothesis and showed them a photo of the codex from the Vatican vault and the clue found in Notre-Dame.

"You ran into the burning cathedral?" asked Copper Beard.

Jacques pulled back his hair to reveal the scar. Copper extended an arm to show a similar burn from a welding mishap.

"They're after the same thing," said Jacques, reminding them of the argument with Darwin and Eyrún back at Emelio's house. "Someone in the Vatican is helping them."

"How much gold?" Black Beard had asked

"Enough that a corrupt King Philip murdered a thousand good men. Imagine the gold that backed six crusades and countless pilgrimages by the wealthy," Jacques said, waxing romantically. He had not told anyone about this pursuit, and it lightened his mood to off-load the secret. He left them in wonder and, taking the second half-full bottle of wine, put €200 down to cover the bill.

In his room, he kicked off his shoes and lay back on the bed. He toyed with visions of gold. *How much did the Templars stash? At least a billion,* came a hopeful reply.

He floated in the fantasy as the gold became his—an elaborate party in the Grand Palais, besuited in fine dark blue and holding a champagne flute. An elegant dark-haired woman slipped an arm in his and whispered a delicious distraction while her fire-red nails stroked the skin under his open white collar. The Duke of Anjou interrupted to thank him for the brilliant vision and work that shifted beliefs for a constitutional monarchy. They toasted to the Sixth Republic of France.

67

Clermont-Ferrand, France

The taxi pulled away from the cottage they rented as Darwin opened the lockbox and then the front door. Eyrún walked through the main room kitchen area and opened double doors. Fresh air flowed around her, its coolness heightening the electric feel of her skin.

"It's lovely," she said, admiring the flowers around a little pond. Soft landscape lights added depth to the small yard.

From behind, Darwin's hands circled her waist, and his lips grazed her neck. She arched back. His fingers slid under her waistband, where they had playfully tried to go the whole flight from Bastia. She had wanted it, but held off when the cockpit door opened at an inconvenient moment.

"Mmm." His tongue played over her bare skin. She swayed, rubbing her ass in his groin. It surged, and she teased with a rocking motion.

He moved a hand across her chest, grasping a breast. She reached back and squeezed. He shuddered and thrust his other hand lower. She gasped as it plunged.

Seconds later, shivering from desire, she pulled his hands away and spun. She met his mouth, tongue projecting the afternoon's pent-up craving. He moved slowly backward as she drove him onto the couch.

A half hour later, Darwin grasped Eyrún's hand and bounced along the sidewalk as if in moon gravity.

"I guess you needed that," she said, tugging his hand in an appeal to walk like a grown-up.

"Yeah. All that tension from the chase. Your demon driving. A whole other secret-sexy-spy side."

"Right. Your imagination runneth over again."

He stopped and kissed her.

"I thought you were hungry," she said when he lingered.

"I am."

They found a neighborhood brasserie around the corner from the cottage, its Sunday-night crowd modest and friendly. A football match on the TV behind the bar attracted a handful of men. Three women at another table shared a bottle of wine, with two small dogs splayed on the floor beside them.

The barkeep doubled as a waiter and took their orders. Darwin asked him which wine was his favorite and ordered a bottle of it. He then ordered a steak and *pommes frites*. Eyrún ordered the same but also asked for an onion tarte with *bleu d'Auvergne* cheese. She shifted her chair around to watch the match as the wine arrived.

"Tell us why you picked this one," she asked, referring to the wine. In Darwin's experience, the locals always knew their wines. Some of the best he ever had came from choices he never would have known to make.

"It's a 2018 Ephémère Gamay from Domaine Miolanne," he said while drawing the cork and pouring. "One hundred percent Gamay grapes are grown on basalt terraces of the Gergovie plateau. It draws essence from the peperite volcanic soils and three months in old Burgundian oak."

Darwin and Eyrún swirled their glasses and sniffed. Bold. They sipped. Darwin's eyes widened. He took in a mouthful and swished it about. A bit pungent, like paprika and pepper with a cherry aftertaste and an aromatic hint of what... Eucalyptus?

"Mon Dieu! C'est magnifique!"

The barkeep smiled and bowed. He told them it came from his uncle's vineyard. Darwin nearly fell off his chair when he learned it was less than eight euros a bottle.

The onion tarte arrived, and Eyrún shared it. Darwin realized they had not eaten since breakfast—in Azerbaijan. Ten minutes later, he went through the steak like a man possessed. Eyrún refilled their glasses and suggested they order a case.

When the football ended, they walked to the cottage, having drunk more wine than intended. Darwin closed the garden doors against the cold. He got glasses of water and found Eyrún already under the covers. He stripped off his clothes and slid in.

"I'm chilly," she said, spooning him.

Fatigue pulled at him, but the memory of their earlier tryst sent a hand searching. She rolled to meet his exploration, and they made long, slow love under the blankets.

68

T heir next morning was full of practical pursuits, with clothes shopping first on the list. They had left Ajaccio the day before with just a purse and backpack. This morning Eyrún found her panties had not thoroughly dried from the quick wash in the sink.

"God, that feels so much better," she said after leaving a lingerie shop. "I need some tops and another pair of jeans."

They split up, and each bought the basics from the stores on a main commerce street. Forty minutes later, they reconnected and headed for a mountaineering shop. Darwin knew the place from a previous visit, and they came away with caving gear, especially lighting and ropes. He also picked up a bendable video camera that could plug into his mobile. The saleswoman demonstrated it by bending it around the corner of one counter.

"What's that for?" asked Eyrún.

"The arrowslits in the walls. We need to see what's on their other side."

With procurement finished, they stuffed the gear and new clothes into backpacks and headed to the cathedral.

The Cathédrale Notre-Dame-de-l'Assomption towered over the old town in Clermont-Ferrand, one of France's oldest cities. While a beautiful example of gothic tradition, the cathedral's distinguishing feature was its shadow-like appearance. The builders had used blocks cut from the lava in the surrounding extinct calderas. Its dark-gray spires pricked the clouds above an ocean of terra-cotta roofs and verdant green mountains.

The cathedral and city were nestled on the Massif Central, a plateau in south-central France that boiled with volcanic activity in past eons. The largest volcano, Puy de Dôme, loomed on the city's western horizon, its last eruption over 10,000 years distant. This entire region was influenced by the volcano geology, its soils rich in crop production and wines flavored from the ancient ash deposited on the land. But something deep below the cathedral was the reason for Darwin's visit to Clermont-Ferrand. He had been here three years earlier to investigate mysterious tunnels.

Following a paper on Roman lava tubes published in 1974, Emelio received a letter from a woman in Clermont-Ferrand who had read it. Her great grandfather, René Giraud, was a research assistant to an early volcanologist studying the area. She had alluded to underground structures in Giraud's papers, but she would not send them, and Emelio never found the time to visit.

Three years ago, she reached out again, and Darwin visited her. This time, at ninety-four, she parted with the old research, saying she hoped they could make something of it. Darwin was stunned by the information. One of Giraud's notes in 1855 described being summoned by the bishop when the cathedral's flooring caved in during a remodel. They discovered an ancient crypt, but the architects and builders did not want to explore the lower levels.

The last letter by Giraud, a confession in 1883, disclosed a cover-up by the bishop. It turned out the crypt contained access to an even lower level of tunnels that led to a lava tube. Darwin used the details in Giraud's letter to break into the crypt, where he found the lava tube but was prevented from further exploration.

Until now.

They reached the bishop's residence beside the cathedral a little before one o'clock. A man about Darwin's age met them, and after a curious study of their expedition-like luggage, led them inside.

"The bishop will join us for lunch in the dining room. Let me show you the room. You can leave the bags there," said the priest, Damien.

Darwin tingled in anticipation. He had been thinking about this moment ever since he had been inside the cathedral three years prior.

69

Bastia, Corsica

Jacques pulled down his window shade and curled into the cramped seat of the Airbus 319. Two cups of coffee and three ibuprofen had done nothing to mitigate his headache, despite seven hours of sleep. Thankfully, the beards sat elsewhere in the plane because of the last-minute bookings. As the flight taxied for takeoff, a woman in the middle seat blathered on her mobile about the beautiful day and how sad she was to be leaving Corsica. The flight attendant put an end to the call.

The next thing he knew, Jacques was being jolted awake by the wheels hitting the runway in Lyon. His head had cleared somewhat during the hour nap, and he trudged to the railway station adjacent to the airport. As the train rolled out of the station, he messaged Franz.

Arrive Clermont-Ferrand 14:07. Any idea where to find Darwin?

Franz called him two minutes later and, after greeting, said, "Clermont-Ferrand? What happened in Ajaccio?"

"Darwin's goddamn grandfather had a shotgun. They got away, and because he's rich, they took a private flight and ditched us again."

"That explains the note my source left me this morning. It said Darwin went to Paris."

"That's why we're following Darwin and not waiting on your source," snapped Jacques. "He's got to be looking for a church. There're ten in Clermont-Ferrand. I don't have the time or the manpower to stalk them all."

"You have others with you?"

"Never mind. Just get your researchers to ferret out churches in Clermont-Ferrand most likely associated with the Templars."

"I'll see what I can do."

"Don't—" Jacques held back the expletives, seeing a young girl peer around the seatback in front of him. "Look, it won't take much. You can probably narrow it down in ten minutes. Text me the names."

He put the mobile on the tray table, reclined the seat, and closed his eyes again.

70

Vatican City

Franz joined John Keenan at two o'clock in the Vatican garden during the cardinal's daily walk for prayer and contemplation. Franz heard Keenan once say he felt most connected to God's world while working the land. Franz shrugged it off. He had grown up in Rome, where God lived in churches, statues, and frescoes.

"The Pope announced the conference for January. We must have that Christ papyrus." Keenan leaped straight into the topic.

Something else is coming. Franz waited.

"I heard Darwin headed back to Paris. Is he going back to Notre-Dame?"

"Our guy—"

"Your guy," Keenan corrected.

"My guy is following Darwin. They went to Clermont-Ferrand, not Paris," said Franz.

"Why?"

"He doesn't yet know but is en route to find out." Franz wished he had more positive news to add.

Keenan took out his mobile, messaged someone, and continued

holding it as they walked. "When will they know this isn't another wild-goose chase?"

"If they don't get a solid lead, it's likely the trail's lost, and we'll never find Christ's papyrus," said Franz.

"You've put a lot of the Vatican's money at risk here, Franz. His Holiness was lenient with you about the missing codex from his library. Evidence of embezzlement would bring dire consequences, don't you think?" Keenan dismissed him.

Franz halted, watching the Camerlengo move away. He breathed deeply to counter an urge to vomit.

The bastard's setting me up for the fall! First, it's "my guy"; then it's the money.

He turned back toward the library. Just shy of the building, he ducked into a small grotto and, finding it empty, sat on its bench before a fountain with Mary holding an infant Jesus. He crossed his arms, pressing them into a gnawing in his gut.

How did it come to this?

He knew, of course. Three years before, Keenan had put in a nice word that got his sons full scholarships to prestigious universities. Keenan had asked for the occasional favor, and Franz had thought nothing of it until the Camerlengo approached him about the Knights Templar codex.

Keenan had also caught him at a time of anger. Franz seethed after having been unfairly removed from a board of directors' position at the new Library of Alexandria. *I was the one whose research had made the discovery of the library possible.* But the corrupt Egyptian antiquities authority had claimed the glory and pushed him out. *Bastards!*

Maybe he had been misguided in taking the Knights Templar codex, but it had lain in the same drawer for centuries. *No one cared about it, and I was going to apologize for the transgression.* He also knew he would not need to apologize if they found the Christ papyrus.

He rocked on the bench, thinking of what to do. The only good thing to come out of this was a loss of his substantial waistline. His appetite had vanished. When his wife inquired about the sudden disinterest in food, he countered with a story about wanting to lose weight.

If this falls apart, I'll lose everything.

Looking at the statue, he mumbled the rosary prayers, fingers moving over imaginary beads. His stomach pain receded as he incanted the Hail Marys. He finished, crossed himself, and looked up. The grotto's objects resolved from shadow with more clarity now: the gurgling water, birds zipping in and out through the bushes, and the stonework's patterns.

Franz stood, the tension flowing out of his shoulders. He started back toward his office, feeling lighter, physically and spiritually. *I didn't become head librarian of the world's oldest library by being a fool.* It was time to turn up the heat on Jacques.

Like you know how, came a recalcitrant voice, and a hand went back to his belly.

71

Cathédrale Notre-Dame-de-l'Assomption de Clermont-Ferrand

A little before three o'clock, Darwin and Eyrún walked from the bishop's residence into the cathedral's north side door. Strong sunlight poured in the triforium windows, filling the eastern end in wondrous colors. The famed workshop that crafted Sainte-Chappelle's stained glass had also plied their talents here. The near-black interior walls looked to Darwin like London's soot-covered buildings until he remembered the builders used the basalt from the volcanoes in construction.

Each of them carried a duffel bag containing a caving kit. Eyrún set hers down to run a hand over one enormous column rising into the transept crossing thirty meters above. "I've never seen an entire building made of igneous rock," she said, wandering around the ribbed column. Darwin thought it not unlike the giant redwood trees in California as she disappeared behind the stone trunk. As Eyrún studied the stone's composition, he put down his own duffel and looked about.

A sea of neatly spaced wooden chairs filled the nave between the massive basalt columns. Large chandeliers hung between the columns, their luminous gold forming a rich contrast against the matte gray rock —a knot of tourists gathered beneath the organ above the west-facing front door listening to their guide. And smaller groups and individuals moved about the cathedral, taking photos and stopping in the side chapels. Ten or so people sat in prayer, mostly near the altar.

All the human sounds were at once reflected by the stone and diffused in the cavernous vaults. Darwin stilled himself and closed his eyes. He knew the sky outside was infinitely more immense, but his juxtaposition with the enormity of the gothic structure humbled him. *There's a spirit in these buildings.* He had tried to explain it to Eyrún once, but words failed. Like hands spinning a centuries-old prayer wheel, the countless generations who visited the cathedral had imbued it with a collective human soul.

Eyrún's hand gently massaged his shoulder. "It's beautiful."

His eyes opened. "Yes. I hurried through it last time. These are special places. I wonder how long they'll last?"

"As long as we want them to," she said, in the calm, matter-of-fact manner of a Zen master.

They picked up the duffel bags, and Damien led them to a red door just right of the exterior north-side door. He unlocked it, and they entered a stone staircase that spiraled down one counter-clockwise revolution before straightening. It continued down a half-dozen more steps before making a ninety-degree turn into a short hall that opened into an underground chapel.

Darwin's heart beat faster than required by a walk downstairs. In the three years since first visiting, he had regularly thought of returning. Now, as the gate groaned open, he walked into the wide chapel and set down his duffel to explore. He wanted to get a proper sense of who built this chapel and when.

Damien continued diagonally across the chapel and unlocked a wooden door. "I believe the ambulatory with the tombs you want is through here. I don't like being underground, and if you don't mind, I'll leave you to explore," he said and moved to the spiral stairs, leaving them alone.

"This is amazing," said Eyrún, when Damien had gone.

The ten-by-fifteen-meter chamber was directly below the choir of the cathedral above them. Eyrún stood with Darwin in the chapel's center. Its long walls featured four openings, two on each side. They had entered from the rear left door, and Damien had opened the front right door. Iron gates sealed the other two openings. Along the walls, between the doors, lay two elaborately carved sarcophagi.

They faced the altar that rose one step. Its wall featured a central arch inset with a stone platform and a pair of niches on each side, holding carved figures. The chapel's back wall was bare except for a collection of tools and supplies left behind by builders. A flat, dark ceiling about three meters overhead made the chapel feel like a stage set in a large theater.

"It's like the archaeological crypt at Notre-Dame. The exhibits felt like they could've been moved from somewhere else," she said, looking at the chapel's chopped-off walls, with alternating smoothed and rough-cut surfaces. Some arches had been filled in with cement.

"You're right. It's an ancient chapel to the untrained eye, but its curators jumbled together reconstructions spanning a thousand years. I researched it while waiting for the Vatican's approval to investigate. You see where the walls cut off?" he asked.

Eyrún nodded, and he continued. "That happened during construction of the first cathedral in the fifth century. Over the next five hundred years, it was sacked by the Visigoths, Normans, and whoever else romped through these parts. The current cathedral went up in the twelve-hundreds, and the giant towers weren't finished until the late eighteen-hundreds."

"That sarcophagus," he continued, pointing to the one on the right with carved saints separated by Greek-style columns, "is fifth or sixth century. They found it during a remodel in eighteen twenty-two. The other one is fourth century and was an altar in the north transept above until the Revolution, when a farmer purchased it as a drinking trough."

"Seriously?" she asked.

"Yeah. Follow me. There's something else I want to show you." They grabbed the duffels and walked into the corridor to the ambulatory that Damien had unlocked. A few steps inside and next to an opening on their left, he pointed to a meter-long stone about thirty centimeters square and broken on one end. Its creators had carved large symbols on one side.

"They look pagan. Are they?" she asked, running fingers over isosceles triangles tipped at various angles and each bisected by scrolling lines. One pattern resembled a fleur-de-lis.

"Dunno. Not like any symbology I've seen. This one may be flower-shaped, maybe an early version of the fleur-de-lis the Merovingians used. And someone could have dragged it here from...who knows. Anyway, I wanted you to see that we archaeologists have plenty of mysteries to solve."

They retrieved their duffels and followed the left corridor. It traced the ambulatory in the cathedral above, curving to the right until they reached a row of tombs that ended with:

GUILLAUME DE BAFFIE

EPISCOPUS AUTEM CLERMONT

AD 1095

"Here we are," Darwin said, standing over a circular metal grate in an alcove to the right of De Baffie's tomb. They dropped the duffels and packs, and Darwin dug out a small pry bar.

"What was here before the church?" Eyrún asked. "I mean, they can't have found this by accident when building the cathedral."

"That's why I wanted that scroll from Ian. Agrippa describes an altar built by the Gauls, the Roman term for the Celtic people in northern Europa. He wrote they built it near a cave so they could come up from below ground for added effect."

"So, the Romans bolted onto the Celts' religious practices and, centuries later, the pagan altar becomes a cathedral," she said, tying a rope around the handles of one duffel as Darwin began descending iron rungs.

"Probably, but most all of the history from that time was written centuries later." His voice faded as he went lower. Eyrún leaned over the opening as he reached the bottom. The shaft, about twice Darwin's height, was bricked with the same basalt as the cathedral.

"Ready," she called down and lowered the first of three bags. Then she moved down the ladder.

They stood close in a lava tube, its smooth walls in black and gray with rust sections. Much like water erosion in a channel, knee-high striations in the walls marked the most recent lava flows. Its floor was churned as if someone splattered concrete about and let it dry.

"It's the upper layer of a braided maze, but it was the first time I was ever in one, and I almost got lost. Here, look at this," he said, pointing to the wall near the shaft.

"That's... an Aquila..." She trailed off, putting a hand to a symbol. Cut lines joined seven points chiseled into the rock to form a bird-like shape. Three close points formed a beak and head joined by a line to the lower four points connected in an upside-down triangle. Agrippa's team had adapted the Aquila symbol from an eagle atop the staff carried by Roman legions.

"Remember when I got so emotional in Iceland?" Darwin said. "I had only seen the Aquila in Agrippa's scrolls. To have found one here, and weeks later in Iceland, was amazing."

"I thought you were a wuss. But, even having seen it in Iceland, this is... I dunno. It's still hard to think the Romans found this."

He laughed. "You sound like me now."

72

Vatican City

Franz made up an excuse to leave early for the day, saying he felt nauseous after lunch. It was true, but his unease had to do with Keenan's threat. He stopped in a neighborhood park outside the Vatican city walls and called Jacques.

"*Bonjour*, Franz. What do you have for me?" asked Jacques.

Franz had forgotten the cathedral search and swiped to a message from his assistant. He forwarded it to Jacques. "I just sent it. Listen, what's your plan? How soon can you find the location?"

"I literally just stepped off the train, Franz. We don't know if Darwin's here or he tried some other bullshit, like changing destination midflight. But *my* plan is to find him."

"Then what?"

"Franz, are you kidding me? If I knew where to go, I'd be there."

"Look, my backer is pressing for a solution. He doesn't trust you and is talking about telling the French police about extorting the church." Franz winced at his awkward assertion.

"That's rich," said Jacques. "Listen closely, Franz. I've recorded every phone call and saved every message from you. I'll go public with all of it, including the clue found under Notre-Dame. Maybe I'm not clean, but hear me, Franz, you and your Vatican will go down with me on this."

"No. No. Jacques. Wait—" The call had ended.

73

Clermont-Ferrand

I diot! Jacques shook off the call with Franz and led the beards to a coffee bar, where they planned how to find Darwin. Then he placed his mobile where they could all see the list of churches.

Basilique Notre-Dame-du-Port
Cathédrale Notre-Dame-de-l'Assomption

"He says these are the only two old enough for the Templar's time," said Jacques.

They searched and reviewed the websites. Each one claimed their crypt predated the cathedral.

"We need to split up," Jacques told the beards. "They'll likely show up at one of these two. Ask the priests if they've seen them. Say you're looking for friends. You're traveling together but got separated."

"They might not buy it. Mobile phones make it hard to get lost," said Black Beard.

"Get creative. We need to find them."

"What about caves in the area? Lots of volcanoes around here," said Copper Beard.

"Needle in a haystack," said Jacques.

"But there's the big one, Puy de Dôme, close to town," said Copper, pointing at the horizon to the dead volcano mounded over the western edge of the city.

Jacques searched it on his mobile. It was hard to tell how it might connect to the Knights Templar, but it had an ancient Roman Temple of Mercury on its summit. His head felt better, but he was in no mood to hang out with one of the beards all day. They split up to cover the three sites and update each other hourly until returning to the hotel at six.

J acques rode a taxi from the train depot to the foot of Puy de Dôme, outside the city. Thick cloud cover looked ominous, but no rain was forecast. While he knew of the Massif Central region of France, he had never been drawn to the outdoors. He boarded the tourist train, a modern urban streetcar but with special cogs to assist climbing the steep grade.

The ascent afforded sweeping views of Clermont-Ferrand and the surrounding valleys, their fields now yellowed and fallow as autumn progressed. Forest skirted the lower part of the extinct volcano; the last eruption had blasted away its crown. French scientists had used the remaining angular plateau for generations to study the heavens.

Twenty minutes later, the doors opened, and a chill wind met Jacques as he disembarked. Most passengers carried long bags and helmets whose purpose became clear as Jacques watched them gather in a large clearing. The side of the mountain, away from Clermont-Ferrand, teemed with colorful paragliders who took flight from the volcano's steep slope.

He went to the large visitor center and read through the displays chronicling the geology and history. There were unlimited locations for caves, as humans had lived in this part of Europe since before Puy de Dôme's last eruption. His mobile vibrated. The hourly update from the beards. He checked it and replied.

Nothing here either

This is a waste of time. Where the hell are they? He crumbled the exhibit map he had taken at the entrance and slammed it into a trash bin. Then he entered the gift shop and stopped at a book display, and stared. After a moment, an employee arranging books asked if she could help him find something.

"Do you know of any large caves in the area?" he asked.

"I don't. Are you a caver?" she asked.

"I've done a little. Is there anyone here who might know?"

"It's all paragliders up here. But, a friend works at a mountaineering shop in town. I think she said they also have caving gear."

74

Lava Tube Beneath the Cathedral

Darwin and Eyrún followed the Aquila symbols, directing them through the maze of tunnels that led downward. It took Darwin a few minutes to reorient himself. The lava from the many ancient eruptions flowed across the Allier valley, building up layers over the millennia. Some of those flows carved channels like rivers and, as they burrowed, their tops cooled and formed ceilings. When the eruption ceased, the lava drained, like emptying a garden hose, and the tubes remained.

Agrippa had found similar tubes and recorded them in his scrolls, but the knowledge was lost in the Roman Empire's demise. Darwin and his grandfather, Emelio, were driven to connect this rediscovered physical evidence with the scrolls to show the ancient Romans moved about in previously unknown ways.

After several hard turns and a more extended passage, they reached a tube just wide enough to walk through. Eyrún shoved the duffels toward Darwin, and he pulled them the rest of the way. She joined him in a circular chamber the size of a small bedroom, but with a curved ceiling. Just off the chamber's center, a meter-wide hole dropped into a dark space.

She touched its low ceiling, and her fingers came away blackened with soot from long-ago torches. Graffiti covered the walls around the hole. Many of the marks were illegible and written over, but one stood out. She had seen it in a photo Darwin showed her three years before in Iceland.

DEUS VULT

ESTIENNE PIERS JEHAN

EUM IRE JERUSALEM MXCVI

"I thought you were nuts in Reykjavík. Even looking at the photo was a stretch," she said.

"You were a pain in the ass. You didn't want to believe anything," he said.

"Because you kept insisting on the preposterous idea of a lava tube going to Europe."

He sensed the conversation was leading to a pointless argument and held a reply. Instead, he focused on setting three cams into the wall gaps, then attached climbing loops to each. He joined the loops with a locking carabiner, attached a climbing rope, tested the hold strength, then dropped the rope in the hole.

Eyrún doubled-checked the rigging, then got on hands and knees to look in the opening. "How far?" she asked.

"It's hard to estimate from here, but I remember it's over twice my height."

"How did they do this during the Crusades?"

"Ladders probably, but long ago removed. Whoever closed up this space didn't want anyone going back."

While the drop posed a low-level technical challenge, Darwin knew from experience the unpredictability of underground lava structures, and they took no chances. They tested each other's harnesses, and Darwin clipped into the safety ropes. He snapped the helmet strap and switched on the light, then backed himself over the edge. Letting out the rope as he squatted over the hole, he looked down before springing off the ledge and releasing the rope.

He used a hand brake to stop just above the floor. "That's a lot better than my first time," he yelled up to Eyrún. The dark space swallowed his light as he spun slowly around the rope. He released the brake and descended the remaining distance, wobbling on an uneven patch and using the rope to balance.

She lowered the other two duffels, then joined him at the bottom. Darwin unzipped one of the bags and set up a bright LED light. Its stark beam cast them as the only figures of color in a world of gray.

E yrún unclipped from the rope and surveyed the tube, roomy enough for two large vehicles to pass each other. The last lava flow had left a great deal of clinker, chunks of cooled lava, that made for rough, awkward walking. The ceiling had a molten appearance, like burned Styrofoam. The superheated plasma above the flowing lava continuously melted and deposited material onto the walls.

She set a gas-monitoring device on the floor that showed tolerable conditions for humans—plentiful oxygen and near-zero carbon monoxide. The temperature at nineteen degrees Celsius meant their light jackets would keep them warm enough, though they had packed down vests for an extended stay.

She broke off a piece of one wall and studied its geology in a jeweler's loupe—typical igneous rock, nothing dissimilar to Iceland. A more in-depth analysis in a lab would tell her its elemental makeup, but that was not their purpose here, and she joined Darwin, who was standing at the southeast-facing wall. While it was impossible to determine their orientation after the meandering route beneath the crypt, her compass picked up magnetic signals.

"That's it?" she asked, studying the basalt blocks that sealed the lava tube. "Why do you suppose it's here?"

"To keep people out or in. Works either way, but I'm guessing to keep out," he said, rigging the endoscopic video camera.

She ran a hand across the blocks, their joints tight enough to forgo grout. Two vertical arrowslits, set about two meters apart, allowed archers a means to defend the walls. The builders cut the blocks on oblique angles to give a wider firing angle but keep the outer face opening to three-fingers' width. She peered in one slit. It was too dark to see anything, so she switched on her mobile's light and held it to the opening. It was not much better. The glare in the tight space limited view on the other side.

"Try this," said Darwin.

She stepped back, and he handed over his mobile. She watched the video as he inserted pinkie-finger-width cable.

"Looks the same. Easy, go slow. It's blurry when you move fast." The picture focused. "That's better. Looks identical to—stop! Go back. Oh, my God."

Darwin held the camera in place as he leaned over and twisted to see the picture. Eyrún held it closer. Three skeletons, wearing armor, lay on the floor. Multiple arrows protruded from the corpses.

75

Clermont-Ferrand

Jacques reached the sporting goods store near Jardin Lecoq. Gear of every kind, much of it in garish colors, lined the shelves and permeated the air with the smell of synthetic materials and glues. One wall featured climbing holds, white with chalk.

"*Bonjour*," said a woman halfway up the climbing wall. Her chestnut ponytail swayed as she glanced between handholds, her broad shoulder muscles straining beneath a tight tank top. She stretched one leg to get a toe on a hold the size of a wine cork.

"*Bonjour*," said Jacques and jumped back as she slipped off the wall. She twisted in midair like a cat and landed on the padded floor.

"Guess that was a little too far. Can I help you?" she asked, standing and wiping hands on her leggings.

"Do you sell caving gear?"

"Yeah, climbing, caving, almost the same stuff. What do you need?"

"I'm looking for a colleague who's visiting town. Might have been in yesterday," said Jacques.

"I was off yesterday. Hey, Etienne. Come here," she yelled to the back of the shop.

A short man with a handlebar mustache joined them, and Jacques repeated the question.

"We get a few touring climbers every day. Can you describe him?" asked Etienne.

Jacques showed a photo of Darwin.

"That guy was in here yesterday with a dark-haired woman. They're our customers of the month after spending nearly two thousand euros," said Etienne, smiling broadly.

"Did they say where they were going?"

Etienne crossed his arms, clamming up.

"I understand. Maybe this would help," said Jacques, placing a fifty-euro note on the counter.

Etienne glanced at the money and frowned, then looked back to Jacques. "He talked about revisiting a cave he explored a few years ago. Near Vallon-Pont-d'Arc, but that's over two hundred kilometers away, so I don't know."

Jacques said thanks and left. He stood outside the shop, pondering his next move, certain the man had lied. *At least we know they're here.* He looked at his watch and headed toward the hotel for the six o'clock meetup.

76

D arwin and Eyrún sat in a brasserie near the cathedral. After finding the skeletons, they photographed the site and examined walls for signs of weakness until their irregular eating over the last few days caught up with them and they exited the tube for an early dinner. They watched people walking by as an autumn breeze tumbled leaves along on the sidewalk two tables away and flapped the sides of the restaurant's exterior covering. Lights came on in the darkened street as evening settled, and the server switched on the heaters.

"Oh, that feels good," said Eyrún. "I never thought about winter growing up in Iceland. I've decided I don't enjoy living in the cold." She moved her chair closer as Darwin scrolled through still photos of the skeletons.

"I'm not an expert on medieval armor, but I'd say these tend toward Muslim soldiers. See how the helmets rise to a point," he said.

"Uh-huh. Any idea how old?"

"Dunno. Seven or eight hundred years, at least. This looks like a staff with a hook. Maybe they were trying to pull down the wall."

"To get in the cathedral?"

"Not per se. More like using the tube to get past the aboveground guards. It would prove the tubes were used long past the Romans.

More data to support my theory," he said, clicking to darken the mobile's screen as their entrees arrived.

During their earlier survey, they guessed from the amount of soot on the ceiling that the Templars or other knights had kept a regular watch. Torches would have been used for bright lighting and cast most of the carbon onto the roof, but they guessed most of the day-to-day light would have come from candles. Eyrún said the torches would have sucked up breathable air and increased carbon dioxide and monoxide.

Once finished looking at the southeast wall's skeletons, they crossed to the northwestern wall that faced Puy de Dôme. The stonemasons had left no gaps in either wall other than the arrowslits, and a search with the endoscopic camera on the northwest wall showed nothing on its other side. Getting through would be a challenge.

"The place needs close going over by forensic archaeologists. It's not my specialty, too tedious, but your friend Pétur would love it," said Darwin, referring to a friend whose passion was combing through the minute detritus to build the picture of ancient people's daily lives.

"Agreed, but if Pétur can't, you must know plenty of resources in France," said Eyrún.

"I've thought about it, but the bureaucracy moves slowly. And Jacques will find us. As you said, there're leaks in the Vatican."

"Then what do we do about the wall?" asked Eyrún, pausing between bites.

Darwin had been gyrating on solutions that did not involve destroying the wall. It went against all his training. Again, he pictured the scroll they had retrieved in Johannesburg and mentally reviewed his notes. Agrippa had written that the local Celtic population knew about the tunnel, but their superstitions prevented them from traveling far. Agrippa's men investigated and reported finding a large chamber one-and-a-half Roman miles up the tube. They described it as being as large as a theater but enclosed over the top and with a curved floor, like a shallow bowl.

Darwin had translated its size estimate to between fifty and seventy meters. What interested him most were the four lava tubes that they said entered the chamber from other directions. *The chamber must be the nexus that Agrippa alluded to in his other scrolls. I need to know where the tubes go.* Anything Knights Templar was a side interest for him.

"I've been thinking about the wall nonstop and can't come up with anything other than to break it down," he said.

"You're sure."

"Yes. I'm sure. The southeast side is intact. We'll leave that one alone, but we have to get through the northwest side. Agrippa's scroll is clear about the lava tube reaching a chamber under the volcano."

"And if the Templar's bank isn't there?"

"Then I've got what I wanted anyway—to find out where the lava tube goes."

Their server arrived with dessert, and they worked the raspberry tarte from opposite ends. "What about that pile of construction equipment in the crypt chapel? Do you think there might be tools we can use?" she asked, forking a stray raspberry.

He zoomed into a photo of the chapel's back wall. "I think that's a pry bar leaning against the wall with the other construction tools."

"Yep," she agreed, looking at her watch. "I'm up for it. Let's go."

They slipped into the crypt door shortly before the cathedral closed at 7:30 and descended to the chapel. Darwin had been right. A pry bar a meter and a half long leaned against the back wall. Eyrún picked up a plastic pail with two hammers and various chisels, and they headed back to the lava tube. Ten minutes later, they reached the wall.

"How do you want to do this?" she asked.

"It's thinnest in the arrowslit, and we can use the slit for leverage," he said, hefting the bar in both hands, its weight about half that of the barbells he used in the gym.

The wall's builders had staggered the half-meter-wide rectangular blocks for strength, using half-width blocks to make a clean gap for the arrowslits. Combined with the angles cut in the blocks for the archers, Darwin figured this was the wall's weakest point. Eyrún concurred.

The arrowslits were four blocks high with the half-width blocks in the second and fourth positions from the slit's bottom. He inserted the chiseled end of the pry bar into the arrowslit against the second-position block and wedged it tight. Facing the wall, he pushed the bar as if performing a chest press. A series of pops sent chips flying toward Eyrún.

"Ah!" she yelled. Darwin paused while she moved behind him. Three more pushes broke off more small chunks. "Stop. Look." A centimeter-wide gap had opened between blocks.

Darwin removed the pry bar from the arrowslit and shoved the chisel point in the gap. Eyrún rapped the pry bar's end with a hammer, causing it to bite deeper. Darwin wiggled the bar and the gap opened. They worked this process of hammering and prying until the smaller block was nearly free. Darwin then rammed the bar repeatedly into the block until it fell away on the opposite side of the wall.

Sweat beaded on both their foreheads and they stripped off their jackets. They looked in the larger opening, but there were no signs of bodies. Eyrún took up the pry bar against the other half-width block. Pushing was more awkward at shoulder height, and Darwin helped until a gap exposed, then she worked the bar in the opening while he hammered. When the block had turned sufficiently, they used the bar together to slam the block out of the wall.

"Wooo! I won't miss the gym this week after all," she panted, hands on knees.

One full-sized block remained in the middle of the arrowslit, sticking out like a sideways tooth. They agreed that removing this last block would give them enough room to pass through. Fortunately, its length created better leverage as it pivoted forty-five degrees with much less effort than required on the first two blocks. Unfortunately, it needed more work to pound it free of the wall, but three minutes later, it dropped behind like the others. They took a break, sitting against the tube wall, and drank from water bottles.

"I need a shower," said Eyrún.

"We went three weeks without one in the Iceland tube," he said.

"Oh, God. That was disgusting."

"Well, we can go back now. Take a shower and return in the morning," he said.

"Are you kidding? No way we'd get any sleep. I'm game if you are," she said, nodding at the opening.

He jumped up and stuffed gear from the duffels into his pack: batteries, climbing kit, water bottles, and energy bars. She joined him and when they were ready, squeezed through the opening. "What's so funny?" she asked, looking at his face-splitting smile.

"I thought of the first time we met. You went underground first. It felt like I was competing to keep up."

"You were. Hand me my pack, slowpoke."

77

Lava Tube

Darwin counted paces and at a thousand noticed more strain in his thighs from the increasing slope. Another 450 paces and a clear edge distinguished the tube wall, exposing a dark void beyond.

"Do you see it?" Eyrún asked. They had walked side by side once Darwin had crawled through the wall.

"Yes, be careful. Agrippa wrote of a drop-off."

They reached the opening two minutes later and stopped. The floor fell away into a vast circular depression, its salmon-red surface full of cracks like a dry lakebed. The ceiling domed four stories overhead, and directly across the chamber, half a football pitch away, another lava tube opened. Looking around to their right, they saw two other tubes that spilled into the space.

"Look..." Eyrún said in wonder, her voice trailing off as she tugged Darwin's sleeve. He turned left to where she was staring.

A broad platform extended five meters into the chamber from its edge, stepping down twice to compensate for the sloping floor. But, what took Eyrún's breath away was a massive wooden door in the middle of the platform. Enormous iron hinges held the door in a frame constructed of basalt blocks. The rock surrounding the portal had been carved in a bas-relief into the chamber's ceiling.

"That's definitely not Roman," said Darwin.

"These aren't either," said Eyrún, walking down four steps cut in the lava tube's edge. She turned and shined her light over them. "These were cut in. The real edge would have been about here." She held a hand at chest height and about the same distance from where Darwin stood on the tube floor.

He stepped down to join her, and they walked across the bowled floor and stepped onto the platform. Beneath a massive lintel, the door was as wide as Darwin's outstretched arms and rose about half again his height.

"The hinges are as big as my arms." He held out one arm.

"Zac's arms, maybe. These things are huge," she said.

The Templars built the door into the lava tube opening with the same basalt blocks as the other walls. Three rows of figures carved in the gothic cathedrals' style ascended each side of the portal and peaked above the door. A single basalt slab formed a lintel and, above it, sat a figure of Jesus Christ, wearing a long-rayed crown covered in gold leaf. In the darkened lava chamber, this bright spot drew one's eye like an oasis in the desert.

"I am the door..." Darwin's voice faded into mystery.

"What?"

"It's a literal depiction of a Christian gospel where Jesus told people he was the gateway to being saved. You're right, I'm sure its modeled after the central portal of Notre-Dame de Paris. See, that's him." He pointed at the carving above the lintel.

On each side of the portal, thin pillars supported three half-height men in full Knights Templar armor. Atop the knights, the rows of smaller figures curved upward and outward, following the chamber's ceiling. "That's eerie," she said, standing within arm's reach of the door and seeing the top figures meet directly over her head.

"Yes, they're classic gothic archivolts, but unique because of the rotunda-like nature of this place. Someone went to great expense to make this."

"Could these be important Templars?" she asked, running fingers lightly over the carvings

"If not, I've no clue who they are," he said, squatting to study the door lock. A four-hand-sized iron plate was affixed to the door's right side, opposite the hinges. Just above a single thumb-sized keyhole, the constructors stamped the metal with two helmeted knights on a single horse surrounded by text: SIGILLUM MILITUM 1292.

"What's it say?" she asked.

"'Seal of the Soldiers' and twelve ninety-two. A date? Dunno what else it could be."

"Where's the key?" she asked.

"That's the question of the day. Unbelievable. What did de Mornay expect us to do?" Darwin stood, one hand against the door, hung his head, and sighed. "This is fantastic. But I can't believe we're supposed to break it down."

"Would it be hard to pick? You know, the kit you have?"

"Too small for this lock, but you're thinking right. We need a bigger version," he said.

"Well, it's eleven-thirty now," she said. "It'll take an hour to get back. We can let people know about this in the morning."

"Agreed. I'm beat as well, but let's photograph everything first."

They spent five minutes documenting the space and retreated from the lava tube back to the crypt. Darwin paused at its opening to look at the chamber one more time before catching up to Eyrún.

78

Clermont-Ferrand

Darwin had slept well but was now awake, staring at the ceiling in the dark room where faint light from the outside lights edged around the draperies. A few minutes later, he tapped his watch. It read 05:13.

He kept going over the lava chamber and the vault's carved entrance. He knew that the Medieval period, far from being a dark age, had produced some of the world's finest architectural creations. Life in the middle ages was difficult, and its less mature technologies were unable to overcome crop failures and disease. Yet there was enough societal abundance to build monuments and wage war.

Rolling sideways, away from the light, he breathed slowly, telling himself it was too early to get up. But behind his closed eyes the door to the Templar's bank resolved, and he focused on the lock. Its seal shouted Templar, but 1292 perplexed him. He felt as if he had seen it before. *So many dates. Where—*His eyes snapped open.

It's on a tomb in the crypt. But which one? He mentally inventoried the row, but the details swam in circles. He had notes and photos. He could hear Eyrún breathing quietly as he slipped out of bed, unplugged the iPhone on the nightstand, and grabbed the wool throw off a bedside chair. He padded into the bathroom where the device's bright screen would not wake Eyrún, pausing once as the wooden floor creaked. Lowering its lid, he sat on the toilet and searched for 1292, which returned numerous possibilities, from phone numbers to addresses. He scrolled to a link for a file that contained, "…date of death 1292" and tapped it.

That's it! The file listed the other tombs in the crypt besides de Baffie's. Three graves over was Thibaud Gaudin 1229–1292. He looked at the note's date—July three years ago—and scrolled back through the photo library. Less than a minute later, he found it and zoomed into the stone. The lighting in the photo was low, and centuries of dust occluded the surface, but just above the dates he could make out a carving of two knights on a horse. *What're the odds?*

Now fully awake, he felt his heart thrumming. He searched Thibaud Gaudin in a browser. All the first-page results linked to articles for the twenty-second Grand Master of the Knights Templar. He tapped one.

"What are you doing?"

He jumped and juggled the iPhone to keep it from clattering on the marble floor. Eyrún stood in the doorway, wrapped in a blanket.

They dressed after Darwin explained what he had discovered and went to the kitchen, where they found Damien and the bishop at a round table. They were also rewarded with the source of the freshly brewed coffee aroma permeating the building.

"Good morning. Are you joining us for the morning service?" asked the bishop.

"Er, yes," said Darwin as Eyrún greeted the bishop and Damien and poured herself a cup. It was not what they had planned, but the 6 a.m. service would get them in the cathedral.

"See you in a few minutes, then. Damien and I need to set things up," said the bishop, pushing back from the table. The two men left.

"What do we do now?" Eyrún asked.

"We go to church. We'll sneak away unless there are few other people and our leaving will stand out. Worst case, it's only thirty minutes," he said, finishing his coffee and moving toward the door.

Night still cloaked the pedestrian street in darkness, three weeks before the autumn time change. They crossed to the cathedral's side door, and Eyrún zipped her puffer jacket tight against her scarf. "I hope it's warmer in the church."

Darwin held open the cathedral's door and followed her in as Damien began the service. They slipped into chairs near one of the massive columns a few rows behind the worshippers scattered in front of the choir.

"Good. There's not a mass," Darwin whispered. "We won't have to walk up, but I don't know if we can get in the crypt door unnoticed." The altar was well lit, and a spotlight on carvings near the door would illuminate anyone passing. They decided to wait.

Darwin found himself lost in the familiar cadence of prayers as he drifted through childhood memories. When the service ended, he whispered to Eyrún, and they moved to greet the bishop and Damien.

"You're getting an early start. Have you found anything?" the bishop asked.

"The many remodels of the crypt make it hard to sort out how the various artifacts and relics come together. Mostly we've looked at what I discovered on my first visit," said Darwin.

"Yes. This part of France has a deep history, going back even before the Romans," said the bishop. "This cathedral is overdue for more thorough exploration."

"Do you need any help?" asked Damien.

"No, thank you. We're just checking the inscriptions on one tomb, then coming back up for breakfast," said Eyrún.

Darwin reached for Eyrún's hand as casually as he could and lightly squeezed a couple of times. He thanked the bishop for an excellent service and said they would catch up later. As they opened the crypt door, Eyrún asked, "What was the hand squeeze for?"

"Caution. Richard introduced us, and we have Papal permission, but we don't know Damien and the bishop." Darwin looking back into the cathedral. He saw the bishop reach under his vestments and take out what looked like a mobile phone.

Merde! He closed the crypt door and locked it from the inside. *It's nothing,* he kept telling himself as he followed Eyrún downstairs. *But why did he ask if we found anything?*

79

Jacques sat reading a newspaper in a café next to his hotel. He finished reading an opinion piece calling for a stronger French pan-European leadership stance outside the European Union's sphere. The author was new to him, and, searching for her background, he found she was young. He smiled in agreement with her position and set down the paper. He refilled his cup from the coffee press, but it had cooled, and he ordered another pot.

"*Bonjour*," said an old man from an adjacent table.

"*Bonjour*," Jacques replied.

"May I have the paper?"

Jacques handed it to the man as the beards walked in the front door and joined him. They exchanged greetings but made little conversation until well into their morning coffees.

"Where are we exploring today?" asked Black Beard.

"They've got to be at one of the two cathedrals. If they're in the crypt, we won't see them unless during their entry or exit. I've asked my Vatican contact, but he's not heard anything," said Jacques, excusing himself after instructing the beards to finish breakfast and each stake out one cathedral. "I'm going to press my Vatican guy into getting us better answers."

80

arwin followed Eyrún across the chapel and entered the corridor toward the ambulatory. He pulled the door closed, squeaking as it met the doorjamb.

"Why did you do that?" Eyrún asked.

"In case someone follows us. I dunno, maybe I'm paranoid, but we've found the way in," he said.

Reaching the tombs, he scanned their fronts, beginning with De Baffie on the far right. "There," he said, kneeling and brushing away cobwebs and dirt. He blew on the remaining dust on the letters:

THIBAUD GAUDIN
AD 1229–1292

He dug into his pack and removed a brush that more effectively cleared the old carvings in the tombstone. Below the numbers, a rounded relief showed a domed building topped with a cross. The text around the circle was challenging to make out, but Darwin knew it from a previous study: DE TEMPLO CHRISTI.

"The Temple of Christ," he said, scrolling his finger around the letters. "It's the other side of the seal on the big wooden door below us." Eyrún squatted next to him as he brought up the picture from yesterday. "The whole inscription reads Seal of the Soldiers of the Temple of Christ."

"Do you think the key's in there?"

"Only one way to find out," he said, pulling a tiny pry bar from his pack and wedging it into the tomb's front stone. He continued talking as he worked the thin steel blade around the rock. "My search this morning showed Gaudin was the last Templar Grand Master before Jacques de Molay, but Gaudin was killed in Cyprus. I think de Molay created this as a clue. I doubt they'd bring Gaudin's corpse all the way to this specific cathedral."

The stone now protruded enough for Darwin to get the bar's bent end behind it. When he opened enough of a gap, they put fingers in top and bottom and pulled. Stone on stone grated as it swung like a door, the left side remaining wedged in place. Their headlamps glinted off a metal helmet. A yellowed skull's empty eye sockets peered toward the heavens.

"I'm not going in there," said Eyrún, moving back from the skeleton.

Thibaud Gaudin, or a convenient body, lay feet first into the shoulder width tomb. Darwin moved his head to illuminate the long dark space. A rotted, once-white fabric lay atop the chain mail–covered skeleton whose finger bones clasped the hilt of a long sword.

"Ew." Eyrún cringed as Darwin extended one arm inside and probed, his face nearly against the helmet's crest. He sneezed, pulled his arm out, and sneezed again. After settling, he rubbed his nose on his left sleeve and then reached back under the chain mail with his right hand.

"I got it," he said a few moments later, after grasping the keychain atop the breastbone. "Come around me. Shine your light in."

She moved on all fours around his left side and adjusted her lamp downward. Darwin had a slender chain in his hand and worked the links slowly between his fingers, like reeling in a big fish on a weak line. He felt the drag. *Almost. C'mon, you bugger.*

The chain gave way as a key popped free of the chain mail, pressing it against the skeleton's chest. It took a few more minutes to work the keychain under the head. Eyrún grimaced as she lifted the helmet, and Darwin worked the chain clear. He sat up against the tomb block and arched his back.

"Ow. My neck cramped, but I didn't want to let go." He held a metal key about a hand's length in size and with a finger-width shaft. The chain looped down, its links made of the same iron as the chain mail draping over the corpse.

"Looks about the right size," he said.

She examined the wide blade. Its flat surface had a cross-pattern notch. "It's not very sophisticated," she said.

"Most lock mechanisms were simple until well past the Renaissance. I think this vault's main protection would have been armed knights."

"But is this *the* key?" she asked.

"Dunno, but I'm hungry. Let's eat," he said, moving back onto his knees and returning the tombstone into place. When done, he brushed away the detritus that had spilled from around the corpse. Then, pausing to examine the area, he ran the brush over the other tombs to make it less obvious that one had been the object of attention. Eyrún pocketed the key as they left the crypt, and, once upstairs, they crossed the cathedral to its south-side door to avoid running into Damien or the bishop. The sun had just touched the city's rooftops as they emerged into the plaza alive with farmers setting up stalls for a weekly market.

81

Eyrún and Darwin sat close to the kitchen to warm up inside a café on the plaza. Before sitting down, she went to the toilet and vigorously scrubbed her hands. The dirt was off in the first ten seconds, but the creepy feeling remained even after drying. Darwin had taken the key to wash it, and it now lay drying atop paper towels beside them on the table. As the server arrived with Eyrún's cocoa, Darwin rolled over the towel to hide the key.

She warmed her hands on the bowl and sipped the cocoa while waiting for their sausage and eggs. As their food arrived, she asked, "Where do you suppose Jacques is?"

"Dunno. I've been thinking about it. Given the leaks at the Vatican, he'll find us eventually."

"Is there anyone else we can contact?"

"Let's focus on what's behind the door first. That'll determine the urgency. If it's empty, we'll look silly calling in the cavalry."

The sun had covered the plaza when they stepped outside after breakfast, and early shoppers swarmed the stalls.

"Can we look around a little?" Eyrún asked.

"Sure, a few minutes. The sun feels good. I'm going to sit on the fountain."

She wandered the vegetable stalls before reaching the cheese vendors. She bought a block of gruyère and some *saucisson* from a butcher, figuring it would be a welcome addition to the dry protein bars. After putting the purchases in her pack, she crossed to the other side of the plaza, beyond the clothing sellers, to the craft stalls. Eyrún stopped at one, enjoying the sun on her back as she looked at silver earrings.

"Those look good on you," said the vendor, a young woman whose fingertips were darkened from working with the gray metal.

"What are these shapes?" asked Eyrún.

"The ancient Celts who occupied this valley. Here, use this." She gave Eyrún a hand mirror to make it easier than bending over the table mirror.

Eyrún held one earring to her right earlobe as she turned her head in the mirror. She caught the sun and pinched her eyes shut until the spots faded. When she reopened them, away from the sun this time, the silver circles glinted in the rays spilling across the plaza. Something else behind her caught the sun. She froze.

Shit! Stay calm. Don't react. She put down the earring and picked up another. The man had moved, but the sun blazed through his copper-colored beard.

E yrún's tone sounded on Darwin's mobile and he set down the coffee cup on the fountain to look at the message.

Copper's here.

> Darwin: Where are you?

Eyrún: Sun side near corner. Coming toward you. Get ready to run.

He stood and followed the tents toward the plaza's corner, scanning the crowd for anyone with a beard. If Copper was here, then Black Beard and Jacques could be as well. *Merde! How did they find us so soon?*

He saw Eyrún moving casually along the stalls and looked in her wake. *There!* Copper Beard shadowed her movement two stalls behind. Darwin scanned around Copper but could see no one else with a beard. Eyrún was now directly parallel with the fountain and turned toward Darwin.

She closed the gap and used her new earring purchase to make their conversation seem natural. "Is he still behind me?" she asked, holding one earring to her ear.

"Yes. He's almost level with the last stall."

"We can head for the cathedral."

"I don't think that will work. They'll know exactly where to go," said Darwin.

"How about the bishop's house?" she asked.

"That works, but—" He seized her hand and began walking toward the cathedral. "He got on his phone. The other guys must be close."

They crossed the plaza, and when they neared the cathedral Eyrún dropped one earring and used the moment, picking it up to look back. "He's closing the gap. Five more steps, then we run to the bishop's. You go around the back. I'll go around front."

"What!"

"Just do it. He'll stop to decide which way to go," she said, counting steps. "Now."

They dropped hands, splitting left and right. Eyrún had the longer distance, and Darwin looked back as he rounded the cathedral's southern end. She had already rounded the front-door spire end with Copper in pursuit. *She's fast.*

He turned back. The sun hit him in the face as he cleared the cathedral. He thrust up a hand to block it. Coming around into Place de la Bourse, he scanned the area between the cathedral and the row of buildings with the bishop's residence. Eyrún was halfway to the house.

"Go right," she yelled, angling toward a street on her left. Copper had only just rounded the cathedral, considerably slower than Eyrún. Darwin merged with Eyrún as they ran on a street perpendicular to the church. Half a block later, she tugged his sleeve. "He's slow. Go here."

Darwin followed her left onto a street that jogged a quick right, then left, then straight. A backward glance ensured him that they could not be seen from the street off the church. Eyrún slowed as they reached the cathedral's front on Rue Verdier Latour and scanned the narrow lane.

"No one behind us." Darwin looked back.

"Good. Let's get back to the bishop's." She sprinted away. Darwin stayed on her right shoulder as they passed the elevated end of Place de la Bourse. She mounted its steps beside the cathedral a second time, and they hugged the opposite buildings until slipping in the bishop's door, where they moved to a front sitting room area. She scanned the plaza outside.

"We lost him." She panted.

"Good thing he was slow."

"It's why I went around front. I'm faster than you and I knew I'd wind him."

Darwin's mouth fell agape.

Eyrún laughed. "We split at the transept door, that's a third to the back and two to the front. We reached the opposite side at the same time."

A bead of sweat curled into Darwin's eye, and he dabbed a sleeve to it. "C'mon," he said, walking upstairs to their room. "I need the toilet, then let's get back to the crypt."

"How the hell did they find us?" she asked.

82

Jacques and Black Beard met Copper Beard at the fountain by the farmer's market about an hour after Darwin and Eyrún got away.

"How did you lose them?" he asked.

"You didn't hire me for speed," said Copper Beard.

Jacques ignored the attempt at humor and looked around the plaza. "It can't be a coincidence they showed up at this farmer's market. Anyway, the crypt in the other cathedral was too small."

He led them into the dark basalt cathedral, quiet on the early weekday. Jacques knew that crypts were typically built beneath the choir and focused their search on the spaces beyond the transept. Three doors and a gate opened off the main sanctuary, but all were locked. He paused and saw a woman with a broom sweeping around one shrine.

"You guys wander off. I'm going to ask that woman some questions," he said. The beards walked around the ambulatory while Jacques drifted toward the woman.

"*Bonjour,*" he said.

"*Bonjour,*" she said, crossing herself after placing a cloth on the shrine and replacing a fresh flower vase.

"It's a lovely arrangement. You have a knack for it."

"Oh, it's nothing. I do my small part for the cathedral," she said, blushing and wiping a water droplet from the marble.

"I wonder if you could help me? I'm an amateur archaeologist studying Medieval frescoes. Does this cathedral have any?" asked Jacques.

"That's the first time anyone ever asked that. To be honest, I have not seen anything like that in the cathedral. But, let me think..." She looked at the shrine as if inspiration would be forthcoming. "Yes, that's it. If there were any, they would be in the crypt. It's ancient," she added.

Perfect. Jacques knew full well from searching last night that Notre-Dame de l'Assomption had a crypt dating back to the 400s. "Is it open?" he asked.

"Not to the public."

"That's a shame. Do you know who I could petition to get special access? It would mean a lot to me," said Jacques.

"I suppose it would be the bishop. I heard he let two people in just yesterday. A man and a woman. They were carrying bags and had a rope, is what I was told. Odd for exploring the crypt, if you ask me."

"That is strange. I wonder what they were looking for." Jacques knew it must be Darwin and Eyrún, and, at this point, he was merely making polite conversation. Unfortunately, the woman took him literally and went on describing how she heard they were looking for a unique tomb. As her conversational claws kneaded his psyche, his eyes darted around for a means of escape.

"Oh, excuse me. They're my colleagues." He gestured toward the beards. "You've been most kind. I have to go." He fished a handful of euro coins from his pocket made a point of dropping them one by one in the offering box of the shrine. When the fifth coin had thumped the bottom of the wooden box, he asked. "Where is the crypt entrance?"

"It's behind the red door. Over there."

He followed her slender finger toward the north transept door. He thanked her again and moved away.

83

Lava Tube

An hour later, Darwin and Eyrún arrived back at the vault door. As he waited, she inserted the key into the keyhole, having won their rock, paper, scissors competition. Her paper had covered his rock, and she took the key from him with the other.

He took a deep breath, his neurons a lightning storm of possibilities: gold, silver, jewels; maybe ancient manuscripts; the Christ papyrus. He stopped on that possibility, imagining the man Jesus dipping a writing implement in ink and penning his thoughts.

It would be beyond precious. We have so little about his life. Then he shuddered, recalling a gospel account of Jesus' life. *Did he really know what was going to happen to him?*

"It won't turn," said Eyrún, bursting his reflection and moving aside.

He stepped up and grasped the key. Something stuck in the mechanism.

"Is it rusted?" she asked.

"Could be, but there's no rust on the outside and no water in this environment." He shined a light in the keyhole. "Can't see anything."

He pushed on the door. Its top half moved a little, but the bottom did not move at all. He dropped on his hands and knees and studied the door's bottom.

"Looks like it's sagging. It's a few millimeters higher on the hinge side. Here—" he said, tapping on the keyhole side. "It's sitting on the stone. I'm guessing the door's tilted and causing pressure on the lock mechanism." He shouldered the door, but it did not move.

"We need a pry bar. Place it about here," she said, showing a gap at the door's midpoint. "Then one of us stands on the end to lift the door, while the other turns the key."

Darwin tried it with a small pry from his pack, but it was too weak to lift the door. Eyrún agreed to fetch the big bar at the broken wall, declining his company, and took off on the forty-minute round trip.

W hile Eyrún retrieved the bar, Darwin explored the lava tubes that emptied into the chamber, beginning with the one nearest the vault. About two meters in, he encountered the rock pile they briefly surveyed yesterday and cautiously moved around it. Beyond it, another section of the tube's ceiling had collapsed, blocking most of its right side and leaning against the wall. It had two arrowslits like the others.

He exited and continued clockwise to the next tube. It entered the lava chamber from a short drop-off. Its ceiling towered overhead, at least the same height at the tube that ran beneath the cathedral. A clear Aquila symbol had been chiseled into the wall at shoulder-level to Darwin. He consulted Agrippa's second scroll, which he had down-loaded to his mobile. Agrippa wrote that they found four lava tubes besides the one they followed to the chamber.

Darwin turned to face the chamber and determined he was standing in the tube that the scroll labeled as heading to Lutetia. He continued inward about ten meters until reaching the wall the Templars had erected. At least they assumed it was the Templars. He could think of no one else who would have a reason. He put an eye to one of its arrowslits. *Lutetia! I wonder…* He visualized the quarries beneath Paris. If this tube went through to Paris, connecting with the underground mines would be a logical connection. *Aya will flip out!*

"Darwin! Where are you?" yelled Eyrún.

He walked out and said, "In here. Checking out the other tubes."

"Come get this thing," she said, sitting on the steps leading down from the tube and shaking her wrists. "It's only about ten kilos, but try carrying it two kilometers.

"You didn't want my help."

"I know. I know. Let's open it." She stood when he reached her. "Thinking about the door kept me going."

Darwin wedged the bar's blade end under the door's midpoint and pressed down. It popped free in a shower of splinters. "Not enough bite. Go farther back toward the hinges," she said.

He pried closer to the hinges and Eyrún tried the lock. "Still stuck." She got the tiny bar from his pack. "Okay, I'll slide this under the middle to hold it up, then you move the big bar here." She said, pointing to a spot nearer the lock. "Okay, press down."

He did. She shoved the little bar in and tapped it in with the toe of her shoe. He withdrew the big bar and moved to the other side of the tiny bar, then pushed the blade in the wider gap.

"It's turning. Push harder," she said, hands on the key. Darwin put all his weight on the bar and a loud clunk reverberated through the oak door.

"It's open!" She turned the key around, and the door moved slightly out from its jamb. He released the bar, and they pulled the handle together. The door was stubborn, moving barely a centimeter at a time as they yanked the handle. But, at last, it was free of the door-jamb, wide enough to insert a hand. They paused.

"You ready?" he asked.

She grinned and swept a sleeve over her sweaty forehead. "Let's do it."

They wrapped fingers around the thick oak—which, now free of the stone, opened with a mighty groan, echoing in the chamber like a foghorn.

84

Vatican City

After a call with John Keenan, Franz opened his office door to find the administrative section of the Vatican Apostolic Archive empty. His assistant and the other librarians had gone on a late-morning coffee break. And, while the thought of an espresso was comforting, his acid stomach had kicked up again.

He walked outside, not aiming in any direction, but finding himself back in the grotto, he sat and looked at the statue of Mary. "What have I done?" he asked.

His fingers massaged his temples as the conversation with Keenan rolled around in his head. Keenan had just told Franz to break contact with Jacques, that his services were no longer required, and to forget about the whole thing. And before Franz could ask why, Keenan had hung up.

What's going on? Franz poured out his soul to the marble figure, but there was no relief this time. The water gurgled and insects buzzed, but it was otherwise still in the contemplative space. Out of the stillness, Franz heard a man's voice coming from behind the bushes. He sat up and peered through the foliage. Keenan was talking on his phone. Franz cupped his ears to hear better against the gurgling water.

"The bishop in Clermont-Ferrand called me this morning," Keenan was saying. "He says there are now two groups of people who have been in the crypt. He went in the crypt this morning and saw nothing, but he said it looks like they went into a deeper tunnel. I told him not to speak with anyone and that you're arriving with a team to take charge of a valuable Vatican relic."

The Camerlengo stopped just on the other side of the hedge, listening to the response. "No. Nothing Franz said this morning makes me think his people have guns, but the Christ papyrus is critical to the church, so it's best to prepare yourselves."

Another pause. *Who's he talking to?*

"No time to drive," Keenan continued. "The bishop's guessing from the frequency of their trips in and out that they found something. Use my account to hire a private flight. The Vatican diplomatic immunity will keep the French from looking in your bags. Get Christ's papyrus. Use whatever force you deem necessary. Go."

Keenan ended the call and resumed his walk. Franz turned back to face the fountain, frozen to the bench as the footfalls receded. *I was told no one would be hurt. Liar!*

"This can't be happening," he said to Mary, burying his head in sweaty palms. "It's gone too far…"

Tell someone, came a thought.

I can't. Keenan will ruin me. My family shamed. Worse, I'll spend years in prison. He shuddered and tried a focused breathing technique his psychologist recommended to relieve stress. *It's not working.* But, as he continued, an idea began to form.

Wait. I can't tell just anyone, but what if I confessed to the right someone?

Franz pictured Richard Ndembele and sat up. *It could work, and I can deny ever having told anyone. The secrecy of the confessional is absolute.* He went back to his desk, where he had left his mobile.

85

Lava Tube

"It's another wall," said Eyrún, looking around the oak door at a basalt block wall a meter inside—an arrowslit aligned directly at them.

Darwin noticed a change in the air. Whereas moments before, the lava chamber smelled like a cement stairwell, a subtle undercurrent now emanated from the opened portal. He had experienced the sensation before, especially the first time he had opened the Box—the long, slow decay of wood, fabric, and metal—undisturbed for years, suddenly wafted by air particles.

"Do you smell it?" asked Darwin.

"Yes. It's a little like old books."

"I call it the breath of antiquity. Like an old museum, but far older. No one's opened this door in seven hundred years." He lingered a moment longer, but Eyrún took a step forward, and he put a hand on her shoulder. "Be careful. There may be traps or other defenses."

"Like what?"

"Dunno, but a false floor that collapses into a spiked pit comes to mind." Darwin peered in, running his light across the floor, paved in the same basalt as the exterior platform. The interior wall with the arrowslit ran to his left, ending in a one-person-width gap. He stepped cautiously and rounded the wall's end to see a second wall behind it, another arrowslit aimed at anyone coming around the corner.

"Brilliant. Even if an army broke into the underground tubes and managed to open the vault, they'd have to go single-file to fight off guards inside." He moved along the second wall and reached a similar narrow opening at its end. He turned its corner, with Eyrún on his heels.

Their lights flashed off a helmeted knight an arm's length away. Eyrún screamed, pulling Darwin back. Both raised their hands in a defensive posture. But when nothing came, Darwin started laughing. "Wait, this can't be like *Indiana Jones*, where there's a knight still alive after a thousand years."

He moved forward and eased into the opening, pressing against the wall. A figure stood before them wearing a medieval helmet and chain mail with a red-cross emblazoned on its white tunic. But, the empty suit draped over a wooden stand, the helmet perched on top.

"Is this some kind of Templar scarecrow?"

"Maybe, or it could be just a place to hang their gear. Look at this." Darwin pointed to a rack with swords and bows standing at the ready near the opening. After inspecting the area for further danger, he led the way through the gap. They entered a long hall where their headlamps fell on thousands of gold bars.

The air shimmered in golden light as a dazzling array of sunbursts flooded the space. Darwin stood speechless, running his headlamp over rack upon rack of bullion. The back of his neck tingled from goosebumps, and he brought up a hand to soothe the feeling.

Eyrún stepped beside him. "Wow!"

Darwin felt like time had stopped, and in the preternatural quiet, he could hear Eyrún's breathing and his own rapid heartbeat as their lights settled on the rack before them. His eyes remained transfixed on iPhone-sized gold ingots, stacked five high and spread across a shelf two meters wide. And this was but one of four shelf units on this wall.

Math was never his strength, but he was satisfied with his brain's calculation—*a lot*.

He put an arm around Eyrún's waist. "Wow," she whispered.

With the initial spell broken, he turned toward her. "I think we found the Knights Templar treasure." She jumped in his arms, and he spun around, yelling, "We found it."

He put her down and studied the hall. The interlocking basalt blocks forming the walls arched overhead—appearing not unlike an underground train tunnel. Taking in the totality of the hall, he said, "This is fantastic!"

He turned to Eyrún as she lifted a gold bar. "It's heavier than I expected." She moved the ingot up and down like a dumbbell. "It feels like the smallest weight my trainer started me on. A kilo, maybe?"

Darwin palmed an ingot. "Seems about right, but the metric system came along much later than the Templars." He examined the flat, smooth bar, its edges rounding to a rougher underside, then flipped it over to see a Knights Templar seal molded into the bottom.

"We need to catalogue what's here," he said.

Let's get to it." She replaced the ingot.

D arwin immediately went to something that drew his attention while spinning Eyrún—a mosaic of golden crosses in the hall's rear that seemed to hang in space. As he moved closer, his eyes resolved to floor-to-ceiling black iron bars that had been affixed with crosses covered in gold leaf, creating the elaborate floating effect.

He wondered if the bars were a prison cell, or maybe a place for the bank's guard. Then its purpose dawned on him. *It's a screen.* He paused at the gate, studying its artistry and function, similar to the medieval cathedrals' choir screens that segregated the clergy from the congregants. He pushed the unlocked gate, the metal squealing in loud protest. Eyrún turned toward the sound and strode over.

The hall extended three meters beyond the gate into a relatively austere section, compared to the elaborately carved portal outside and the precious metals in the main section. The area was devoid of furniture, and nothing hung on its walls. Darwin stepped on a platform jutting out from the rear wall and moved toward an arched alcove set into its center.

A statue of Mary holding a baby Jesus stood on a faded royal-purple cloth. Eyrún joined him on the platform as he examined the carving, wiping away a thin layer of dust with a finger. Its milk-white marble glistened in the bright LED light.

"This is exquisite," he said. "Medieval art lacked realism. But, this is modern, worked in a style befitting the renaissance—somewhere between Donatello and Michelangelo. Look at its flowing lines and the polish; how the sculptor captured the delicate features of a mother's expression gazing lovingly at her child. But where did this come from? The Templars sealed this vault before thirteen-oh-seven, but this artist? They must've found an early genius. I can already hear the art historians salivating."

He paused, as if tallying possible answers, before running his fingers over the fabric and folding it back to reveal a white marble slab. The delicate cloth ended in a gold border that partially concealed a wooden cabinet below the slab whose wood had hardened and darkened with age.

"Do you think that's where the Christ papyrus is?" asked Eyrún.

"It looks easy enough to open. How about you video this while I open it to look in?"

She began recording as Darwin carefully folded the purple cloth onto the shelf. The cabinet's two front doors had no knobs or obvious mechanism, and Darwin fumbled at opening it. Eyrún restarted the video once Darwin determined that the doors slid apart. He placed hands on each panel and leaned to the right so Eyrún's camera could see, then moved the panels until they hit built-in stops.

The shoulder-width opening revealed an unfaded deep purple velvet lining the cabinet's interior. A dark-gray cylinder about the size of a tall beverage can lay on its side in a carved wooden block. Darwin put on cotton gloves and reached in, gently picking it up. He brought it toward Eyrún's camera as he narrated, "This is heavy, about as much as a full soda can, and looks to be made of lead. Each end cap is soldered shut, so there is no way to tell what's inside. But if we believe the document written by de Molay, then it contains the papyrus written by Jesus of Nazareth."

He returned the cylinder to its place, where he knew it would be safest, and examined the cabinet's inside. Finding nothing else, he closed the doors and folded the purple cloth back in place.

N ext, Darwin began shooting photos and video from inside the Christ papyrus section and moved back through the gate. He closed it, snapped a few photos, and turned his attention to the left wall, where a weapons cache filled the device's screen. He froze. *Mon Dieu. They're Roman.*

He stopped the video, pocketed the device, and examined a pristine stack of Roman broadswords on the top shelf. He stooped to look at a row of helmets on a lower shelf, one with a centurion's plumes, which he lifted. "Eyrún, look at this."

He lowered the helmet onto his head as she came over. "Wait," she said. She snapped his photo, and he replaced the helmet on the rack. Meanwhile, Eyrún knelt to look at the lowest shelf. "What's this?" she asked, pointing at three forearm-length bronze tubes, deep green with age and exposure.

Darwin squatted, his heart beating as if it would punch out of his rib cage. "Oh, my God! I've been searching years to find this." He grasped one tube, its diameter fitting neatly in his hand, and ran his fingers across the letters SPQR stamped on its side.

"You know what they are?"

"Roman military scroll cases. SPQR is for Senatus Populusque Romanus, roughly meaning 'in service to the senate.'" He worked the end cap from the tube and looked inside. Wooden dowels held a papyrus scroll in place. He showed it to Eyrún.

"Can you take it out?"

"Hopefully. It's nearly two thousand years old. If I had to place a bet, I'd say these scrolls document precisely what the Romans did in these lava tubes. The Templars must have found this Roman military kit and stored it. Perhaps honoring another warrior tradition?" he speculated, replacing its end cap and examining the other two bronze cylinders.

After a minute, he stood. "Let's get this first inventory done. How about you count the gold bars, and I'll video that opposite wall." She agreed and walked to the vault's front as Darwin turned to the left wall to resume videoing.

Like the opposite side of the hall, the first three racks contained the gold ingots, while the fourth rack held ceramic pots with gold and silver coins. Each jar of coins had been sorted by size: the smallest about the size of a one-euro-cent piece compared to other coins that filled his palm. A codex lay next to each container labeled to match its adjacent pot. He flipped through one and roughly followed the Latin description of deposits and withdrawals.

Beside the fourth rack, a stout lectern held a thick volume. Its cover read "Clermont-Ferrand." He opened it to find a detailed transaction ledger complete with depositors' names. Closing its cover, he looked at other volumes on the lectern's lower shelves and read their spines: Acre, Antioch, Aragon, Genoa, Jerusalem, and Tripoli. He lifted the Jerusalem volume onto the lectern and carefully opened it.

"*Merde!*"

"What now?" asked Eyrún, walking over.

"These are the bank's ledgers. Look, this one's from Jerusalem. It shows withdrawals by pilgrims who had made deposits in another Templar location—say, Genoa—before sailing to Antioch. This historical value is beyond precious. Archaeologists will spend years studying these. What did you find?"

"I counted the gold."

"How much?"

"Well, each shelf is stacked five high, three rows deep, and twenty stacks across. That's three hundred bars and five shelves: fifteen hundred per rack, and there're six racks."

Darwin ran his hand in a circle as a hurry-up motion.

"Nine thousand bars. Remember last month when our banker gave us a prospectus on gold at sixty euros a gram?" He nodded. "If these bars weigh a kilo, then we're looking at half a billion euros. And, that's not including the coins."

Darwin whistled. "No wonder that Philip tortured de Molay to find to this place."

"What do we do now?" asked Eyrún.

86

Cathédrale Notre-Dame-de-l'Assomption

Jacques caught up with the beards in the cathedral ambulatory, and they moved casually to the crypt door. "It's locked," said Black Beard. Jacques and Copper scanned the few visitors as Black Beard picked the lock, and a minute and a half later, they were in.

Wall sconces lit the spiral staircase, but they had to use their mobile device lights in the corridor. Before entering the darkened chapel, Jacques turned and put a finger to his lips. The beards nodded. They entered the empty chapel, and Jacques checked the gate opposite the entrance. Locked.

Copper Beard waved his light to get their attention after pulling open the wooden door that Darwin had closed. Black Beard crossed from the other locked gate, and the three of them went in, traversing the crypt's ambulatory to the left. They reached the dead end, and Jacques examined a row of tombs. "Where did they go?" he asked.

"Look at this," said Copper, who was kneeling over the grate at the far end of the row. They gathered around, and he shined his light on the rungs. "Someone's been using these. The rusty iron is smoothed. See how it's different in the rung's centers?"

Jacques sat up. He wanted to pull up the grate and get after them but knew their lights would give out. *What was it the old lady had said, bags and a rope? That's why Darwin went to the caving shop.*

"We need better lights. Let's go up," he said. They closed the doors in the crypt chapel as they found them, including locking the upper cathedral door. While Jacques and Copper went to the sports shop, Black Beard stayed in case Darwin and Eyrún came out. "Get food and water bottles," he said as they left. "We might be down there a while."

87

Lava Tube

After registering Eyrún's question, Darwin's hand went reflexively to his mobile, but stopped, knowing there was no signal here, his hand dropped back to his side. We *need to tell people. But where to start?* His brain raced through possibilities, and all his training compelled him to create a systematic investigation. To accomplish that they needed to protect the site and bring in resources.

"We need to let the world know about this place, and get more archaeology resources engaged."

Eyrún concurred and added, "We'll need evidence to back up our call to action. Let's take some coins and a gold bar as proof."

Each of them selected coins from the various jars. By Darwin's eye, the coinage had been minted across Europe during the centuries before 1307 when Philip ended the Knights Templar order. As they gathered the coins, Darwin dawdled, paging through the ledger atop the lectern.

"Let's get going," Eyrún admonished. "We don't have years to secure this place.".

Darwin turned two more pages before closing the ledger and

moving toward the exit. They pushed the vault door closed, using the pry bar to leverage it into the jamb, and locked it. Darwin laid the bar on the platform, and they headed back to the cathedral.

88

Cathédrale Notre-Dame-de-l'Assomption

J acques and the beards returned to the crypt chapel after purchasing better lights and rope. They opened the grate, and Black Beard descended first, followed by Copper Beard, and then Jacques. "What is this place?" he asked, reaching the bottom.

"It's a tunnel," said Black Beard. "Not human-made, that's for sure. Volcanic, maybe."

"Where are they?" asked Jacques.

"Hell if I know," said Black.

"It splits up here," called Copper, who had gone in first and was exploring about ten meters distant. They reached the junction where Copper stood and agreed that Jacques would remain at this point as the beards investigated which direction Darwin and Eyrún had gone.

Jacques had been in a storm drain as a kid, which he thought was the closest experience to where he stood now. Except this tunnel undulated as if manufactured organically *like the bowels of some creature.* He shuddered and shoved the thought aside but ran a hand over the rock as if to be sure it wasn't alive.

"Nothing that way. It narrows down to this," said Black Beard, holding his hands in a head-sized circle.

They turned in the direction Copper had gone and met him a short way later, coming back toward them. Over the next half hour, they eliminated false junctions until they reached the round chamber where Darwin and Eyrún had rigged the ropes into the hole.

"I'd say Darwin knew exactly what he was doing," said Black Beard.

"Meaning what?" asked Jacques.

"He didn't randomly drop into that mountaineering shop and buy gear. I'd put money on him being in this lava tube before," Black Beard retorted.

The realization slapped Jacques like a wave. *Precisely! It's why Darwin put that string on my map, but he must have needed the scroll in South Africa to confirm something. What?* He looked around at the graffiti as the beards knelt and peered in the hole.

Jacques joined them and stuck his head in the hole. *Doesn't matter. He's down there. The treasure's down there.* He gasped at the size of the tunnel below and leaned farther in, hands slipping off the edge, pitching him into the void.

89

Lava Tube

Darwin laid a hand on Eyrún's arm, and they stopped. A light showed ahead in the tube where there should not be any. They switched off their headlamps. The edges of the opening they had made in the wall stood out against the blackness as a light source on its other side moved about. Something passed across the light source, temporarily blocking it.

"Shit," said Eyrún. "It's them."

"We can't be sure from this distance, but I think it's safe to assume it's Jacques and the beards."

"What do we do?" she asked.

"Dunno, but we can't fight them here. Let's get back to the vault. We can think about it on the way."

They moved away as fast as they could manage on the rough lava floor. Only a few places were safe enough to jog, and five minutes into their retreat, Darwin called a halt, where they switched off their lights to look back. "Nobody following," he said, turning on his light again.

"What if we hide in one of the other tubes off the chamber? They'll focus on the vault door," she said, walking beside him.

"I thought about it. But they'll explore the tubes, leaving no way out for us."

"What if we hide, and then run out as soon as Jacques gets to the vault."

"They might break it down in the time we're gone. We can't let that happen," he said.

No solution seemed optimal, and Darwin's biggest concern was protecting the treasure inside. He reasoned the best way to do that was from inside the vault. A few minutes later, they crossed the chamber, and Darwin keyed the lock open while Eyrún worked the pry bar under the door.

"What if we can't get out?" she asked when they had gone inside.

"Bring the pry bar. The door pushes outward. I'm sure we can work it open."

A handle on the door's inside allowed them to pull it shut, but the bottom edge caught on the jamb. As much as Eyrún worked the pry bar, and Darwin yanked on the handle, they could not get it fully closed. Darwin stood back, running a hand through his hair while studying the centimeter gap between the door and jamb.

Meanwhile, Eyrún followed the interior defensive walls inside, and a few moments later, Darwin jumped at the sound of metal scraping stone. He turned to see a sword's tip tracing up and down the arrowslit. "We have weapons," she said through the stone gap.

90

J acques's legs swung awkwardly during the descent. Black Beard took hold of them and guided his feet to the tube floor. Not ten minutes earlier, he had grasped Jacques's waistband, preventing him from going headlong down the hole. As his feet contacted the rocky ground, Jacques knew the fall would have been fatal. He unclipped from the rope, and his attention was drawn to Copper standing at the southeastern wall, face pressed against an arrowslit. "What's in there?" asked Jacques, walking close.

"Can't see anything," said Copper. "But they went through the other wall." He turned and walked toward the northwest wall. Jacques looked in the gap for a moment, saw nothing but blackness, and followed Copper.

"Through here," said Black Beard, standing next to the wall with the broken-out blocks. "You're the smallest. Think you can manage it without killing yourself?"

"Fuck off," said Jacques, and navigated the rough opening in the wall. One rear jeans pocket ripped as his butt caught a jagged edge.

Copper Beard pushed through next, his jacket scraping against the rock but managing it. He looked back through the opening. "Might be tougher on you," he said to Black Beard.

Black Beard passed their packs through and worked his way through the opening with less trouble than Jacques had. They shouldered their packs and followed the tube.

91

Vatican City

Franz sat in the back of a chapel in the library complex, watching dust dance in the noonday sunlight. A few minutes later, Richard Ndembele entered, knelt next to Franz, then crossed himself and turned toward Franz. He nodded, then walked to the confessional. Franz followed and sat in the confessional.

The wooden partition opened, leaving a thin purple drape between them. Franz began, "Forgive me father, for I have sinned. It's been a week since my last confession."

After the formalities, Franz launched into the situation. Richard listened and asked questions. After ten minutes, Franz stopped. All was quiet and he kept pushing down visions of arrest and humiliation, when Richard asked one more question.

"You're sure you don't know to whom the Camerlengo was speaking?"

"Yes. I mean no," said Franz, confused. "No, I don't know who it was."

After nearly a minute of silence, Franz asked, "Father?"

"I'm still here. I was thinking of an email I received this morning from another troubled soul."

"What about? No one can know I told you about this—I'll be ruined." Franz kneaded his palms.

"Nothing that should worry you. The sanctity of the confessional is absolute. I do not know who you are except a man confessing his troubles and that another man may be in peril. Think about your actions. Pray for forgiveness and the safety of those you have put in harm's way."

The partition closed. Franz's body shook and tears flowed onto his hands.

92

Lava Tube

"How far does this go?" asked Black Beard.

"That's what we're going to find out," said Jacques, walking on the uneven surface. One awkward step while he looked at the ceiling caused him to stumble into the wall, and he kept his attention on the floor from then on. The beards engaged in a conversation about caves where Black described a mission in Serbia routing insurgents out of an old railroad tunnel.

After a quarter-hour, Jacques called a halt to listen. "Turn off your lights." They did. Jacques's body immediately felt he was tumbling and put a hand on the sidewall. The darkness was total, and he lost all sense of direction. *Breathe.* The air rushing in his nostrils seemed to roar with the loss of any visual sensation. He steadied himself.

"Christ! It's pitch-black," whispered one of the beards.

"Shhh." Jacques admonished. He strained to hear and peered into the void. *Is it ahead? Where is ahead?* He shuddered. His heart thudded as cold sweat beaded on his face. He fumbled with the light switch, finally turning it on and the brightness blinding him. It took a minute for spots to dissipate.

"Looks like that didn't go well," said Black Beard, staring at him.

"Shut up. Let's go." Jacques began walking and wiped his forehead with the back of one hand. *What if I got stuck in here?* He repressed the thought and kept going.

The lava tube's curve almost closed off at the headlamp's infinity-point, making it seem like Jacques was walking in a giant circle. Then the tube straightened as a substantial dark chamber unveiled, and he stopped at the steps cut into the floor. His headlamp swam across the space, intersecting with the beards' lights.

"There!" said Copper Beard, whose light had settled first on the vault door. They turned to look and flowed down the steps as one.

"Wait," said Black Beard, withdrawing a pistol from a jacket pocket.

"Where did you get that?" asked Jacques recoiling as if it were a snake.

"Buddy who lives in Clermont-Ferrand. We were in Serbia together."

"Put it away," said Jacques.

Black Beard stepped over and looked down at Jacques. "I don't know if they're armed, and I'm not taking any chances. We get the gold and get out of here. Understand?"

Jacques nodded.

"Over here," said Copper, standing by the door. They joined him as Copper ran his fingers along the door's edge. He gently pulled it but met resistance.

"Are they in there?" Jacques whispered.

"Don't know, but they could also be in one of the other tunnels," said Black Beard, swirling his headlamp across the chamber. "You wait here. We'll check it out."

Jacques sat against the door and watched the two beards move across the bowled floor. Black Beard looked in the smaller and larger tubes across from the vault. Copper Beard checked out the tube on the left. A short time later, they both walked back.

"There's a wall in that one," said Copper.

"Same in the other two," said Black.

"Maybe they went out before we came in, and we missed them," said Copper.

Idiot. Jacques shook his head. "Not likely. They wouldn't have left the door open."

Black Beard waved a hand at them, and they stopped talking. He pointed to the door, then put a finger to his lips. Then he pointed between the door and one ear. It took Jacques a few moments to understand the pantomime: he guessed Black Beard was telling them Darwin and Eyrún were listening.

Copper grasped the door's edge with his fingers and pulled while Black lifted the door handle. Copper's fingers slipped off twice, but on the third try, the massive door opened.

What!? Jacques looked at another wall less than a meter inside the doorframe. An arrowslit faced them. On instinct, they all folded against the door's outer wall and turned off their lights. Black Beard peered around the darkened frame and turned back to them. Switching on his headlamp, he said. " I'm going in. Wait here."

93

Darwin and Eyrún had figured on a half hour to arrange their defenses before Jacques and the beards arrived. The walls inside the vault door would force the intruders into single file, which, along with the arrowslits, would give Darwin and Eyrún an advantage. They moved the swords and shields away from the corner of the second wall and discussed the differing possibilities—settling on decisively disabling the first person by hitting him with the pry bar.

"That leaves two of them and two of us," said Darwin.

"But, what if they have guns?"

"It's hard to get handguns here, and they didn't have any in Corsica."

With their defense set, Darwin paged through the accounts book. Not quite a half hour later, voices outside the door heralded Jacques's arrival. Darwin and Eyrún pressed against the second interior wall and turned off their lights. Shortly after, the vault door's hinges groaned, and its bottom edge scraped against the stone. Light spilled in through the arrowslit nearest them, and they heard whispered conversation before the outside lights went out.

"Get ready," Darwin whispered close to Eyrún. He held his breath and wiped his sweaty hands one at a time on his pants, keeping hold of the pry bar. *Merde! I can't see. How close are they?*

Grit crunched just in front of them. "Now!" Eyrún switched on her light, catching Black Beard full in the face. Swinging the pry bar, Darwin saw a glint of dark metal. "Gun!" he yelled, adjusting the bar in mid-swing and hitting Black Beard's forearm. The gun barrel exploded and flew out of Black Beard's hand, bouncing across the floor. Eyrún karate-kicked Black Beard's gut and tumbled away.

Darwin steadied himself, his ears numb from the gun blast, surveying the scene like a silent movie. His momentum had carried him deeper in the vault. Eyrún had swept up the gun as she rolled and now sat aiming it at their attacker. Black Beard stood, his palms outward in surrender, in a sea of gold coins that had spilled from a shattered pot.

The shouting slowly registered as the searing ring in Darwin's head faded. "Don't shoot! Don't shoot!" Black Beard was repeating.

"Stay against the wall." Eyrún stood and moved toward Darwin in mid-vault. "Jacques, get in here. Now," she yelled. A moment later, he and Copper Beard walked around the wall, lining up next to Black Beard.

———

D arwin picked up a Roman spear leaning against the back wall, since the pry bar had rolled under a rack and he did not want to risk looking for it. Eyrún, holding the gun with both hands, covered Jacques and the beards, while Darwin assessed their overall position. *We have the weapons advantage, but we're stuck with our backs to the wall unless they leave voluntarily.*

As if sensing Darwin's thought, Black Beard asked Eyrún, "Are you willing to shoot your way out? You don't look very confident with that thing."

"My uncle taught me to hunt. At this range, it's hard to miss," she said, dropping one hand from the gun and shaking it to relieve tension.

She doesn't have an uncle, thought Darwin, keeping his breathing steady. Copper lifted a gold bar. "Stay away from that," Darwin shouted.

Suddenly, Copper backhanded the bar at Eyrún. She twisted to block it with her gun hand. Darwin's eyes reflexively followed the flashing gold. Copper followed the toss, shoving Eyrún while grabbing the gun as Black Beard rushed Darwin, wrenching away the spear.

It was over in seconds. Eyrún and Darwin both looked up from the floor at the sharp ends of the spear and pistol.

94

Darwin and Eyrún sat against the rear wall by the statue while Jacques and the beards studied the gold and silver in the vault. Eyrún snatched her pack from Copper Beard after he had searched it for weapons. She checked that her belongings were intact, and in the process, rummaged out a *saucisson*. Ripping off its wrapper, she tore a piece between her teeth and chewed noisily. Through a mouthful, she said, "I hate these morons. How're we going to get out of here?"

"Dunno," said Darwin. "I don't think the beards want anything but the gold. Jacques is supposed to get the Christ papyrus. Maybe we work out a deal. They take the gold—"

A harsh metallic rasp sent shivers up her spine. Black Beard had hefted a Roman sword and scraped its edge across a Templar sword in his other hand. "Nice weight on this one," he said of the Roman blade, tracing a slow figure eight with it.

Copper picked up another Templar sword and touched blades with Black Beard. The clank of metal on metal rang in the chamber as they slowly sidestepped each other, then faster, tapping blades in mock combat.

"Cut it out," said Jacques.

Black Beard turned to Jacques, bringing the Roman short sword's tip under his chin. Jacques pressed against a shelf with jars, the rack creaking. His head stretched back to get away from the blade, and Black Beard followed his movement with its tip. "I've had enough of your arrogance, Professor Dickhead."

Jacques's eyes went wild with fear. His hands shook. "I…"

"You what? Here's what we're going to do. Gold was worth fifty thousand euros a kilo when I looked it up this morning. But we have to fence it. That will take time and might lower its price. But I figure about sixty kilos each should be enough," said Black Beard. He looked at Copper on his left.

"Three million sounds good to me," said Copper Beard. "I live frugally."

Black Beard stepped back and lowered the sword. Jacques's hands went to his neck.

"And, I'll take this too," said Black, waving the sword. "It'll look good over my mantel."

Eyrún glanced at Darwin, watching the swordplay. *He's about to say something.* She kicked his foot gently and wiggled her head, side to side, mouthing, "no." They had tormented these guys over the last few days, and Black Beard's threatening Jacques was a good example of their frayed nerves. *Best not to test them further. Let the tension pass.*

"It's a sherpa exercise," said Black Beard to Copper and Jacques. "We deposit this load by the hole near the crypt, come back for a second load, then move it all up through the cathedral."

"What about the Christ papyrus?" asked Jacques.

"Get it on the next trip. I don't care what you do with it after that," said Black Beard.

Jacques moved to the cabinet, and Darwin and Eyrún moved aside to watch him. He slid open the doors and reached for the lead tube.

"Be careful with it," said Darwin.

Jacques glared at him but used both hands to pick up the cylinder. He stood up and slowly tipped it from side to side, listening for anything inside.

"How much are they paying you to get that?" asked Eyrún.

He laughed. "My Vatican contact is a moron. He paid me up front and said I could keep whatever treasure I found. Maybe I'll just leave the papyrus here? People sidelined the gnostic gospels and the Dead Sea Scrolls. I'm sure this one will cause nothing but more arguments."

"Jacques!" Black Beard called him after loading the packs. "Put this on." Jacques skulked away from Darwin and slipped his arms into the pack's straps. Black Beard added five more ingots, stopping when Jacques complained. The beards had each taken thirty.

"What about them?" asked Copper, pointing to Eyrún and Darwin.

"We lock them in until we return," said Black Beard.

Eyrún and Darwin looked at each. "Then what?" she asked.

Black Beard turned in their direction. "Then we get the next load, and Jacques can get his papyrus."

Eyrún watched the vault darken and, moments later, heard the clunk of the lock. Part of her wanted to scream, but the engineer side knew they would be back. *They're too greedy.*

95

Eyrún was up the moment they heard the door lock mechanism fall into place. She went to it but returned, finding the beards had also relocated the swords and spears outside. But they had ignored the pry bar, and she crawled under a rack and removed it.

"We can break through the door," she said Seeing that Darwin had opened a Roman scroll, she asked, "What are you looking for?"

"Evidence to back up a thought..." he trailed off. He sat propped against the back wall and looked up at her. "I was puzzling over what Agrippa wrote. Including the tube we walked through from the cathedral, the chamber has five tubes, not four. He only wrote that the tubes go toward Lutetia, one to Germania, and the other to Hispania."

"So..."

"Either the Templars cut this vault into solid rock, or it's the fifth tube and goes somewhere beyond this wall—maybe to a local outlet? I had this thought—what if the Templars created a back door to this vault? A way out or for defense."

She laughed. "What, like a secret latch and the wall opens? That wall looks damn solid to me."

"It's plausible."

"You're a dreamer, Love. But have at it. There's nowhere else we can go until they get back."

Darwin returned to reading the scrolls, finishing one and opening another while Eyrún explored the shrine above the cabinet. She carefully folded the purple cloth's edges under the statue of Mary, and the polished white marble slab shined in her headlamp. She displaced the statue and, on impulse, looked under the fabric.

"Oh, my God. Darwin, look at this!"

He jumped up to see an Aquila symbol carved into the marble.

96

Jacques's hips and knees ached as they neared the broken wall. The uneven floor, along with the heavy gold, caused his body to compensate in ways his joints hated. Besides, the pain between his shoulder blades felt like someone had whacked him with each step.

They had stopped seven times so far to rest, but no more than a minute each time. The beards had joked about a workout they called a farmer's carry where a heavy weight was moved from one place to another, simulating work a farmer would perform. Black Beard also talked about carrying twenty-liter petrol containers in the army.

It's like a competition with these idiots. What's the point? thought Jacques as they started up again. He repeated the mantra that had kept him going: *The gold. The gold. There're a million euros in gold causing my pain.*

Finally, the wall reflected in their lights, and his thoughts shifted to visions of moving back into his big house. They had moved a fraction of the gold bars in the vault, not even clearing one shelf. *Moving it all's going to be a bitch.*

97

"What does it mean?" Eyrún asked about the Aquila.

"I'll bet money that it means the Templars read these scrolls and used Aquilas to mark the ways in, just like the Romans," he said, rolling the fabric back and replacing the statue. He knelt, slid open the wood doors, and removed the lead container, placing it carefully away from them on the platform. He then leaned in the recessed cabinet and felt around. All the sides, the back wall, and bottom were covered with velvet. Only the marble slab's underside was left rough.

He felt around. *Cut marks.* "Something's here." He twisted to look at it. "It's another Aquila," he said, sliding out and stretching his back. "I'm going to see if the back comes off. Hand me the small pry bar."

She did, and he stretched back inside, working the bar around the fabric in the back corners. Slowly, a false wall peeled away, the ancient purple material tore in places. He winced at its destruction but kept moving until his neck cramped, and he backed out.

"I'm smaller. Let me try." Eyrún leaned in and worked her fingers around the top section. Darwin held his light on it from the side. She strained, grabbing the panel with both hands while using her chest to brace against the cabinet's bottom. The board pulled down a little, and she withdrew, massaging her neck.

"Ow." She kneaded her cramping muscles.

Darwin grasped the panel's top edges, pulling it free and exposing a bare wall cut from a single piece of rock. Another Aquila was carved in its center.

98

Jacques and the beards reached the wall and passed the bags and packs through. When they came to the hole in the ceiling, they sat against the tube's side and rested.

"What do we do with the man and the woman?" asked Copper Beard.

"They don't know our names. We get five more loads like this, leave them locked in, and leave an anonymous tip for someone to get them out," said Black Beard.

"But they know me, and so do the police. I say we lock the door and walk away," said Jacques.

Black Beard laughed. "Look at you. I thought it was just the wine talking in Corsica when you got tough about a treasure that's *rightfully yours*. Maybe we should leave you with them on our next trip."

Jacques went rigid against the wall. Black Beard leaned in almost touching noses and continued, "People kill for this much gold, Jacques. How do you think the Templars got it? They weren't shaved-head monks wearing sacks. They were men-at-arms who built a wealthy franchise. Then their bankers took over, extracting money by more legal means, just like today. You disgust me." He suddenly swatted Jacques's temple, knocking him out.

99

Darwin pushed the cabinet's back, and its upper left corner moved slightly. "Is there a piece of wood handy?" he asked, looking backward.

Eyrún grabbed the end of a wooden object protruding from the closest rack and handed it to him.

"Where did you get this?" he asked.

"With the Roman stuff, behind the pots. Why?"

"It's a crossbow shaft," he said, moving to the rack, and reaching behind the pots, where he pulled out another wooden shaft and two metal bows. He looked around the space, lifted the lid on a tall pot, and pulled out a quiver of short arrows that still appeared dangerous.

The crossbow shaft was arm's length, square in cross section, with a groove scored on its topside. A notch on one end fitted the metal bow, and the shaft's other end was cut into a hand-sized handle. A metal mechanism near the handle end would hold the taut bowstring until released by a trigger on the shaft's underside. Eyrún laid an arrow in the groove. "All we need is a string," she said.

"Not these." Darwin held pieces of cord that had fallen apart as he lifted them.

She took them and studied the knots, then went to her pack and removed a coil of three-millimeter nylon twine. "I'll bet this would work."

"We don't have time to test it. They'll be back in—" he looked at his watch "—thirty or forty minutes. We need to get through this."

"Use the pry bar," she said.

He took up the bar, then began tapping the rock along its top edge.

"It's moving," she said, kneeling and peering in the cabinet. "Keep working it back and forth." After a minute of steady tapping, the rock fell away, crunching as it hit bottom on the other side.

"That didn't sound good," said Darwin. They both looked in the opening, their headlamp beams disappearing down the lava tube on the cabinet's opposite side. Eyrún moved, and Darwin wriggled in, poking his head out the other side, then came back. "The cabinet back's shattered, and ten or so basalt blocks stacked to one side, but nothing else."

"You're sure this intersects with the next tube over, the one with the collapsed ceiling?" she asked, referring to the tube that entered the chamber to the right of the vault. "And it has a wall. How do we get out?"

"I might not bet my life on it, but what else are we going to do here? I didn't like the sound of being locked in."

They surveyed the chamber, Eyrún suggesting they take all their gear to throw Jacques off track. Darwin went through first, and she passed through their packs, followed by the wooden stand for the Christ papyrus, then, finally, the lead tube. Darwin had moved the basalt blocks and restacked them to hide and protect the priceless relic.

Eyrún next passed through the cabinet, then reached back and slid the cabinet doors closed. Darwin held the cabinet back in place, and Eyrún used the big pry bar's blunt end to tap it home. They kept the backing in place by stacking two basalt blocks and replacing the broken stone.

"It won't keep anyone inside from pushing through, but they'd have to know to do it," said Darwin. "Ready?" he asked when they had gathered everything. Eyrún nodded, and they began walking.

100

Jacques came to and looked at his mobile: 17:33. *How long was I out? Christ, they left me.* He looked around. His pack was gone. A chill wave of dread coursed through his limbs. He looked around the tube, stopping on the swinging rope and lights shining through the hole above.

"Hey," he yelled, wincing at the sharp stab in his temple and putting a hand to the spot. *No blood.* But he pushed his hand back to feel good-sized welt. "Hey!"

Copper Beard leaned into the hole. "You're awake. Good. We're moving this lot of gold out. Then going back for more."

"Where's—" the pain cut short his question.

"He's fetching the car," answered Copper.

Jacques went to the rope. "Pull me up," he said, knowing Copper Beard was the more pliable of the two. "I'll help move the gold, and then we can come back for the rest."

The light from above shined down on Jacques's face, and he grasped the climbing rope. As the line moved upward, Jacques's hands slipped. Copper let the rope go slack, and Jacques tied a loop and put one foot in it. Copper then pulled Jacques through the hole.

They moved the packs and duffels to the shaft, and Copper

ascended to the crypt level to pull up the bags. Jacques's head throbbed each time he bent to tie the rope around another bag's handles and, finally, he climbed the rungs himself. Black Beard had returned as they ferried the last of the bags from the tombs into the chapel. He frowned at Copper, who shrugged.

A few minutes later, Jacques carried a pack outside the cathedral's side door, where he found the cool damp soothing. Black loaded Jacques's pack in the rented car as Copper brought the last bag and dropped it in the hatchback.

"What about bags to get the rest of the gold?" asked Jacques.

"We empty these at the hotel, then come back," said Black.

101

As they walked to the hoped-for junction, Eyrún asked, "Where in Spain do you think this goes?"

"Agrippa's scrolls didn't say, but imagine exploring all the tubes coming out of the chamber. Where do we go first? Spain, Germany, or Paris?"

"I'll settle for getting out. Let someone else do the long turn underground." To pass the time, Eyrún talked about the large chamber as once being the top of a caldera and the lava flowing outward, forming the five tubes.

About seven minutes into the downslope walk, the tube converged with another tube that came in at a thirty-degree angle from their right. Eyrún stood in the junction. "The angle's right for it to go back to the chamber," she said and began the upslope trek. They reached a basalt block wall—identical to the others, down to the arrowslits, in just under ten minutes.

"Give me a few minutes." Darwin set down the heavy pry bar and drank some water.

Eyrún joined him and continued working with the crossbow, studying the loops on the old bowstring. Then she fashioned a simple loop on one end of the nylon twine, measured the distance across the metal bow, and tied another loop. After testing the release mechanism, she tried to arm the bow. But it was far too tight, and she set it aside.

They went to work on the wall. The first block at the arrowslit bottom was full-sized and refused to move. The second block , half-sized, turned with relative ease. Darwin worked it back and forth with the pry bar, and it tumbled free of the wall in a couple of minutes.

"One more should do it," said Eyrún, sizing up the hole. "We're only going through once, so we can manage a tight squeeze." She left Darwin to work on the wall and refocused on the crossbow.

He grunted while working the stones, but when all was quiet a moment, she looked up. Her brain suddenly registered a problem—the blocks were stacked differently in this wall. The half-block lay under a full-sized block that leaned dangerously out of the wall as Darwin pushed the bar. She realized that when he turned the half-block, the wall would come down.

"No!" she screamed, diving at him. The wall's left side tipped as she hit Darwin broadside, spinning him as her momentum carried them both to the right. The wall tumbled into the chamber with a deafening roar, bringing a weaker part of the ceiling with it.

Seconds later, they lay in a heap, Darwin pressing Eyrún into the floor. She grimaced from something sharp under her hip. Darwin's face contorted in a mass of pain, and he breathed heavily as if holding back nausea. "My leg!" he groaned.

102

Eyrún cut off the bottom of Darwin's pants leg to clean a gash in his calf. Fortunately, he was only hit by a sharp-edged block, not crushed by the wall. She helped him limp to the side of the lava tube, where he leaned and sucked air between his teeth as she poured water to clean the wound.

"You'll likely need stitches in this," she said, tearing the pants fabric into strips. She unbuttoned her top and pulled a cotton camisole over her head, and folded it into a pad. "It's not sterile, but it'll have to do for now. Hold it here." She moved his hand to the makeshift bandage while she tied the strips around it.

"Not so tight," he said, grimacing. She loosened the knot.

"Let me know if your foot feels numb; I'll loosen it more. How does my shoulder look?" she said, turning toward him.

"There's an angry abrasion on your shoulder blade," he said. "Thanks, doctor Stephansdottir."

"That would be my sister," she said, putting her top back on and buttoning it. When done, she told him to stay sitting while she determined the damage. The rubble had buried the pry bar and most of Darwin's pack—water pooling on the lava from the crushed water bottles.

The crossbow and her pack lay a meter free of the rock pile, though she had no memory of tossing them. The entire wall left of the arrowslit had come down, as had part of the ceiling, but the tube was open, or at least looked open. She would have to climb the two-meter pile to size up its stability.

"Didn't anyone ever tell you not to pull the bottom block from the Jenga tower?" While she meant it as a joke, she realized it was exactly how Darwin lived his life.

"We can go back around to the chamber," he said.

"I doubt you can walk that far, and then we're locked inside the vault. No, let me try this first. I've seen worse." It took three minutes to pick her way up the loosely packed sharp-edged basalt pile. "From the top, it goes through. The ceiling looks okay."

103

Cathédrale Notre-Dame-de-l'Assomption

An hour after stashing the gold bars in one of the hotel rooms, Copper Beard dropped Jacques and Black Beard back at the cathedral's side door. They went inside to avoid a light rain while Copper Beard parked the car.

Black Beard picked the lock to the crypt stairwell but left the door closed, and sat in the side aisle waiting for Copper's return. Still angry from being whacked in the head, Jacques studied a painting in an alcove by the crypt. He placated himself with thoughts of the gold. They had decided that moving all of the gold would take days, and each trip increased the possibility of being caught. *One more trip and we're made. I'll walk away with five million. Good enough. Besides, I can always come back.*

The side door opened, and he glanced back, expecting to see Copper Beard. Three men, dressed in black with heads bowed like priests, walked into the cathedral. He turned around to the painting, but, a few moments later, he felt a presence. Two of the men in black now stepped into his periphery, about an arm's length away.

"*Bonjour*, Jacques," came a voice directly behind him.

Jacques turned to see a dark-haired man, face in shadow because of the spotlight behind his head, pointing a compact pistol at his chest. The man brought a finger to his lips, signaling quiet. The gun barrel looked oddly fat. *Shit, a silencer.* His mouth went dry. He looked toward Black Beard and opened his mouth to speak but snapped it shut when he heard the gun's hammer cock. He looked frantically around the cathedral—empty except for them.

"Take us to the papyrus, Jacques."

"What papyrus?" Jacques's face broke out in a cold sweat as he caught sight of Black Beard standing and disappearing into the shadows.

"Where's Darwin?" asked the man.

"Help!" Jacques yelled, then gasped at a sharp punch to his ribs. The men yanked him toward the crypt. He resisted, but while they were about his height, they had considerably more strength. Mashing him between them, the first man opened the crypt door. Jacques rapidly moved his feet over the steps, almost being carried into the chapel below. Once out of the short hallway, the men released his arms, and he had to run three steps to catch his balance.

"Who are you?" said Jacques, turning as the man with the gun entered the room.

"Miguel Suarez, head of Vatican security."

104

Lava Tube

Eyrún sat on the downslope of the rock pile as Darwin worked his way up the other side. She adjusted the cord's length and restrung the crossbow. She rolled the catch into position, cocked the string, and pulled the trigger. It thrummed like a double-bass, but the metal bow popped out of its slot in the shaft.

"How're you doing?" she called over the pile to Darwin.

"Just—" He yelped as his cut leg slipped.

"Can I help?"

"Not really. I'm going to ease my way down this side. I can hold my leg up." Darwin reached the top and blew out between his cheeks as he worked through the opening, sweat running down his temples.

She moved off the pile and watched him lift his butt up, move down a little, adjust his good leg and arms, and repeat the process. Then she focused on the crossbow and a hole cut horizontally through its shaft. She wiggled the bow back in its slot. *I get it. The extra cord we found lashes it together.* The decayed bowstring had been coiled with another, thicker line. She cut a length of climbing cord and passed it through the shaft and around the bow, fastening them together.

"Will it work?" asked Darwin, now next to her at the bottom of the pile.

"Only one way to find out." She cocked the bow again, laid the arrow in the groove, and notched it. The new string was thicker but workable. She aimed at the opposite tube wall three meters distant.

"Maybe we should look away," said Darwin.

They both turned, and she squeezed her eyes shut—the trigger released. A loud crack, followed by the sound of tiny pieces landing around them. She flinched as something hit her face.

"Holy shit!" she said, looking at the wall. The arrow had disintegrated, and she held a tiny piece of wood that landed in her hair. She went to the wall and found the arrow's point bent beyond reuse and handed it to Darwin.

After he examined it a minute, she suggested they test his leg. He stood with most weight on his right leg. "It's not as bad as I expected," he said, walking with Eyrún as a crutch. "I'm not running a marathon this week, but I think I can walk out of here."

"How long has it—wait." She switched off her light and waved her hand to quiet him. When his light was off, she moved to the tube's opening. "Darwin, stop," she whispered as he hobbled after her. Four distinct lights emerged from the cathedral tube.

"There're four now? Who—" Darwin whispered.

"Shhh."

The group passed across the floor and platform to the vault door. One person bent to open the lock while another trained a light on the figure. *Blond hair.* "It's Jacques," she said. Two others stepped to lift the door's handle. "But those two are smaller than the beards."

Jacques turned to face the man who had stood back while the others opened the door. "You got what you wanted, now let me go," they heard him say, his light fully on the other man's face.

"What! It can't be," said Eyrún. "Why would Miguel be here?"

105

J acques unlocked the vault and stepped back, handing the key to one of the men. Miguel stood to the side while his men grunted, working the door open. He had holstered the gun earlier, but Jacques figured it would take but a second to pull it out. He kept picturing Black Beard walking into the shadows, and his chin dropped. *The bastards abandoned me.*

For the entire journey through the lower crypt and into the lava tube, Jacques had expected the beards to follow them. *Maybe they are.* But, he knew that fell on the wrong side of reason. *One gun against three, and they got out with nearly three million each. Putain!*

He thought back to Miguel's interrogation as they walked through the lava tube on the way to the vault. If there was a glimmer of hope that the beards would come back, he needed to keep Miguel from thinking there were others.

"How did you, one guy with no weapons, overpower two people?" asked Miguel.

Jacques told him Darwin and Eyrún had agreed to work together with him once they found the vault. "We want different things. Darwin and Eyrún want the scroll for you people. I want the gold."

"And they just let you lock them inside."

"No. I panicked. I didn't trust them. When Darwin put the key down on a rack, I grabbed it, slammed the vault door, and locked them in. I had the gold in my backpack and moved it to my hotel room."

"How many bars?"

"Twenty."

"Then why were you in the cathedral when we arrived?"

"I was exhausted after moving the gold and went to eat something. It bothered me thinking of them in the vault. I decided I couldn't leave them to die and came back to let them out."

Miguel grumbled something incomprehensible and asked no more questions for the rest of the journey.

While he waited for Miguel's men to open the heavy wood door, Jacques ran through scenarios in which he could get away. *Make some kind of deal. Darwin knows where the Christ papyrus is. That makes him their enemy.*

Miguel's voice jerked him back to reality. "Jacques. What's it like in there?"

He described the two defensive walls, but said that Darwin and Eyrún had no weapons unless you counted throwing the gold bars.

"You didn't tie them up?"

"No. I had no rope. Besides, where were they going to go?"

"Darwin! Eyrún! It's Miguel Suarez," said Miguel. "We have Jacques in custody. It's safe to come out." There was no response, and Miguel waved his guys in. "Two of us are coming in. We mean you no harm, but we are armed,"

Jacques had a sudden horrific vision. *Shit. What's to stop them from taking the scroll and locking us all in the vault. Whoever sent these men won't want anyone to know about this place.*

"It's empty," yelled one of the men from inside the vault.

"What!" Miguel grabbed Jacques and pushed him into the vault ahead of himself.

Jacques rounded the second wall, seeing one guard standing near the back wall and the other on his hands and knees shining a light under the racks. "No one's here," said the guy in the back.

"Where are they?" Miguel spun Jacques, pressing him against the front wall.

"I have no idea. Where could they go?" Miguel's forearm pushed into Jacques's neck. Hard pain in his throat brought tears. "I—" he gagged. Miguel let up slightly. "I… They were here, I swear." Jacques's eyes searched wildly, as if Darwin and Eyrún were hiding.

"There's a keyhole on the door's inside," said the guard who had knelt on the floor.

"Did they have another key?"

"I don't know. I didn't search them," said Jacques. His eyes darted around the chamber. *What the hell? Did one of the beards come back while I was knocked out?* "They were here. I left them right there. He was reading one of the Roman scrolls he found on that rack." Miguel having released him, Jacques pointed.

"Open it, Gino," said Miguel to the Vatican guard nearest the cabinet. Gino fumbled for half a minute before sliding the empty cabinet open.

"Dammit," said Miguel and turned to the other guard. "Marcus, go out there and look around. Be careful. Those weapons on the platform are old but still dangerous."

"Wait," yelled Gino, his body a third inside the cabinet. "This has been opened."

"What! Marcus, stop. Watch him." Miguel nodded toward Jacques and squeezed in beside Gino, who pulled at displaced purple fabric, revealing wood and broken stone. He pushed on the backing, and it fell away into the wide lava tube behind the vault.

"Holy Mother Mary," said Miguel.

106

E yrún and Darwin had crossed to the vault after the four men entered. When they heard Miguel tell Marcus to go out and look around, they rushed behind the open vault door. Eyrún waved Darwin in behind her. His face was screwed up from the pain, but he stayed silent. Eyrún loaded an arrow in the crossbow's groove and held it ready to fire.

A moment later, Miguel yelled again for Marcus to come back. Eyrún moved around the door, Darwin shadowing her. They could hear Miguel and his men talking about the cabinet back. Eyrún moved to the arrowslit in the first defensive wall but could only see the second wall. She led with the crossbow to the wall's turn, her heart running like a cheetah. Nothing.

She looked through the arrowslit in the second wall to see Jacques, to her right, standing halfway through the vault. One man stood across from Jacques, gun pointed. Miguel backed out of the cabinet as the man next to him, crawled through the hole.

"What did the Christ papyrus look like?" Miguel asked Jacques.

"A gray metal cylinder about this size," said Jacques, holding two fists, thumbs together.

"Anything like that over there?" asked Miguel.

Eyrún heard a muffled "no." Then Miguel asked Gino to find out where the tube goes. "No more than five minutes, then come back."

She motioned to Darwin to go back outside. Once away from the door, she whispered, "I need you to stay out here. Get one of the spears or swords. If I have to run out fast, hit whoever's behind me."

"What are you going to do?"

"I don't know yet, but if I can disable one of them and you get another when they run out, that will give us a chance."

"Is that thing accurate enough?"

"Yes, pretty sure it went straight when I fired it," she said, taking a deep breath and closing her eyes as she exhaled. Darwin kissed her and went to the weapons pile to get a spear as she went back inside. Once in place, she checked the crossbow, careful to stay out of the light pouring through the slit. Her hands started to shake, and a feeling of dread made the crossbow seem suddenly heavier. *I don't want to do this.*

She remembered a conversation with Zac from the previous year when he described going into life-threatening situations as a US Army Ranger. "Sometimes, attacking is your best survival option," he had said. "You hate doing it, but you have to survive." She thought of Darwin outside the vault and of wanting to see her family again. Her breathing steadied, as did her arms. *We're getting out of here alive.* She lifted the crossbow as Miguel yelled from inside the vault.

"What?" Miguel backed up from the open cabinet as Gino's face came into view.

"It goes a couple hundred meters and joins another tube. I think it connects with one of the other tubes that dumps into the big chamber," said Gino.

"Okay, we know they're in there," said Miguel. "Time to flush them out. Marcus, get in there with Gino. I'll go around to that other tube in case they've figured a way out. I don't care what happens to them. We get the Christ papyrus and lock the vault. Then seal up the crypt under the cathedral."

"What about—" Jacques crumpled to the floor as Miguel hit him with a taser.

Shit! Eyrún jumped back but settled again. She decided to shoot Miguel after the two guards disappeared into the tube. They could then lock the vault and get help. But Miguel moved behind the racks after taking down Jacques, so she had no clear shot. *C'mon, move.* Eyrún willed him back to the room's center. The second guy, Marcus, was halfway through. *Oh, fuck!* She shifted aim to his thick legs. She pushed down the urge to be sick and pulled the trigger. The arrow fizzed across the vault, burying itself in the man's butt. He screamed—body shooting upward in the cabinet.

Eyrún ran outside the vault, screaming, "Darwin, it's me." She ran around behind him. A moment later, Miguel came through the door. Darwin swung a spear like a bat, catching him in the chest—air burst from Miguel's lungs, and he slumped.

"Run," Eyrún yelled. "Back to the tube." Twenty seconds later, she stopped at the tube's edge. Darwin hobbled along, wincing with each step. Miguel was getting to his feet. Darwin would make it before Miguel, but she needed to be ready to shoot. She jumped into the tube and ran around behind the first rock pile. She pressed against the lava tube wall and cocked the bow as Darwin ran past—climbing the rock pile against the collapsed wall. A gun fired outside the tube. He went down.

Darwin!

107

The shot missed, and Darwin rolled into a sitting position, one palm torn from his stumble into the rocks. He pulled at his left knee—calf burning like someone stuck him with a branding iron. Out of the corner of a watery eye, he could just see Eyrún squished in behind the other rock pile nearest the tube entrance. Miguel moved inside the tube—gun barrel smoking from the shot. He stopped facing Darwin, but not far enough in to see Eyrún behind his shoulder.

Darwin turned toward the opening behind him and shouted, "Stay in there, Eyrún." Then he turned back to Miguel. "You asshole." He tried to stand but fell back.

"This isn't personal, Darwin. The church wants the Christ papyrus."

"THE church. What makes you think your twisted dogma speaks for all Christians?"

"Save your humanist bullshit, Darwin. Where's the cylinder? Jacques said it was there earlier."

"It was. He took it with the other gold."

"He said you took it," said Miguel.

"Of course he would, the lying fuck. He left us here to die. Ahh." He winced at a wave of pain coursed up his leg.

"You're lying, Darwin. That greedy asshole doesn't care about anything but the gold. Where is it?" Miguel took the sound suppressor from his pocket and began screwing it on the barrel. "No one will come running at a gunshot down here, but it's too damn loud, and I value my hearing."

He leveled the pistol at Darwin. "Eyrún. I know you can hear me. Maybe you're even watching me." He glanced at the intact arrowslit. "Darwin says he won't tell me, but I'm hoping you will. How much do you want him to live?"

"Jesus, Miguel. It's a piece of papyrus. A long-forgotten gospel. We probably can't prove beyond doubt that Christ wrote it anyway," said Darwin.

"You'd be surprised how the right relic motivates people. What's it going to be, Eyrún? I'll count down from three... two..."

Eyrún kicked a rock. Miguel stepped toward the sound—too late to see the arrow that ripped through his right arm, below the shoulder. He dropped to his knees, gun clattering on the rock floor. His other hand squeezed the damaged arm—blood pumping through fingers, looked blankly at Darwin, and tipped sideways.

They were on him in a flash. Eyrún flung the crossbow, and they rolled Miguel on his back. "It hit the brachial artery," yelled Eyrún. "Get your fingers under here." She pushed Darwin's hand into Miguel's armpit. Blood pumped freely from the wound.

Miguel twisted in agony, his face white as a ghost, but he still kept trying to get up. Darwin held him down. "Miguel, stop fighting. We're trying to save you." He turned to Eyrún. 'How bad is it?"

"Bad." She retrieved the crossbow and undid its bowstring. "This'll work as a tourniquet. We can get the bleeding stopped, but considering where we are, he could die."

Miguel's eyes rolled up in their sockets. Darwin slapped his cheeks. "Miguel, Miguel. Stay with us."

Suddenly, the lava tube flooded with light—its opening blazed like the sun. Voices shouted, *"Arrêtez. Mains en l'air!* Hands up!" Darwin saw red crimson dots appear on Eyrún's chest and looked down at two more on his.

108

Darwin stared in stupefaction as four heavily armed figures fanned around them. "Who are they?" yelled Eyrún, fashioning a tourniquet around Miguel's arm.

One figure stepped closer, weapon lowered. "*Quel est votre nom? What's your name?*"

"Darwin Lacroix. She is Eyrún Stephansdottir, my wife," said Darwin. "This man needs help. Who are you?"

"*Baissez vos armes.*" The lead soldier ordered the three others to lower their weapons, then he turned back to Darwin. "I'm Lieutenant Corbet, Commandos Marine. Is there any other danger here?"

Darwin told him about the man who went in the lava tube and might come out the opening behind them. He also told them about the other injured man and Jacques in the vault.

"We secured the vault," said Corbet. He gave orders, and two of the soldiers worked their way up and over the rock pile. Then Darwin heard him bark orders for a medic.

Eyrún spoke soothingly to Miguel. The bleeding had slowed, but his pallor looked grim. A minute later, another soldier knelt next to them, pulling a first aid kit from her pack. She packed gauze into the wound, stopping the bleeding. Eyrún let the medic take over.

"What happened here?" asked Lieutenant Corbet.

An hour later, Darwin sat on the platform steps. The medic had bound his leg after Miguel had been stabilized and confirmed Eyrún's guess that he would need stitches. But Darwin was in no danger. The medic had said a former team member of hers had walked three days with a similar injury. He had smiled at the reduced seriousness but had no intention of channeling his inner commando.

Other military arrived to set up a recovery operation, and Miguel and Marcus were being stretchered out. Eyrún was relieved to learn that an arrow in the man's gluteal muscles did not threaten his life, but he would not enjoy sitting for quite a while. Gino surrendered himself in the lava tube in the face of overwhelming force and was conscripted to carry Miguel's stretcher. Jacques had recovered from the taser bolt but required assistance from two commandos during the hike out.

When Jacques and Miguel's men were gone, Eyrún crawled through the hole with Corbet and another soldier to supervise moving the blocks. She lifted the Christ papyrus cylinder with great care, passing it through the hole to one of the other commandos who placed it on its stand in the front corner. She then crawled back herself.

The chamber had quieted following the departure of the injured. The initial four members of the special forces unit, including Lieutenant Corbet, asked Eyrún to explain the lava chamber and then for Darwin to explain what the Romans and Knights Templar built. The modern warriors were especially intrigued by the actual combat weaponry of their ancient brethren.

"C'est fantastique," one of them said when Eyrún demonstrated the crossbow. She left them to explore and joined Darwin on the steps, where he was leaning back on his hands. She drank from a water bottle and patted his closest hand.

He turned and smiled. "How are you, Love?"

"Better, knowing I didn't kill them," she said.

"Can you believe it was Miguel?"

"No. It makes no sense."

A light emerged from the cathedral tube as a deep voice boomed. "Darwin!"

109

"What are you doing here?" asked Darwin at seeing his friend Richard Ndembele.

"It's nice to see you too." Richard laughed, hugging them both before sitting on the platform steps, where he continued, "It seems I've again caught you breaking into my cathedral. And I see you chose expediency over methodology. When will you learn to be a proper archaeologist?"

Darwin's mouth fell open, and his cheeks flushed. He looked at Eyrún, then at Richard, who began laughing again. Darwin smirked but could not hold it and joined the laughter. Eyrún followed.

"God, that felt good," said Darwin a minute later after the infectious outburst settled.

Eyrún wiped her eyes with a clean part of her sleeve. "Thanks, Richard."

The big man put an arm around her. "Everyone is okay, Eyrún. I talked with the medics on my way in here. You did what you had to do to defend yourselves and save this magnificent place. Now, tell me what you found."

Darwin ran through the discovery, from breaking down the walls to opening the vault and finding the secret escape route in its back wall.

Then he finally asked the question that had been burning since Lieutenant Corbet burst on the scene. "How did you find us?"

"Let me answer by backing up to the beginning. It will make more sense. And, there are some things I can say and some things I cannot." They nodded, and Richard continued. "His Holiness suspected several people were threatening his Papacy, which was why he asked you to help. By the way, Darwin, you have made a powerful friend. You too, Eyrún," he said, looking at each in turn. They smiled.

"Anyway, we followed Franz closely. He is a competent librarian, but not so much a criminal mastermind. Working with you allowed us to follow the snake's tail to its head, but it turns out it's more a hydra. His Holiness suspected corruption in the Vatican bank and created a special investigation team of internal and external resources. He asked me to liaise with the outside financial auditors to keep their scrutiny hidden from Keenan.

"As Camerlengo, he had oversight of the Vatican bank, and his ultraconservative views had him in contact with wealthy Catholics. Keenan directed that flow of donations toward vigorous Papal opposition but we couldn't connect it to any wrongdoing. As a follower of one such conservative group, Miguel ended up doing much of Keenan's dirty work. Unfortunately for you, he played Jacques against you to find the treasure."

"Bastard! I should have shot him somewhere more vital," said Eyrún.

"I doubt you would want that on your conscience, Eyrún, but I can understand the sentiment. Anyway, Darwin, your messages allowed me to monitor Franz and Miguel, which led to a lucky break. This is the part I cannot share, but suffice it to say, we got access to hard data that exposed Keenan's misappropriations." Richard wrapped up with, "John Keenan has decided to retire back to his farm in Alabama for health reasons."

Darwin whistled, then asked, "What about Franz?"

"He's also taking early retirement from the Vatican. I hear he's been offered a consulting job with the new Library of Alexandria."

"But how did *you* find us here?" Eyrún asked.

"When you messaged me about Clermont-Ferrand, I knew there

was only one place that meant. Your text from earlier today that you had found something that needed urgent protection got me moving. Fortunately, I have unprecedented access to His Holiness, and he called the French president, who called in his military elites."

Darwin and Eyrún sat quietly. After some time, Eyrún asked, "Do you want to see it?"

"I thought you'd never ask." Richard said, grinning.

They stood, and Richard helped Darwin get his balance. Eyrún went ahead to turn on the portable lights in the vault. Darwin led Richard around the defensive walls and stopped next to Eyrún as Richard entered the vault.

"Good heavens," said Richard, his wide eyes roaming the golden chamber.

Darwin chuckled at his usually verbose friend's sudden economy of words.

"How much is in here?" Richard finally spoke again.

"I counted while we were locked in. About nine thousand bars— each weighing a kilogram," said Eyrún, watching Richard's mouth fall open and finished, "Four-hundred fifty million euros, give or take."

"But that's not the real prize," said Darwin. "What you seek is over there."

Richard walked to the step along the back wall where Darwin and Eyrún had replaced everything in their original positions. Richard paused, saying a prayer before the statue of Mary and Jesus, then knelt, grunting as his large frame settled on the stone. He reached out both hands and slid apart the cabinet doors.

They heard him take in a massive breath, shuddering as he exhaled. He reached into the cabinet and grasped the cylinder's edges. He cupped it reverently and bowed his head while lifting it out.

"Oh my." His deep voice shook.

The End

EPILOGUE

Paris

S now whispered through the darkened streets of Paris and across
Notre-Dame's protective covering. The ice crystals swirled in the
holiday lights, still up a week into the new year, as the city settled into
its post-holiday flow.

Inside the Richelieu Amphitheater at Sorbonne University, several
hundred people had gathered for a lecture on the discovery of the
Knights Templar bank. While the gold story was old news by Decem-
ber, three days prior to tonight a raft of articles was published on
global news sites, and the academic presses published longer papers.
These offered detailed evidence on the Roman military use of lava
tubes and included photos of previously unseen artifacts and scans of
second- and third-century codices.

In addition, leading archaeologists and journalists, and a podcaster
with a multimillion-subscriber following found prepaid air tickets and
hotel reservations included with their invitations. The event promised
unprecedented access to artifacts unearthed in the discoveries and a
significant announcement. For those who could not physically attend,
the event would be live-cast on several social media platforms.

In the months following their discovery of the Templar's bank, Darwin and Eyrún hired a team of writers and researchers to complete Darwin's body of work and push it through peer reviews. After the political infighting that followed their Iceland and Egypt discoveries, they wanted an overwhelming body of evidence to garner public support for exploration. In the days following tonight's presentation, a flood of social media posts would bring alive the discoveries.

Even before the publications, archaeologists had joined forces to study the lava tubes and their connections across Europe. The Puy de Dôme and Clermont-Ferrand sites were nominated as global heritage sites. The French took pride in these new cave networks that joined Lascaux and Chauvet as testaments to human ingenuity and achievement.

Sadly, when researchers opened the lead tube, the Christ papyrus was crumbled due to its antiquity and poor preservation in earlier centuries. However, it was being restored by a team of forensic archaeologists and gospel scholars. The Holy See had opened its doors to a cross section of Christian sects and ancient document experts to study the fragments. The team announced it would release scans in the spring to enable global participation in reassembling the text into its original form.

A s the crowd filled the amphitheater, Darwin stood off-stage, watching the attendees file past the display cases. Like the Roman papyrus scrolls, most objects lay under plexiglass, but Darwin and Emelio insisted the Box scarred by Vesuvius's pyroclastic surge be uncovered.

"History is alive and real. Let them feel its wonder," Emelio had said to the curators.

People ran fingers over the Box's pockmarked surface before looking at the scrolls it had saved. Some tried on the centurion's helmet and lifted a Roman gladius, waving its broad blade. Twenty gold bars from the Knights Templar horde were the most popular objects, as people held them for photos. The French state claimed the gold as legal owner of both the land and cathedral; however, it granted Darwin and Eyrún a ten percent finder's fee. The president pledged the remaining amount to restore Notre-Dame de Paris and preserve the Knights Templar vault under the Clermont-Ferrand cathedral. Jacques was given a suspended sentence for breaking into Notre-Dame de Paris during its fire in exchange for cooperation in finding the gold taken by the beards.

An announcement that the talk would begin in two minutes motivated the crowd to their seats, the voice over the sound system assuring them that the objects would still be on display after the talk. A few minutes later, Darwin took to the stage and began by projecting a photograph of an alluvial plain in Iceland that overlooked the ocean. Shrubs and ground-hugging vegetation clung to life in its rocky volcanic soil, with no signs of human occupation.

"Imagination. Wonder. Curiosity. These are the requirements for exploration. We follow leads, sift through the dust of ages, and..." he paused, "beg for grants."

The archaeologists in the audience roared.

"And, sometimes, it's just stupid luck."

He clicked to the next photo of the same plain, but with a truck, its front wheels sunk to the axle, exposing an underground chamber. The entire audience laughed.

After pausing a moment while the laughter settled, he continued, "But, it's the raw determination to explore that leads to a significant discovery." A photo of Herculaneum filled the screen, its excavated ruins a level below the modern dwellings of Campania, Italy. "Tonight, I'll take you through one such journey that began in eighteen sixty-seven."

Over the next hour, Darwin led them through his three-times great-grandfather finding the Box in Herculaneum; Emelio's early research and development of his theory on Roman lava tube use; and his own discoveries in Iceland and Clermont-Ferrand with Eyrún.

Darwin touched on Emelio's humiliation at being shouted down decades ago while presenting an early theory, and admonished academia to be more open-minded to changes in the status quo. "After all, science does not deal in beliefs. It uses independently verifiable methods to interrogate ideas."

"With that in mind, we have an announcement. Eyrún, if you would join me." He waited while she walked onto the stage next to him.

"We did not seek riches when we chased our ideas. While we worked hard, the diamonds we found in Iceland and gold in France were not the treasure we sought and, certainly, more than we need. We are explorers, and we want others with similar passions to join us. Eyrún," he said, stepping back as she moved to center stage.

The screen showed a black-and-white photo of a volcano spewing a towering cloud of ash. Eyrún began, "While Mount Vesuvius is most famous for its eruption in the year seventy-nine, here it is erupting again in 1944. We owe a debt of gratitude to a Roman scientist named Agrippa, who wrote about Mount Vesuvius and other volcanic structures. His studies and documents were preserved for our future analysis in the box behind me, but there is still much to discover. Imagine what else is out there," she challenged the audience and paused to let it sink in before continuing.

"Darwin and I were lucky that our dreams also brought us wealth. Today, we're giving most of it away."

The projection switched to the harbor city of Ajaccio, Corsica.

"We are founding the Agrippa Center for Archaeology, a research institute and museum, to be based in Ajaccio, Corsica," she said. "In addition, we have established a substantial scholarship trust for interns from countries that lack the resources to train archaeologists."

The crowd applauded enthusiastically, and when the applause subsided, Darwin stepped next to Eyrún.

"And one more thing," he said, channeling a legendary presenter whom he admired. "These discoveries in Iceland, London, Paris, and Clermont-Ferrand would not have been made without the determination and courage of a man who persevered with a controversial theory. Emelio, Please join us."

Emelio sat up sharply, his eyebrows arching as he looked around in surprise. He stood as Eyrún waved him on stage, meeting him at the side steps, where they walked back to the lectern together.

Darwin continued speaking. "Words cannot do justice in expressing my gratitude and love for my grandfather, Emelio. His undying pursuit of the truth and personal sacrifices led to this night. His refusal to compromise led to career setbacks that were harsh blows to him and his family, but he never failed to show us his love and challenge us to be the best we could.

"Every prominent leader shows us what is possible, and when we finally see the light, we forgive their shortcomings. The honor you give me tonight is rightfully his. Let me introduce someone who will properly remedy the situation," said Darwin.

Emelio's eyes went wide as the president of France walked in from the wing and joined them on stage. Emelio looked back and forth between Darwin and Eyrún and the president.

After shaking hands, the president took a step back as an assistant carrying a small box moved in beside him. Darwin leaned and whispered something into Emelio's ear. The old man's chest swelled as the president spoke.

"Emelio Lacroix, your conviction and sacrifices have brought honor to the Republic of France. In a tradition established by Napoleon Bonaparte, a native son of your Corsica, I award you the Légion d'honneur."

The president lifted a five-pointed cross from the opened velvet case and pinned it on Emelio's lapel. He stood back, applauding as Emelio beamed. The medal glinted in the spotlights, and its red ribbon on Emelio's blue suit and white shirt formed the *tricolore* of the French flag.

The audience rose and joined in the applause.

———

Following a reception at the amphitheater, the extended family gathered at Darwin's and Eyrún's suite at a hotel just off the Champs-Élysées. Darwin's sister Marie, her husband Julien, and their two children were in from Lyon. His parents joined from London. And Eyrún's mom and sister had flown in from Reykjavik, each with their fiancés. Emelio showed everyone his medal, and Darwin's niece,

Chloe, proclaimed loudly that she would get a medal when she grew up.

Stevie and Zac were the only non-family members attending the party. Back in October, they had been underground at the time Eyrún messaged them for help. But they were able to reach Clermont-Ferrand the day after the fight with Jacques, Miguel, and the commandos to witness the vault's discovery. After Darwin led a toast, the family settled into eating and conversation, while the four friends found a moment together on the balcony. The brisk January air felt refreshing to Darwin after the overly warm suite.

Zac proposed a private toast. "To our next adventure. Whatever. Whenever." They clinked glasses and drank. Zac had flown to France to celebrate New Year's Eve with Stevie after spending the Christmas holiday with his family in Oakland, California.

"We have an announcement," said Stevie. "Zac's company was acquired, and he's moving to France to live with me."

"*Magnifique!*" exclaimed Darwin, hugging Zac and then Stevie. They toasted again.

"At least I can pronounce the town—Orange," said Zac. "I'll work remotely to tie off the company transition. And then? Who knows."

Darwin's dad, Olivier, came outside to find him. "There's someone at the door for you," he said. Darwin and Eyrún left Olivier with Zac and Stevie and went to the door, where they were surprised to find Adolfo from the Vatican waiting for them in the suite's entry.

"Monsieur and Madame Lacroix," said Adolfo, "Nice to see you again. His Holiness sends his congratulations to you and your grandfather. He also is most grateful for your help in finding the Christ papyrus and asked me to deliver this as a token of our appreciation."

Darwin took the half-meter long rectangular box and raised his eyebrows as if asking what was inside it. Adolfo shrugged. Darwin peeled the tape on one end.

"Be careful. I'm told it's fragile," said Adolfo.

Darwin set it on a table in the entry and folded back the flaps. He glanced in and pulled out a plastic tube. "*Mon Dieu,*" he said. The tube's special end caps created a hermetic seal to protect its contents.

Darwin had commissioned hundreds of these tubes to transport the ancient Library of Alexandria scrolls found in the Siwa Oasis.

A letter bearing the symbol of the Holy See was fixed to the tube. He opened it.

Dear Darwin,

I would have liked to give this to you in person, but when Richard Ndembele explained your selfless act to honor your grandfather tonight, I thought it appropriate that you receive my gift more quietly.

Twice now, you have shown the moral courage to do what is right. Please accept this scroll, written by Alexander of Macedonia, as thanks for your notable accomplishments. I'm told it has special meaning for you and Eyrún. Franz helped me locate it, and I persuaded the Egyptian president to give it to the Vatican Apostolic Archive. May it contain all that you hope it does.

In closing, there are other mysteries in the secret vault. It is time to remove them from the dusty drawers and bring them into the light of discovery. I am creating a select archaeological investigation branch of the Archive reporting directly to me. It needs a gifted, uncompromising leader.

Might you be interested?

Alexandria, Egypt

E arly the next morning, Nahla Al Mahwi stood at her penthouse window, gazing at the Mediterranean Sea beyond the broad roof of the New Library of Alexandria. As patient as a viper, Nahla knew that victories in her business sometimes played out over years.

Her original plan to get Alexander the Great's treasure scroll had failed when the Egyptian antiquities director, Abbas Kamal, was sacked. But serendipity offered a second chance when she had recently learned of the scroll's gift by the Egyptian government, and her Vatican insider relayed that the Pope was giving it to Darwin.

What goes around comes around. Nahla smiled as her assistant set down the tea service on a nearby table.

"Did Darwin get the scroll?" she asked.

"Yes. It was delivered to him last night in Paris," said the assistant.

"Good. Keep following him. My source there said he was up to something in Azerbaijan."

AUTHOR'S NOTE

Thank you for reading Templar's Bank. I hope you enjoyed it and would love to hear from you at dave@davebartell.com, and please write a review on Amazon.

The prologue took shape as I stood on the Pont Saint-Louis in early November 2019, looking at Notre-Dame just as Eyrún and Darwin did in chapter 18. I had taken a mini-break in Paris at the end of a business trip, telling my wife, "you never know when we'll be back." Never have such words felt so right.

While Templar's Bank is a new adventure for Darwin, it brings closure to his longstanding quest to prove that ancient Roman's used lava tubes to travel in secret across Europa. During my writing of Hypatia's Diary, the scene where Darwin finds her diary needed more details to bring the secret room of documents to life. On a whim, I added the Templar codex, and the seed of this adventure germinated.

Many great stories have been written about the Knights Templar and the legend of their lost wealth. One of my favorites is Steve Berry's: *The Templar Legacy*. But I decided on a different story track, one where the Knights Templar ran a banking empire in addition to being warriors. All the military movement and pilgrim travel across thousands of kilometers of unfriendly terrain would have made it dangerous to carry large amounts of gold. So, I added money exchange to the travel protection services the Knights Templar provided. Their bank would have been like any other bank, with gold and silver held in reserve to back the transactions.

But the Templar's legend was not all about money. Rumors abound of them finding a relic in Jerusalem so powerful, and it kept them independent of kings and Rome for hundreds of years. And, since Darwin lives to dig up the truth and share it universally, I dipped my pen into the digital inkwell to tell his latest adventure.

Templar's Bank presents a consistent Darwin fulfilling his initial quest begun in Roman Ice. It's Eyrún who we get to know better in this story as she transcends her life as a hard-working provider for others to rediscovering old passions. Also, she and Darwin begin building their life together in Corsica. Their new home and the Agrippa Center for Archaeology open doors to many new adventures

Zac and Stevie took a back seat in Templar's Bank to allow Darwin and Eyrún a chance to grow. Will they be back? We shall see?

Please write a review as we authors thrive on recommendations. If you found anything amiss in the book, please email me directly, and I'll fix it. While I worked with a translator, developmental editor, a copy editor, and a proofreader, to err is human.

Again, THANKS, and I invite you to learn about the next Darwin Lacroix Adventure by joining my mailing list at davebartell.com.

ACKNOWLEDGMENTS

Thank you, Doctor Denis Sadone, for checking the French and Corsican translations. While I have traveled regularly to Europe, my small bits of French and Spanish fall far short of fluency.

Tightening a story's flow and dialogue as well as validating details and consistency makes any novel better. Thank you to my copy editor Mark Rhynsburger.

As this is the third Darwin Lacroix adventure, character development becomes a more critical piece of the series. We all naturally age and grow wiser, and our relationships mature. Thanks to Annie Tucker, my development editor, who helped refine Eyrún's growth and rediscovery of lost passions in Templar's Bank.

Every book deserves a great cover and, thanks to Patrick Knowles Design, Templar's Bank has one. This is our second collaboration as he also did the cover on Hypatia's Diary

And, thank you to Diane Bartell, my wife, best fan, and most important person in my life. She will soon be asking, "Got anything new for me to read."

Onward to book four: Tuscan Hoax!

ABOUT THE AUTHOR

Imagine the wonder at being the first person to open King Tut's tomb? Dave Bartell loves reviving lost history and his novels breathe "thriller" into archaeology.

As a kid, he was frequently found tinkering in his parent's garage. His insatiable curiosity to understand how things work led him to study biochemistry and, later, fueled a career in high-technology. His what-if mindset and life experiences combine to make his fiction plausible and feel realistic.

Dave lives in Los Gatos California, a small town tucked into the edge of Silicon Valley. He enjoys hiking in the hills behind his home, where beauty is still analog.

He hopes you enjoy his stories and invites you to share your thoughts at dave@davebartell.com. And, visit davebartell.com to get a sneak peek of upcoming projects.

[a] amazon.com/Dave-Bartell/e/B07KN8HPYP
[BB] bookbub.com/authors/dave-bartell
[f] facebook.com/DaveBartellWriter
[g] goodreads.com/davebartell
[o] instagram.com/davebartell
[y] twitter.com/davebartell

Made in the USA
Middletown, DE
06 July 2023

34647813R00208